S0-FQW-150

If ASHEEL
WON'T
BURN

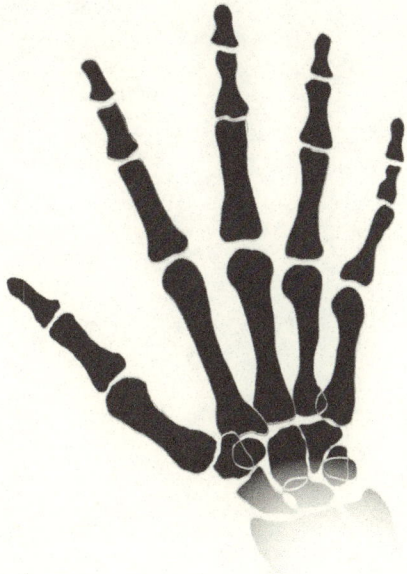

© 2021 by Jenn Jarrett

First edition published December 10, 2021

This is a work of fiction and all references to people, places, or events are coincidental.

This book may not be reproduced in any form, including electronically or in print, without written consent from the author.

Bible quotation from English Standard Version

ISBN (ebook): 978-1-7375112-1-2

ISBN (paperback): 978-1-7375112-2-9

Content Warnings: fantasy violence and death, abductions of children and adults

Typography: Garamond, PenultimateLight

Cover Design, Interior Design, and Editing by Jenn Jarrett

JennJarrettEdits.com

". . . for whatever one sows, that will he also reap . . .
And let us not grow weary of doing good, for in due
season we will reap, if we do not give up."
Galatians 6:7–10

If Asheel Won't Burn

Won't

Burn

JENN JARRETT

CHAPTER 1

A sheel had sniffed every person in town, and some of them reeked. The stench of their stained hearts, like the town's compost heaps, permeated through her small office in the council building, and after breathing in the fumes for hours, her lungs ached for fresh air.

Meager gifts decorated her desk and consoled her slightly. The people of Seshnia brought the bribes as if she were an actual deity with power over their fate. Most were worthless to her—a small pile of underripe fruit, a fraying skein of yarn—but some were nicer and what she'd expect if she had any real control over it.

Asheel lifted an embroidered handkerchief from the pile and blew her nose to try to rid herself of the stench, but the odor followed her ceaselessly, never fading like regular scents. All magic came with a price, but she would have taken any other price than having no way to turn it off.

She crossed her arms over the desk, nudging her knife away

from where she'd whittled in the worn wood, and laid her head on her forearms, her wavy black hair falling around her. It did a pitiful job blocking out the stench. Just a little longer, then she'd be allowed to leave and gulp the fresh air outside, crisp and freeing. She'd spend her life outside if she could, away from the townspeople, but shouts and pounding feet reminded her of the Reaper Guard practicing downstairs. The clean air would have to wait.

Her lids drifted closed, and she pressed her nose against her perfume-soaked sleeves. Only hints of a citrus aroma remained, a slight relief, but she coughed when her own odor seeped through the fabric.

A floorboard creaked, and one of the council apprentices peeked inside. "Are you okay?" he asked.

"Just ready for this to be over," Asheel said into her sleeves, muffling her voice and hopefully her frustration.

"The last family is here. Are you ready to see them?"

As if she had a choice. She didn't lift her head, and the apprentice left.

What had Seshnia done to prepare for the reaper before discovering her ability? What did the other towns do without someone like her, gifted to sense who was next? She couldn't be that much of an anomaly if her friend, Lana, had a similar talent. No matter how atrocious someone's heart became, Lana could sense any kindness that remained. If the two of them existed, more people like Asheel had to exist, too.

Footsteps thudded through the hall followed by laughter, and the Farson twins ran shrieking into the room, almost knocking over a basket of incense at the door. Asheel groaned but sat up to do her duty.

Their mother knocked on the doorframe after her children and swept inside draped in a flowing silk gown. She adjusted a cloak draped over her arm, then snapped her fingers. "Calm down and show you have manners."

The twins, carrying their own beautifully dyed cloaks, quieted but still giggled on the other side of Asheel's desk, facing her with gap-toothed smiles.

"Sorry we're late," the mother said. "I almost decided not to bring them after buying your special incense." She winked. "Mind making this quick?"

Asheel rubbed the sleeve creases imprinted in her forehead. "Special incense?"

"The incense you blessed for your father." From her satchel, the mother pulled out three thin sticks covered in cinnamon bark that Asheel had helped her parents grind two nights ago. The mother waved them in the air, stirring up the noxious fumes in the small room. "I got the last few."

Asheel would have to talk to her dad about his lies. Blessed incense? She didn't have powers like that. His heart had only the earliest hints of danger, deception and greed, wafting from him like stale cologne, but if he kept this up, the reaper would come for him soon. Asheel closed her eyes and breathed deep through her nose to get to work.

The mother exuded a bitter but sweet scent, she would be safe, but something rotten soured the air. The twins were eleven, a little young to smell so bad but still older than Asheel had been when her gift became apparent. She squinted at them and breathed deeply again. One child reeked from across the room. Each person the reaper took was a tragedy, but for him to target a child tonight, that proved he was heartless himself. Surely children were safe from him, but the odor was undeniable. She stifled a gag and pulled her lips between her teeth to hide her grimace.

She barely took another breath to double-check that the odor didn't drift from the Farson mother, and while blinking through the fumes burning her eyes, she declared their fate. "It's one of them tonight."

The Farson mother gasped, then grabbed her children's shoulders and forced a smile. "You can't be certain from that distance." Her voice shook, and she nudged her kids around the desk. "Kady, Berice, let Asheel check you out."

This was the worst part of the whole, simple procedure. Asheel covered her nose with her sleeve and leaned back in her chair, away from the approaching kids. "Please, no. I don't need a better sniff. I'm certain." She couldn't hide her gag the second time. "I'm so sorry," she muttered through her sleeve and pointed at the slighter of the twins. "It'll be Kady."

Kady's face paled beneath her freckles, and Berice reached for her hand.

"You're wrong." The Farson mother pulled her twins back from Asheel and tucked them into her sides. "My babies are good, not a rotten bone in their bodies." She frowned and held the twins tighter then glared at Asheel. "Take it back! Don't you dare put your curse on them."

The denial, the blame—the part Asheel dreaded. She should have asked the mother to leave while she checked the kids, but it was too late. She shook her head and lowered her arm from her nose. "I don't control it. I don't know why, but the reaper's choice will be Kady."

Trembling shook the mother's full cheeks, and a red flush spread across her face. "You vile . . ." She pursed her lips then spat over the twins' heads. The glob splattered around Asheel's hovering arm and sprayed across her cheek.

Asheel froze, stunned, while the woman grabbed the remaining citrus incense and dragged her children from the room.

"The incense doesn't work," Asheel muttered and scrubbed the slime from her cheek, but the woman and her children were gone. If the incense gave them some comfort, some hope of the reaper making another choice, then she wouldn't steal that from them. Hopefully they didn't hear her.

Sympathy and resentment tore at her evenly, bubbling in a frustrating mixture that tightened her throat. She knew it was hard to accept, seen the denial every month, but the blame didn't get easier. The frustration settled as tension across her shoulders, another burden from the town.

She rose, ready to disappear into the night without checking in with the Reaper Guard, but Lana, tall and slender, ducked into the office, glancing over her shoulder. "What did you do to the Farsons?"

"I didn't do anything," Asheel fell back into her chair, "but she's probably storming through the town now telling everyone I summoned death to her home." She motioned for Lana to step inside.

Floral hints of Lana's kind heart drifted to Asheel with each step her friend took across the room, settling the residual stench from the smaller twin. Lana grabbed an apple and slid into an empty seat while eyeing the gifts. A faded brown eye patch, contrasting her gentleness, covered her missing eye. "So, the reaper will take one of hers?" she asked while chewing.

"Kady."

"The little one? Wow." Lana swallowed. "Isn't she too young?"

Asheel nodded. The reaper had taken younger kids before, but he typically took adults, sometimes teens. She tilted her head back against the chair and stared at the ceiling. "I'm not doing these checks next month. They can't force me."

"But your apprenticeship."

"What apprenticeship? Who's my mentor?" Asheel flung her hands up and gestured around the room, then let them fall to her lap. "Apprenticing for the council, sure, they're all my mentors. But this part of it . . . no one's here to teach me how to handle angry mothers. I can't do it anymore."

"We need you." Lana grimaced and shook her head. "I mean, we can make guesses who might be taken, but no one has the nose for it like you do."

"But it doesn't help." Asheel took her knife from the desk and stuck the blade in the carving she'd started earlier. "It doesn't stop them from being taken, so why make me suffer for them?"

"It helps. It gives their family in denial a chance to say goodbye."

Asheel squinted. "That's not what the ones in denial do." She jerked the knife harder than necessary, and a chunk of wood flew over her shoulder. "Do you know what the Farson lady did to me just now?"

"I can imagine." Lana crunched into the apple, juice glistening down the last sliver of green peel. "She's upset. Don't take it personally."

Asheel scowled at Lana. "She spat on me." With the knife tip, she pointed to her damp sleeve. The memory of the woman's vile spittle made Asheel gag again. It wasn't the first time she'd been spat on, but that didn't make it any less hurtful or disgusting.

Lana finished her apple and tossed the core into a trash bin. "Like I said, she's upset. Wouldn't you be?"

"I wouldn't be upset at someone who can't control it."

"They don't know that."

Asheel shook her head, her hair falling across her cheek like a curtain. "They should. I tell them every month. At least she'll still have the other twin."

"That doesn't make the loss of her daughter any easier."

"I know." Asheel poked the knife back into the desk's surface. She imagined how her parents would feel if the reaper stole her or her little brother in the night. They'd be devastated regardless of which one he took, but they wouldn't spit on someone who had nothing to do with it. She sliced the knife through the desk again. "I wish they wouldn't blame the reaper's choice on me. They're the ones who stink."

She dusted wood splinters from the desk, wanting to wipe

away her frustrations as easily as the flecks that fell to the floor. Lana was sympathetic, but she couldn't understand how exhausting the burden was. Her apprenticeship was satisfying, helpful. "How was everything at the care-home today?" Asheel asked.

Lana straightened and grinned. "Harv recognized me today!"

"Harv?"

"You know. The retired blacksmith from Kemnuk?" When Asheel shook her head, Lana rolled her eye. "The one you said had a heart that smelled like feet and I told you he smelled like that to everyone."

"Oh, him!" Asheel leaned back while the man's craggy face flicked in her memory. "He was so confusing." His mind was already so far gone when he'd arrived at Seshnia a year ago that Asheel couldn't understand how his heart had a smell at all. Lana cleared up the confusion before Asheel stuck him with the other Seshnians at risk of being taken by the reaper.

Lana nodded. "He asked if I could sing him the song I was humming yesterday, and when I asked him which one, it was actually one from yesterday!" She grinned. "I know his memory will never be the same, but he's so sweet. He thanks me for every little thing."

"That must be satisfying," Asheel scraped her knife along the desk again, "knowing they appreciate you."

"Don't be jealous." Lana reached across the desk and patted Asheel's shoulder. "You're so much more important to the town than me."

"I don't feel that way though." The memory of the spittle dappled her cheek again. "I just wish someone would say thank you. No one ever thanks the person who tells them they're the reaper's next target." Instead, they brought her gifts as if she'd change the reaper's mind and fled from her in the streets as if she'd curse them with her presence.

"Can you blame them?"

"Yes, I can. I deserve some thanks for putting up with all of them."

After a final jab at the desk's surface, Asheel leaned back to examine her finished masterpiece. Jagged curves formed a lopsided skull, and the triangles that she had meant to be fire surrounding it looked more like spearheads. She wasn't an artist, but it was obviously a rough outline of the reaper.

Lana stood and frowned at the motif. "Your heart's turned hard," she looked up at Asheel with her eyebrows raised, "and you're going to be caught."

Lana was probably right, but what could anyone do about it?

"They started me on this path long ago. How am I supposed to change it?" Asheel asked. "None of it's my fault, and I can't go back in time and tell five-year-old me to hide her gift." She couldn't remember the older kid's face, but she'd never forget the putrid smell that seeped into his heart. That night, the reaper took him, and Asheel's life changed forever.

Lana sat back in the chair, shadows from the lamp stretching across her prominent cheekbones. "Remember how fun it was at first? Be happy you can help."

"Being the pride of the town was fun before my predictions made every family my enemy," Asheel agreed, "but it's been a long time since I could call this fun. Not since the parents started hating me and our friends feared me." She threw her arms up in defeat. "Now the whole town disregards me." Only kind-hearted Lana had taken pity on her and befriended Asheel, the town's curse.

A crash from the guards practicing shook the walls, causing the two girls to jump. Asheel sighed and frowned at the door.

Lana's sepia forehead crinkled at Asheel's reluctancy. "Go join them." She prodded Asheel with her knuckles. "They're probably almost finished anyway."

"I guess I'll make an appearance." Asheel stood and squeezed her eyes shut. "I feel like I've given everything to this town, and what have I gotten back but duties I can never escape?" No one had her power to fill the role. "These gifts don't make up for what I've lost." They didn't make up for the childhood friends that ran from her. She'd never forget the sound she'd made while they fled with a barely whispered "she's coming." She bit her bottom lip to keep back the tears threatening to fall.

"Oh, come here." Lana stood and held her arms open for Asheel who dove into them. "The hard part of today is over, and you can figure out next month's reaping night later."

Lana crouched a little to hold Asheel tighter, and Asheel rested the tip of her nose against Lana's smooth neck and breathed in the sweet, floral aroma of her friend's untainted heart. It soothed Asheel. For just this moment she could relax without the town's stench choking her, and her tears fell freely, soaking into the spirals of Lana's hair while Lana patted her back. If their gifts were reversed, Lana would figure out how to cleanse their whole town with her power. She'd even lost her eye while trying to protect one of the grown men who'd been taken.

Lana shushed Asheel's sobs and squeezed her tighter. "I know it's rough. Remember how much good you're doing for everyone."

But Asheel had been sniffing the people for almost fifteen years with only hate and blame in return. "I want to be normal." Asheel's lips brushed against Lana's neck. "I didn't ask for this magic. I didn't ask for this job. I want a choice."

But she didn't have a choice, and she had to face her duties. She took one more deep breath of Lana's beautiful, clean heart and leaned out of her arms. The smell of decay and rot, the stench of bitterness and resentment, filled her lungs again, following her like a shadow, inescapable. A smell from her own heart. But she wouldn't tell anyone how bad she reeked herself. What would they say when they found out she could be taken, too? Lana claimed Asheel was doing good, but if she really was, why did she smell so awful herself?

Lana held Asheel's shoulders then wiped tears from her cheeks with calloused but gentle fingers. "Go get practice over with and protect that little girl tonight," she said and shooed Asheel out the door. "I'll take these presents to your house."

Asheel left her office. The stench in her heart pulled at her, wanting release, wanting revenge on the whole town, simmering like the first embers of a fire in her core, but she pushed it down.

She walked through the council's two-story, expansive complex while listening for the Reaper Guard, brushing her shoulder along the stone walls, staying close to them in case a guard darted through, but even the muffled voices had quieted. Anyone not needed for the practice had left to get ready for the annual Gate Feast. She peered into the auditorium where a handful of people sat on benches, nervously chatting or lost in their own thoughts. They were the ones she'd warned could be taken before she'd been certain Kady would be the reaper's target. Two hulking men, a young lady pruning herself in the reflection of a guard's spear, two teens practically sitting on top of each other, and the Farson mother with her twins.

Not wanting to disturb the tension balanced over the sprawling room, large enough to hold half the town, she motioned to a guard at the door. "Are you in the middle of a run?" she whispered.

The guard shrugged. "We just got the signal we're starting soon and were about to lock up the room. You might be able to catch them at the main entrance."

Asheel thanked the guard and slipped through the quiet halls to the reception area. Scorch marks still scarred wooden pillars from previous attempts to stop the reaper, barely visible in the darkened hallway, and when the coattails of a guard disappeared behind one, Asheel dropped her eyes to her feet so she wouldn't have to talk to anyone. An occasional clank or whisper from the darkness revealed guards setting traps or wedging themselves out of sight. At the reception area in front of recently replaced double doors, a small group huddled together in the entryway between two wide, polished pillars.

The leader, Stevart, an amber-toned, lanky fellow who never filled out his clothes enough, noticed her and shouted across the reception area. "About time you made it." He motioned for her to join them, his arm breaking up the setting sunlight streaming through the doors. "Did you hear the new plans for this reaping night?"

Asheel shrugged. "Are they much different than last time?" They had new plans to capture the reaper every month, and each month, they failed. They were a waste of time, which would be better spent at home with their families, holding their loved ones that could vanish in a few hours.

"Really?" YoAne, a squat but graceful woman just as pale as Asheel, scoffed at her. "You don't show up until the end of practice and you haven't even reviewed the plans? Why even show up at all?" She turned to Stevart. "We don't need this rat. Let her go home."

Asheel clenched her fists but took a deep breath and remembered what Lana said. The town used her as an outlet for their hurt, but Asheel's warnings helped. Even if she couldn't see how they helped, they helped. Still, the vengeful side of her would like to see YoAne live every day with a rotten piece of flesh tied under her nose, be forced to sniff filthy people, and then still show up for pointless practices, which they obviously didn't need Asheel for. She spun to leave, but Stevart grabbed her wrist.

"Shut up," he told YoAne then turned to Asheel. "We could actually use someone who doesn't know the plan. Want to be our reaper for this last run?"

Asheel's eyebrows shot up. She'd never been offered the role before. "You want me to pretend to be the reaper?"

Stevart nodded. "It'd be helpful. We need someone who doesn't know where everyone is hidden to see if we got the traps laid out right."

The idea, playing the villain, intrigued her. "Is it dangerous?" she asked. The group around her towered over her, a short height she got from her dad, but even if she were taller, she'd never be as tough as the well-muscled guards they usually picked. She'd seen the traps they'd set before, and several had been dangerous enough to hurt their typical role player.

"No, I don't think so." Stevart glanced down the hall as if looking at the ambush areas through the walls. "We have safety elements in place, but we'll call it off if anything goes wrong."

Acting like the fiery skeleton, the curse everyone considered her a part of, sounded like a good way to get out her frustrations. Asheel agreed to take the role.

Stevart told her to give them a few minutes then try to get to the auditorium. He handed her a torch to indicate her as the reaper, and then the small group of guards disappeared into the darkened building. Away from her. Like her friends had. She closed her eyes. She'd just turned twenty, old enough to leave town and start fresh somewhere else. Too old for her childhood trauma to keep haunting her. She needed to get over it, but no matter how hard she tried, she couldn't forget. A new city wouldn't heal her heart.

After giving the guards a few extra minutes to find their positions, Asheel stepped into the dark hallway. The shuttered windows lit the complex enough to navigate without the torch, but the complex felt different now than it did when she'd walked through it just minutes ago. Shadows thrown from the torch danced around her, the pillars, benches, the occasional statue, and she jumped, ready to fight, every time one looked faintly human.

She wouldn't be much help to them if she were stopped only minutes into the practice run. She needed to think like the reaper.

She closed her eyes and listened for anyone nearby, but the crackle of the torch hid any heavy breathing or shifting clothing. She could easily imagine that she was alone in the complex. She breathed deep. Stench from the people she'd checked faintly reached her, rancid like the time she hid a dead mouse under her bed. She, of course, knew where they were already, but her focus on them proved that if they wanted to hide the smell from the reaper, they would need much heavier perfume. She breathed in again. If the people smelled that bad, surely the guards with their mostly kind hearts . . .

And there. The concoction of sweet aromas paled in comparison to Lana's, but the first round of guards was close. The pull of the Seshnians she'd warned came from straight ahead, tempting her to follow it to finish the practice quickly, but the reaper had proven he had brains. He wouldn't fall for the ambush, so she wouldn't either.

Asheel ducked down a side hall, keeping her footsteps light, and passed the dining hall with its echoing emptiness and then a few of the council's offices. She pushed open an office door that had a backdoor into the next corridor and peeked inside. No one.

But a shout from the other end of the hall startled Asheel into the room, and she dashed through the office and to the door on the other side, knocking a chair and a stack of papers to the floor. She couldn't be caught yet. A new desire, to prove she could be a decent reaper, fueled her, and she sprinted through the second corridor and turned down a third.

The massive doors to the auditorium with the putrid people inside loomed ahead. She would take one. The foulest. She would take the Farson child with her.

Her need to prove herself shifted to an odd desire that pulsed through her, so pleasant she didn't try to ignore it, tickling the simmering embers of rage, jealousy, and pain in her core. She'd strike a real terror in the woman who spat on her. Revenge would be so satisfying.

And under her rage, her own stained heart's stench flared to rival the odors ahead of her.

Just before the auditorium, Stevart's voice echoed out. "Now!"

Two sides of a metal cage, the size of a wagon, flew at Asheel from opposite sides. The torch in her hand flared bright as she held it out while running. The metal casings slammed against the torch but bounced from their protective rubber, and Asheel dove through the crack before the cage clanked together again. She pelted down the last stretch of hall and smashed into the locked doors, which shoved open. Had she always been so strong? An ache shot through her shoulder, belated pain she'd definitely feel in the morning.

Berice and Kady shrieked and scrambled for their mother. The teens ignored Asheel's entry, and the two men startled from their discussion. Pruning girl didn't even flinch. The third wave of guards shouted at them to remain calm, but Asheel didn't pause, her gaze focused on the little girl with frizzy brown hair and freckles coating her cheeks—Kady.

But mere yards away from Kady, a weighted net slammed into Asheel from the side and knocked her to the ground, the torch sliding across the floor. Tiny chains woven together, a rope of metal instead of flammable fibers, anchored her to the ground, trapping her like an animal. Chained. Captured. She flailed but couldn't get out from under the metal bands.

"Are you okay?" Stevart jogged up behind her then shouted over his shoulder, "You guys could have hurt her. Didn't I give you a regular rope net to practice with?"

"Sorry, boss. It doesn't fall as fast," a bumbling voice shouted back.

Another guard from the auditorium joined the shouting. "We thought it was going to be one of you guys. No one mentioned Asheel was our practice reaper."

"Doesn't matter who it was. You shouldn't have been throwing a metal net at any of us." Stevart lifted the net from Asheel. "Are you okay?" he asked again.

She rolled onto her back and stared up at the lead guard. Berice had fallen into hysterical crying, but everyone else had calmed after her explosive entry. The first two waves of guards fumbled into the room, some huffing at missing her and others rolling their eyes at the pathetic attempt that didn't even work on a small human girl. Someone shouted an "I told you so" about the door's bolts being worn, and another shouted back that no one cared.

The aches from her flight through the complex already quivered through her limbs, but Asheel was okay. She nodded to answer Stevart's question. The drive of the game released its grasp from her chest where her heart pounded with excitement. She'd had more fun than she'd had in years, exhilarated by the freedom to tear through the building, but she didn't want to admit that she enjoyed her short time acting as the reaper. That would give them even more reason to keep her with the Reaper Guard when she wanted away from it all. She refused to believe that was her fate, that her whole life would be spent focused on the reaper.

Stevart held out his hand. She glanced at it, took it, and sat up with his help, and he let go of her like he would catch whatever cursed her.

Still, his kindness shone through in his smile. "Don't be late for lookout duty." He gave her a wave while jogging towards his guards. "Let's consider more sentries in the corridors," he shouted. "Add someone with a fourth metal net at the cage and disperse the first wave more, but I think that's all we can do tonight without exhausting ourselves too much. Reset the traps, replace those busted locks, and head to the feast."

The guards whooped, and the endangered people hurried from the room. Asheel stood and followed them at a distance, lost in her thoughts about how tempting revenge had been. She walked back through the building past the guards resetting the traps, retrieved her cloak, and stepped out into the chilled night air. Songs and laughter from the Gate Feast clawed at her ears from the next street over. The town was laid out like tree rings. Shops, entertainment, eateries, and homes encircled the council's complex, the central point of the town. Fruit orchards of reds and purples and fields of ripening green and orange vegetables filled the outermost circle. Beyond that, larger livestock filled meadows, and up high on the plateaus, safer from predators, quieter livestock grazed.

Asheel darted from the complex's entryway and ducked into an alley between a glass shop of sparkling rainbow flecks and the embroiderer's house covered in curtains and tapestries. She leaned her back against the glass shop and slid until her rump met the cobblestone ground.

She wouldn't hide in the alley all night. She just needed a break from everyone and the burden they put on her. Just a few minutes to herself without the eyes of the council and townspeople watching her every move. A deep breath of fresh air replaced some of the rotten smells from her nose with mouth-watering aromas of smoked hog and heavily buttered bread. Her parents and little brother were already at the Feast, celebrating, along with Lana's family.

The music from the Feast echoed throughout Seshnia, an odd contrast to their typically morose reaping nights. This was the first time she could remember their Gate Feast being on the same day as a reaping night, and surprisingly, the council had voted not to change the celebration day for this year. They told the citizens that it could add cheer to such a gloomy time, but during the meeting when they voted, it had been because they didn't want to disrupt the trade schedule.

She'd join the feast in a minute, after the song, to give them a few more moments without her presence spoiling the celebration and let her prepare to pretend their looks didn't hurt. They pleaded for her input into their safety but ignored her own pleas for her wellbeing, ignored how worthless she felt. How could anyone understand that always being right about who would be taken felt more like a failure than a success? To Asheel, wanting to help meant protecting the people, keeping them from being taken by the reaper. But her fortune telling was the opposite, and they were right that it made her just as horrible as the reaper himself. She might as well have been dragging people to the Reaper Gate for him.

Her magic alone indicated her status with the people, but it didn't make her higher or mightier than them or to deserve their praise. It showed that she didn't belong. But everyone belonged somewhere. She had to have a purpose, and she'd find her place away from the Reaper Guard and the council. Maybe away from Seshnia entirely.

She closed her eyes and listened to the upbeat music whose lyrics contradicted its happy melody. She hated the song, most people did, but they still sang it as tradition. Its lyrics hit even harder since this was a reaping night. When it ended, Asheel whispered the last line back to the darkness. "When the ash-crowned reaper comes tonight, who's left mourning in the morning?"

CHAPTER 2

In the last few rays of the setting sun, Asheel hurried to her family's table at the Gate Feast. Fires flared to life, but the impending reaper visit marred the normal festive atmosphere. Still, musicians filled the open space with notes of practiced joy, songs about the Reaper Gate, the man who created it, and the safety and peace it brought to the world, and dancers spun in rippling costumes, swirling hypnotic displays of color.

Her mother, brother, and Lana's family stood around a red stone table, the fire swaying in the middle of it, while her father wandered from family to family selling incense with false promises of safety for the night. He wasn't the only opportunistic person. Besides the butchered herd beasts, some of the farmers sold special treats from their crops, puffed rice with drizzled sauces, sticks of spun sugar, skewers of scorched fowl, and palm-sized fruit pastries made with the bursting, citrusy fruits of Yulgerre.

"I was about to send Lana to track you down," Willa said

when Asheel stumbled to the table. Her mother slid a cooled plate of ham and vegetables to her. "How was practice?"

Asheel shrugged and shoveled food into her mouth to avoid answering.

Coby, her younger brother, nudged scraps of his meal across his plate and thankfully changed the topic. "I'm done. Can I go play with Berice and Kady now?"

Across the feast area, the Farson family huddled together at their own table, all with understandably sullen faces. Asheel shifted closer to Lana to put their table's fire between her and the Farsons and hide from her guilt.

Willa peered over the hand Coby blocked his plate with and shook her head. "Take another bite of squash. Then you can play until the skit."

"But the gravy's touching it!"

"It wasn't earlier." Willa scraped the gravy to the plate's other side with his fork. "If you didn't want them to touch, you shouldn't have been playing with it."

Lana elbowed Asheel and nodded toward the merchant handcarts. "Did you see the turnout?" she asked.

Asheel glanced at them while she chewed. Travelers from Novoshna and Kemnuk, who usually overshadowed the Seshnian merchants, speckled the edges of the celebration, distant from their Seshnian counterparts. Some who'd been out earlier in the day had already packed and left to get far from Seshnia before the reaper arrived, though distance wouldn't stop him. He'd taken one on the road before.

"It's a shame the council didn't change our feast night," Lana's father muttered.

Willa coerced another bite down Coby. "Imagine how many more we'd have if we'd waited another day."

"I know." Lana's father stacked his plate on his wife's. "But the council was right, look how much happier everyone is for this reaping night." He gestured toward the dancing teens. "Though I wish we'd had more traders than this."

"Why any come here for the Gate Feast instead of Novoshna, I'll never understand," Lana's mother said, staring at a jewelry cart that glittered even from a distance.

"Some people don't like the big city as much. Too many people, too noisy. I heard they've started handing out candy to the children who dress up in costumes."

"In Novoshna?"

"Yeah. The kids love it. Maybe we could do that next year."

Asheel imagined children dressed as monsters running through their capitol. She'd only seen its packed streets once when she was younger than Coby, but the city had almost doubled in size since then. Many families from smaller towns like Seshnia and Kemnuk moved there, hoping Novoshna's new metal wall would protect them from reaping nights.

Lana's parents rambled on about bringing the new tradition to Seshnia and Willa continued bargaining extra bites into Coby. They'd all already finished eating, except Coby, and watched the younger couples and single youths on the verge of adulthood pairing off to dance around the stage, filling the feast area with laughter. Their rapid breaths of exertion puffed into the chilly air and swirled above them a few inches before vanishing with the smoke from the many fires.

Asheel nudged Lana's elbow and nodded to their peers. "Why don't you join them?" she asked.

Lana watched the writhing teenagers, most wearing vibrant coats threaded with lavish, sparkling embroidery. "And have a repeat of last year?" Lana had gotten sick from the swirling auras only she could see that had engulfed her in the dance area.

"Close your eye," Asheel said. "Then you won't see them."

"And step on everyone else instead? Not worth it." Lana faced Asheel, and the light from their table's fire glinted off her eye's black depths. Asheel stared at it, lost in it, as if Lana could see straight into her mind. Lana grinned and threw her own question back at her. "And why don't *you* join them?"

Asheel stuck her tongue out then shoved a too large bite of squash into her cheeks. "Because I'm still eating."

A part of both of them wanted more acceptance by the young adults they grew up with, but their gifts drove the "normal" kids away early on. Asheel and Lana latched onto each other after that and became inseparable.

"Come on." Lana grabbed Asheel's last bite of ham and ate it. "Let's check out the stalls before they pack up."

"Be back before the skit," Willa called as they wandered away.

Fewer than a dozen travelers called to the Seshnian crowd, beckoning them to purchase foreign goods. The two girls wove between their wood stalls, enjoying anonymity to the merchants. A few coins weighed Asheel's pocket from her workday, but the idea of moving away from Seshnia kept growing, and if she wanted to move away from home, she'd need to save more. She could move across the ocean where no one knew her, but she didn't know those languages. Or she could become a traveler, selling and trading incense, but she'd need to practice making the sticks more. Even Novoshna's new metal walls called to her, a physical barrier between her and the reaper who'd ruined her life. No one had to know about her magic there. She could start over.

"Only the finest silvers from Kemnuk," a woman shouted from her small stand of shimmering buckles, necklaces, and cuffs.

A girl with the same dimpled chin and arched brows as the woman pranced to Asheel and draped a bracelet across her wrist. "Stunning! Look at how the shine flatters your complexion."

Asheel shook her head and twisted her hand to slip out of the bracelet. Even if she had enough to buy jewelry, she didn't want silver and gold to attract more attention from the townspeople. It wasn't worth the extra strife.

The girl moved to Lana and looped a thin chain over her shoulders. "And look at how it draws the eye to your graceful frame. Exquisite!"

Lana also gently removed the jewelry and followed Asheel a few steps to a larger cart. A handful of people gathered around it where a merchant chortled to the sky like a wolf. "I told you Seshnia was all farmland," he yelled to the jewelry woman. A sparse row of sickles, shovels, and rakes leaned on the cart behind him. "They don't want none of your fancy weights." He shook his head and turned back to his customers. "Wife had a bet that she'd sell double than my stock if I let her bring her trinkets." Though his teasing seemed rude, a sweet berry scent wafted from him, no nefarious intents, just fondness for his family.

A farmer laughed with him while testing a sickle along a scrap of leather. "It's not like you have much stock to outsell her. And these prices. This is nearly double what my parents' tools cost."

"Prices rise. Inflation, my boy." The merchant shrugged. "And it's been a tough year. Most smiths went the easy route and sold their metals to Novoshna for that useless wall."

"So you think it won't keep the reaper out?" The farmer pressed the edge of the sickle with his thumb.

The merchant scratched at his beard. "I can't say I'm optimistic about it. The thing is impressive, though. I'll give them that. The panels," he grabbed a shovel and ran his hand over the back of the spade as if it were the wall, "so smooth not even the rodents can climb it, and so tall only the birds can fly over it."

"You've seen it?" Asheel interrupted the conversation. "The wall?"

The farmer jumped at her voice, glanced over his shoulder, then put the sickle back and bid the merchant safe travels home. Lana placed a hand on Asheel's stiffened shoulder, a reminder that she had a friend, that the farmer's avoidance didn't matter.

"Of course." The merchant straightened and chuckled, though his brows lowered as he watched the farmer walk away. "Only reason I'm here and not there is my ware. Didn't want to answer the officials as to why I didn't donate the metal to their wall, as if they weren't using some of it for their own use." Another Seshnian approached the cart, and the merchant turned his back on the girls.

"I can't imagine it," Lana said and led Asheel to the next cart with painted ceramics from the gulf city where Lana's parents were from. "Huge sheets of metal, feet thick and towering over the treetops . . . it sounds like something out of a fairytale." She smirked. "A land with impenetrable walls and secrets to hide."

Asheel rolled her eyes. "You realize people would say our gifts belong in fairytales too, right?"

"Not yours, they believe you every month. But mine maybe." Lana lifted a squat mug from the cart and traced its floral design with a finger. "A visitor at the care-home was talking about someone who sounded like me in Kemnuk. He could see auras. The visitor said they didn't believe him, thought he was crazy, seeing things, and considered shipping him to our care-home, but someone from Novoshna came to get him."

"I know what you see is real." Asheel touched her friend's hand. "It's not a fairytale." She could see Lana starting to spiral into memories of their peers teasing her around when Asheel's magic had been discovered. Asheel had the same moments, and they were so hard to pull out of. "So you don't think the wall will work?"

"I don't doubt the wall is massive." Lana put the mug back on its shelf. "I just think people are overexaggerating it."

If the wall really did keep the reaper out, how long would the fiery monster circle the city before returning to the Reaper Gate without a victim? If it worked, everyone would want to move there. Did they leave enough space to build more houses? Every few years, even Seshnia added another ring of streets to keep up with the demand for bigger, better, more modern homes, adding indoor plumbing and new gadgets. The farms of the outer circles invaded the surrounding forests, pushed outward by the new buildings. Maybe Novoshna would add to the wall when they ran out of space inside. Or have cheaper land outside the border, maybe land Asheel could eventually afford.

A stall of assorted objects from overseas had the largest crowd who watched the owner crank the bottom of an electric lantern.

". . . and after three minutes," she released the crank, flipped a switch on the side of the metal casing, and a bulb lit with a quavering glow, "you have enough charge for an hour of light. No fuel needed."

The crowd gasped at the ease. Electricity was a luxury only a few people had in Seshnia, but the option of a single, portable lantern could be what finally brought it in mass to their small town.

What other wonders were across the sea or even in their neighboring cities? Bitterness filled the back of Asheel's throat about being stuck in Seshnia, forced into her role, and the stench of rotten eggs drifted from her breath.

They finished their lap of the trader's stalls and stopped at the last one to taste samples of a traveler's jerky, salty and seasoned with hot peppers. Asheel coughed from the heat and stepped away from the cart, shaking her head and waving her hands, Lana and the trader laughing at her spice intolerance. While Lana tasted another flavor, Asheel glanced back at the stall with the electric lantern, trying to stifle the jealousy still rising. She wanted out, wanted to travel where no one knew of her curse. Wanted the freedom she felt while talking to the travelers who didn't know of her ties to the reaper.

By the lantern stall, a Seshnian Asheel had checked early that day chatted with two women, visitors she hadn't seen at any of the carts. Matching cropped jackets clung to their broad shoulders and Novoshna's emblem, three squares interlocked, embroidered the sleeves in a blocky design. The Seshnian nodded to whatever the women had said and pointed directly at Asheel, and the duo turned to meet her gaze and cross the sparse street to her.

What would Novish officials want with her? She hadn't left Seshnia in years, and she hadn't done anything much worse than vandalize the desk in her office . . . and maybe a little petty stealing and pranks, but nothing worth a visit from officials.

"Are you the one with the gift?" the taller of the women with crisscrossed, thin braids asked.

The shorter one rubbed her rosy, windchilled cheeks. "He said her name is Asheel."

Asheel stepped back and glanced over her shoulder where Lana had wandered to the far side of the jerky cart, but the taller woman held up her hands in peace.

"Wait," she said. "We just want to talk."

"I haven't done any—"

"No, no. We're here off the records, special request to investigate the rumors," the taller said. "I'm Maleen, and this is Vimi." Her many shoulder-length braids slid along her neck as she tilted her head toward her partner.

The odor from Maleen was both sweet and sour, a frustrating, sickly mixture that had Asheel craving for the ability to read minds to know what foulness touched Maleen's heart. Having orders off the record couldn't be good. Vimi's odor wasn't much better, so with the soured smell engulfing Asheel, caution was her best choice.

"What rumors?" Asheel crossed her arms.

Maleen lowered her hands and adjusted her sleeves. "We've had a recent surge in new citizens at the capitol, all of them bringing tales from their homes. Of course, by the time the stories reach the ears of the palace, we have no way to know how true their origins are."

"What rumors?" Asheel repeated but tried not to sound pushy with the officials. Her magic wasn't a secret in Seshnia, but she'd seen envy for her powers before and knew what greed could cause. She wanted people to forget her magic, so she wasn't about to offer explanations to a few who might not know.

"A girl with the reaper's eyes," Vimi said and arched an eyebrow, studying Asheel.

"And what? You're supposed to cut her eyes out for protection potions or something?" Asheel gestured to her face. "As you can see, my eyes are normal. You have the wrong girl."

Asheel turned to find Lana, who'd wandered back to the pottery stall.

"No, wait." Vimi touched Asheel's back but didn't grab her. "We're to protect you if anything."

Asheel paused. Protection wasn't a new idea for her either. The council didn't want her wandering into the forests alone, though she usually ignored their requests for guards.

"I don't have the 'reaper's eyes.'" She watched Lana, who had the "eye" if anyone did. "And I don't know anyone who does."

"Then why did that guy tell us you're the one?"

Asheel shrugged again.

"The queen will pay good coin for someone who can see who the reaper will kidnap."

Asheel turned back to the officials. "Pay?"

"As well as a spacious room and fantastic meals, of course."

Asheel chewed her bottom lip. A way to leave Seshnia without being homeless in a strange town. But if she were to move there because of her gift, that wouldn't exactly be starting over like she wanted, leaving the hatred of her community behind. It'd all happen again. She'd be treated like royalty, then spat on again within a year.

"We'd need proof, though." Maleen eyed Asheel's bland cloak. "We can't bring any random girl to the palace."

It was so close to what Asheel wanted, but if she gained as many enemies as she had in Seshnia, she couldn't imagine handling the hatred without her family and Lana to support her. With the way out of Seshnia suddenly so palpable, she didn't want to take it. But what if Novoshna didn't hate her? What if people in the big city could understand her magic better than her small town and could see her as more than a curse?

"Why would the palace want someone with evident ties to the reaper?" Asheel asked. "Haven't you heard the other rumors? That she marks his next victim for him?"

Maleen gave Asheel a knowing smile. "Maybe that's the rumor that won her an invitation to the palace."

"So the palace wants a weapon." Asheel refused to be used like that even if she could control her magic.

Vimi shook her head. "The palace needs every protection it can find."

"Why? What about the wall?"

"The queen doesn't trust it."

"So the king wants to make the queen more comfortable?" If the job were only checking the royal family, Asheel could handle that. The likelihood of one of them being taken out of everyone in Novoshna was miniscule.

"The king is gone," Vimi whispered, glancing around them.

"Vimi!" Maleen clapped her hand over her partner's mouth.

Vimi jerked away from Maleen's hand and rolled her eyes. "Relax. She's obviously the girl we're looking for."

"We're on strict orders—"

"And I'm sure the queen will be happier that we brought her the girl rather than tiptoed around the truth. People will find out soon enough. There were witnesses."

Maleen lowered her hand. "I'm not sticking up for you again."

Vimi turned back to Asheel. "The reaper got him last night."

Asheel's certainty that the royal family would be safe shattered. If she'd warned them the king was next, then they'd have blamed her just like those in Seshnia. "Why haven't we heard about it?" she asked and glanced to the celebrating Seshnians who'd started returning to their tables. The only sadness that touched them was the general dread for their own reaping night.

"We left Novoshna before dawn at the queen's order. I'm sure the news will get here in the next day or so." Vimi tugged at her jacket and the sour smell stung Asheel's nose again. "All we need is some proof that you're the girl with the reaper's eyes, and then we can escort your back to the palace."

"What kind of rumors have you heard to make you think those powers will be any help?" Asheel asked.

"Like you said, we've heard you can mark the reaper's target," Vimi said and cut Asheel off when she opened her mouth, "and we've been told even if that's not the case, that maybe the girl can be taught how to use her magic like that."

"By whom?" Asheel scoffed. No one in Seshnia could teach her, and she couldn't expect any different at the palace.

"Our gifted." Maleen joined the conversation again. "We only have two—wait, three in the palace, one's in training. They're very different from your supposed talents, but I'm sure they can help you refine your abilities."

The palace was collecting people with magic. A collection of people with abilities like hers, who could help her. Questions sputtered on her lips.

"You'd be respected like them, held in high regard, given lavish accommodations." The sour part of Maleen's scent unfurled almost visibly and hit Asheel hard enough to know she was lying. Asheel covered her nose.

Vimi elbowed Maleen in the ribs and shook her head. "You'll be feared but protected," Vimi said. "The royal advisors—the other people with magic, we call them advisors—have a whole palace wing to themselves with their own servants."

"Do they get harassed when they go into the city?" Asheel asked.

"No, that's never—"

Vimi cut Maleen off. "They stay in the palace. They're too valuable to let wander, but every necessity is provided for and it's very spacious."

While Vimi rambled about the palace's glory, Asheel closed her eyes and took shallow breaths to keep from gagging from the sour smell. She'd never be allowed outside. She'd always be surrounded by foul odors if she decided to live in the palace. Even if she had the whole wing to herself, she'd be no more than a prisoner in a fancy room. And all of that away from her family, maybe never seeing them again. And then what if she couldn't expand her ability like the queen wanted, to place the stench on someone else for the reaper to take? How long would the queen give her to learn more control? Would she be hung or beheaded the moment she failed?

"So," Maleen placed her hand on Vimi's arm to cut her off, "all we need now is for you to show us your magic."

Asheel opened her eyes, and Maleen and Vimi watched her expectantly. "How?" Even if she decided not to go to the palace, she'd still like to gain more control over it. Maybe be able to turn it off sometimes. "How do your 'advisors' prove it?"

"Do your eyes glow when you use it?" Vimi asked.

Asheel shook her head. "It has nothing to do with my eyes. How did the others prove it?" she repeated.

Maleen looked at Vimi and gestured toward Asheel, but Vimi grimaced and pulled her lips into her mouth. Then she gritted her teeth and blew out in a sweeter breath that stifled Maleen's sourness.

"I guess trust has to start with one of us. The oldest advisor has magic based on hearing." Vimi tapped her ear. "He can know what you're thinking if the thoughts are directed toward him. He learned how to hear beyond that though."

Maleen grabbed Vimi's wrist and shook her head. "Don't reveal everything."

"What?" Vimi raised an eyebrow toward Asheel. "She's obviously the girl. If she has magic too, she can do just as much as them." She turned back to Asheel. "The other can compel you to do what she wants." She shook her head and ran a hand through her light brown hair, lifting it and letting it fall limply back in place. "She doesn't do much directly, but her potions and tonics work wonders. Just don't ask what's in them or you'll never want one. I don't really understand the trainee's magic, but he's been close to the queen since he arrived."

So the others had different abilities than she did. It sounded like something they actively chose to do rather than how the smells just came to Asheel. And the queen expected Asheel to be locked away in a wing of the palace with those disturbing abilities?

"No way." Asheel stepped back from the officials, her feet skidding across a few pebbles. "Live with people who can control me against my will and know what I'm thinking? That's terrifying!"

A pungent stench of manure wafted from Vimi as she reached toward Asheel. Her brows were lowered and eyes widened. "They're not bad people." She took a step forward while Asheel took another back. "Wait! What would convince you to come with us?"

"Nothing." Asheel stepped back again, and Lana ran back to her side.

"Come on," Lana said and gave the officials an apologetic smile. "The skit is starting."

Asheel looked from the officials to Lana grinning at her side. Even if the palace didn't sound miserable, it didn't have Lana. But what if Lana went too? Was that an option? Maybe there *was* something that could convince her to go to the palace. She wouldn't reveal her friend's magic, but she needed to know how open the invitation was.

"What if I change my mind in the future?" she asked. "What if in a few months I decide I'd like to go to Novoshna and try to use my ability for the queen? Is this a now or never deal?"

Vimi's frown flattened slightly, and she looked at Maleen whose eyebrows had raised. She shrugged and Vimi nodded slowly as if to her own thoughts rather than Asheel's question.

"It's not now or never."

"You don't seem certain." Asheel studied their scents, but their response didn't seem like a lie.

"I'm certain enough," Maleen said. "The queen didn't mention it, but she'd welcome a gifted soul anytime, even if the king hadn't just been taken. You can think about it tonight and give us your answer tomorrow. We'll be at the inn for a few days."

"My answer is no. At least for now." Asheel grabbed Lana's hand to stop her tugging at her arm. "But I can't say for how I'll feel years from now. A lot can change."

"And a lot can change in months," Maleen said and placed a hand on Vimi's shoulder. "We'll tell her majesty that you're still considering, and we'll come back in a few months, four or five, to see if you've changed your mind. Is that long enough?"

Asheel nodded. She didn't really think she'd change her mind in only months, but Maleen was right. A lot could change in months, weeks, even from day to day.

Teachers calling to the kids to start the skit dispersed the crowd around the traders' stalls, and Asheel pulled Lana away from the officials.

"You should have lied—" Maleen's voice faded into the Feast's noises as Asheel wove back through the people.

Lana glanced over her shoulder while Asheel lead her back to their table.

"What was that?" she asked.

Asheel chewed her lip again. "An invitation to Novoshna's palace."

"The palace? Why?"

"They want my gift to protect them."

"Did you tell them it doesn't do that?"

Asheel shrugged. "Kind of. And they still want me to go."

"But you declined?"

"I declined." Asheel grasped her friend's hand tighter.

CHAPTER 3

A sheel's dad, Kee, finally returned from his soliciting at the other tables, his basket empty and a platter of sweets in his hands.

"One for everyone," he said and stretched onto his toes to peck his wife, nearly a foot taller than him, on her cheek. Willa snatched a pastry while he set the platter on the table. "Save one for Coby."

Coby was near the Farsons' table playing a hand slap game with Berice, their teacher calling to them, while Kady pouted beside them. It was so unfair. Kady was tiny and had the sweetest face. What kind of selfish desires had seeped into her little heart to make her the reaper's next victim? Coby would be devastated when his crush vanished in the night.

How different would this night be if they didn't know Kady was next? Asheel could imagine her laughing by Coby, creating a night filled with joyful last memories instead of shaking with fear with her parents hovering over her every move. Maybe leaving for the palace would be for the best.

The music quieted, and the dancing teens huddled around a few tables near the center of the gathering. Then the younger kids, including Coby, followed their teachers to the center, and the musicians modulated their songs, preparing for the skit. The kids dug through baskets and pulled out cloaks with jagged spikes and droopy wings, hats with horns and wiggly antennae, shoes and gloves covered with claws and tentacles. They circled around the stage, facing their audience.

After chasing down a few of the higher energy children, a balding teacher with a booming voice shouted to the crowd. "Many, many years ago, longer than our history can recount, our world was ravaged by monsters."

The kids roared, held their frightening limbs in the air, and slashed at the crowd. A few fell into a fit of giggles, and Coby snarled, his missing teeth anything but intimidating. His brown curls stuck out from a fuzzy hat. Asheel dropped her gaze to her hands clenched together on the table. Kady stood beside Coby, unmoving, shivering.

"What's wrong with the Farson girl?" Kee asked. "She looks like she got a whipping."

Willa whispered in his ear, and his eyebrows rose with a glance of pity at Asheel who dropped her head to the table.

"It's not your fault," Lana whispered and looped her arm through Asheel's to pull her out of her guilt.

"The Farsons don't think that." Asheel nodded toward their table where the mother dabbed at her tears with a handkerchief.

Lana hugged Asheel's arm tighter and rubbed her shoulder, but she found herself watching the fire more than the skit to avoid looking at Kady.

The balding teacher described the monsters that used to torment the land, while the children ran around the stage when their monster was called, then he continued through the history of their country, Loshgow, and how the great Cay, a man from Novoshna with immense power, sacrificed himself to lock away the monsters.

"All that remains from that time is the Reaper Gate. We respect it, and we thank it for its protection." The teacher bowed, not mentioning the terror of the reaping night that would start in a few hours.

An older child in a red skull mask wove between the tables. He returned to the center with the rest of the kids who all swarmed him. A few children giggled again while they piled on the older child. Then the skit was over, and the kids removed their costumes and returned to their families.

"You did so good!" Willa grabbed Coby in a tight hug, burying him in her wavy black hair that matched Asheel's.

Coby escaped his mother's arms and darted around her to Asheel and Lana. "Did you see I got to be a cat monster this time?" he asked.

"You did great!" Lana patted his head.

Asheel hugged him and praised him too. His curls tickled her nose and smelled of smoke, sweet pastries, and all of the innocence of the world.

"I think Kady's mad at me," he mumbled to Asheel.

"No, curly." Asheel pulled his wool cap back onto his head. "No, she's mad at me." Asheel might have been burdened with all the hatred of the town, but she wouldn't let Coby blame himself.

She glanced to the table where the Farsons had been and caught a glimpse of their backs as they left the feast.

CHAPTER 4

After dousing the Seshnians she'd identified as endangered with perfumes from boiled flowers, Asheel slipped the opaque bottle into her pocket while no one was looking, a stolen payment for dealing with foul Seshnians, and climbed the steps to the council building's roof. The other two spotters hadn't arrived yet, giving Asheel a chance to breathe in the refreshing wind. It whipped her hair in a chaotic display that matched her warring thoughts and smelled like pine and approaching rain. Behind a thin cloud, the moon glowed like a halo.

Despite knowing the perfume did nothing to hide the odor that called the reaper to them, Asheel patted the remaining drops from the bottle onto her own skin, mixing her noxious fumes, like rotten fruit, with the flowery scent. It was a pointless effort just like the incense that did nothing to hide the smells of the endangered. But a little reprieve was better than none, and she rubbed perfume residue along her upper lip.

"Hey, don't put too much of that on." Another spotter, the oldest by a decade, climbed through the roof hatch. He had some breathing troubles and couldn't fight more than a minute before collapsing in a fit of coughs, but the eccentric career advisor still let him join. More than an arm's length from Asheel, he sneezed, which flung his long black bangs into his face. "You're polluting my air."

"We're outside. It can't be that bad," Asheel said. She held the bottle upside down and shook it. "It's too late, anyway."

He sneezed again. "You knew I was spotting with you tonight. Why did you have to use the whole bottle?"

"It was only a few drops."

The spotter coughed then held his hand against his chest while he wheezed. "Just stay on your side of the roof." He pulled his jacket around him and stomped toward the opposite side.

Asheel walked to her assigned corner, reminding herself to be sympathetic. Everything she did made everyone angry. She just wanted everything to be good, be perfect, but that wasn't how life worked. Couldn't people see how hard she was trying?

Would the same career in Novoshna's palace be any different? The officials had said something about her doing more with her magic. How? It wasn't a conscious decision. The smells drifted off everyone, and the worst smelling people were taken. If she couldn't even turn off her magic, how was she supposed to learn how to force it onto someone to mark them for the reaper?

Her post looked toward plateaus that flattened the mountainsides where Seshnia's herds grazed. Across the street, the doorframes of the market, freshly painted the previous week, became muted greys in the darkness. The market had been wooden stands with cloth awnings until a few months ago. After back-to-back tornadoes destroyed the stands multiple times, the council voted to build sturdier outlets for the shops.

The candlemaker had saved their tattered awning, woven

purple and yellow stripes that blended with the night's other greys, and hung it above their door as a reminder of the community coming together to build the new market. A loose shred of the fabric fluttered in the wind, waving at Asheel like another mocking Seshnian.

Asheel *tsk*ed at the fabric and nudged a scrap of debris off the edge of the council building where it fell in a satisfying plummet. She set the empty perfume bottle on the edge and considered kicking it to see how far it'd go, but the hatch opened again.

"Sorry. Sorry." A volunteer with a flower tucked behind her ear climbed through the hatch and left it open. "I'm not late!" The volunteer glanced across the quiet expanse between Asheel and the other spotter. "Cheery bunch you two are."

"This isn't a post-feast party. It's serious," the spotter shouted from across the roof and pointed to the empty side. "Get to your post." He stood on the corner that faced where the reaper usually descended the mountain.

"Sorry!" the volunteer yelled back. She jogged to her spot and plopped down like a bird in her nest.

Asheel, left to herself, fiddled with her dagger while staring into the night. Waiting for the reaper was all that remained. He rarely approached the town from her side, but it was possible. Near the edge of one of the plateaus, a flicker of a shepherd's fire kept catching her eye. She'd have to say something to the council about the distraction. Maybe the shepherds forgot what night it was. How did they track the days during their extended time away from the town?

Her thoughts circled back to a job at the palace and fantasies about getting anything she asked for if she could control her magic. She studied the streets and shops below her imagining herself in a palace window watching a population who didn't fear her.

No one walked in the streets on reaping nights. Most people hid in their homes with their doors locked tight, probably lying awake worrying about their family, and anyone not in their house hid throughout the council building, prepared to fight for the endangered, or waited on horseback on the outskirts of town, ready to chase the reaper when he succeeded.

She squinted through the darkness until she found her dad's incense shop, a few shopfronts down from the candlemaker. He'd said the inside was bigger than it seemed with rows and rows of fragrances, but Asheel hadn't visited it yet. She would. Eventually.

The candlemaker's tattered awning fluttered again, and Asheel shook her head then focused back on the mountains to watch for the reaper's glowing form. Minutes felt like hours. Her eyelids grew heavy, and the frogs croaking in the distance became a lullaby.

The oldest spotter's shout startled her from a half-asleep trance. "He's coming!"

Asheel jogged across the roof to get a glimpse. Trailing down the mountainside, the pinprick glow of the reaper's fiery footsteps flickered, broken sporadically by tree cover, and at the end of the trail, approaching the town, the terrifying monster ran with inhuman speed. With a wheeze, the spotter stumbled past Asheel and dove down the hatch.

"The reaper is at the edge of town and moving fast! Get ready!" His call echoed down the line of guards, each passing the alert to the next.

The reaper was in a full run by the time he reached the front of the council building. The recently replaced front doors splintered from his impact with a crack that echoed through the night and shook the building. Guards shouted inside, and Asheel could imagine the destruction the reaper ravaged.

The other woman on the roof, the volunteer, shrieked. "Is he always this aggressive?"

"No," Asheel shook her head. "Sometimes it almost seems like a game to him, but he's rushing through this tonight."

"Maybe he knows about the traps." The volunteer quivered beside Asheel.

"Of course he knows. We always set traps."

More shouts erupted and a shriek gurgled to an abrupt end, followed by more shouts. Smoke plumed out the shattered door.

"We have to get off the roof!" Asheel shoved the volunteer down the hatch. "Hurry! Head to the back exit."

They both coughed while climbing down the stairs, and Asheel's eyes burned. Smoke filled the building, dimming the lights, but Asheel had spent enough time in there to know the layout and dragged the volunteer down the corridors, straight for the rear doors.

As planned, the guards who'd been placed there had left to help with the fight when the reaper hadn't come through their way. Asheel pushed the door, but it didn't budge, and she squinted through the thickening smoke to find the wood barricade still lowered into its slots.

"Help me!" Asheel shouted to the volunteer who coughed and rubbed her eyes. Asheel grabbed her shoulders and pulled her to the door. "Help me lift this. Pull it straight up, got it?"

They tugged and the barricade lifted slightly, but the volunteer fell into a coughing fit before it cleared the slots. Each breath brought in more of the haze, and with her sides heaving, Asheel crouched to leverage the beam with her shoulder. They tried again, and the barricade shifted out of its slots with a groan. Still coughing, the volunteer opened the door and ran out with the smoke billowing around her. Asheel, kneeling on the entryway, gasped at the clearing air. She was almost out of this mess. She'd never help with the reaping night again. She'd leave Seshnia and those expectations behind her.

Screaming pierced through the corridor, and Asheel turned just as a glowing figure skidded around the farthest corner and into the hall. The reaper. And he held Kady, a tiny shadow in the smoke.

She beat his face with her little freckled fists while he struggled to grab her arms and ducked his head from her strikes.

In those few seconds, Asheel ran through her options. Something inside her screamed for her to run out the door and to the inn where the officials waited for her, to flee into the night with them, and another something in her heart yelled that this was her chance. She braced herself and pulled out her knife. This was it. She'd finally be some real help.

When the reaper, still struggling with Kady, was feet away, Asheel lunged and collided into him, knocking them to the ground and shoving her blade between his ribs. Her weight pinned the reaper, and Kady skidded across the floorboards with a pained sob.

"Run, Kady!" Asheel screamed, and the little girl clambered up and darted back into the smokey hall.

This was the closest Asheel had ever seen the reaper, a frightening array of scorched features, shriveled scraps of skin that clung to his cracked bones glowing with fire. The smoke that swirled around him, creeping from his bones, filled out a mottled leather vest and pants. Black coals in his eye sockets stared at her, and the scorched bits of flesh around his eyes lifted in a look of disbelief. A shimmering sliver of blue smoke wove between his teeth like stitches holding his jaw shut, and tendrils of smoke danced from his scalp and dropped ash to the floor. The fire from his bones, uncomfortably hot, lapped at Asheel's skin, blistering her arms where they touched his shoulders and searing her clothes, but she still pinned him to the ground.

He sighed before shoving Asheel off him. She slid across the floor, her back crashing against the doorframe shooting numb tingling down her legs, and she screamed from the pain. The reaper jumped up and darted back down the hall, and in seconds, he returned through the smoke with whimpering Kady thrown over his shoulder, the knife still jutting from his ribs.

Asheel couldn't move, and half her body blocked the door. She screamed and struggled and tried to pull herself out of the way. Finally, she got one leg jerked under her and sat up against the frame.

He paused in front of her, the smokey wisps from his skull floating across his shoulders, and she scrambled farther along the wall.

"Just go!" she screamed in the reaper's face. "I don't care anymore."

The reaper tilted his head, and instead of running away with his capture, he bent, studied Asheel, and grabbed her wrist. His bony hand seared her while his gaze passed between her and Kady.

"Help me!" Kady screamed. Her large, teary eyes pleaded.

Asheel clenched her teeth, her own stench strengthening with her anger at the situation. Would the reaper take her, too?

Guards shouted and coughed and turned down the corridor.

The reaper dropped Asheel's hand and tore his gaze from her to glare at the guards, Kady yelling for help from his shoulder. After one more glance at Asheel, he ran out the door and disappeared into the night with Kady's sobs echoing through the streets. Most of the guards ran straight out of the building into the fresh air. A few went back down the corridor either to help the remaining people escape or put out whatever fire the reaper had started, but one squat woman stopped in front of Asheel.

"You didn't try to stop him?" YoAne yelled over the chaos, inches from Asheel's face.

Tears brimmed Asheel's eyes. "I tried," she whispered. She'd failed yet again. "My knife did nothing!" she shouted back.

"I wish he'd have taken you. You're just as bad as he is." YoAne kicked Asheel's leg then ran out of the building with the others.

Asheel winced from the bruising setting in over the aches from practice. She'd tried, and as usual, all it got her was being yelled at. Tears fell down her cheeks and onto her sweat-soaked shirt.

A muffled cough drew Asheel's attention back to the corridor, and Stevart emerged from the haze while pressing a cloth to his mouth.

"Are you okay?" he asked with one eye shut tightly and the other squinted. The smoke at the entryway had dissipated into the night, and he used the cloth from his mouth to wipe his forehead.

Asheel shrugged. "I don't know."

"Are you hurt?"

"A little." She dropped her eyes to her lap.

Stevart leaned against the other side of the doorframe, sweat dripping down his amber cheeks. "Can you stand?"

Asheel didn't look up while she drew her legs under her and lifted herself using the doorframe. Although shaky and still dizzy, she seemed stable enough. The jolt from hitting her back had faded to a weird buzz.

Stevart coughed into his cloth then wiped his face again. "Go on home. I think we're done here for tonight."

"What about the fire?" Asheel glanced back into the building. She needed to help with something. Needed distraction from the fumes that reeked off her and to feel like less of a failure.

"They got it under control. The records room is a total loss. That's what caused all this smoke. The rest of the building should be fine." He jerked his head out the door. "Go on. There's nothing left to do here. Get some sleep."

After ducking her head and ensuring she wouldn't fall when she let go of the doorframe, Asheel limped from the building and into the night alone. Most of the chaotic shouting had died down, and she strained her ears to listen to the horsemen. If they'd been able to catch the reaper, she'd know by now. She kept her eyes on the pebbly street while she walked. A few volunteers also heading home passed her, but none of them said anything to her or even to each other. No one needed to. They'd all failed.

The sounds of the night grew quieter and quieter, everything going back to normal, until Asheel reached her house and stumbled inside. Her parents, waiting at their table, sat straighter when she limped in.

"Is it over?" her dad asked.

Asheel nodded. They didn't ask if the reaper got the child or who he took. The details didn't matter; the result was always the same. Her mom held out a cup of water, and Asheel drank it to cool the burning the smoke had left behind. Her parents stood silently, and Kee walked to their bedroom while Willa examined Asheel's seared sleeves.

"Are you okay?"

She pulled up her sleeves to check her burns, which had bubbled into small blisters.

"Keep those clean, but they'll heal fine." Willa pulled her into a stale cake-scented hug. "I'm glad you're safe," she mumbled into Asheel's hair. "Go sleep. I'll wake you before the council meeting."

Willa followed Kee, and Asheel put her cup in the sink, then slipped into her shared bedroom, trying not to wake Coby.

He had his covers pulled over his head, but a few of his brown curls peaked out from under the blanket. His bed was against the wall opposite the door, a clear view to their home's entrance, and hers was in the corner on the other side with a tall cabinet between them. She walked lightly to her side of the room, but when a floorboard squeaked under her, Coby sat up with a scream.

"Shh," Asheel hushed him and hurried to his side. "It's just me." She climbed into his bed and hugged him.

"I thought you were the reaper coming to get me," Coby whimpered and hid his face in her soiled clothes. She twirled a finger in one of his curls while his shoulders relaxed. "Did you get him?"

She shook her head and the tears pooled again. She'd opened the door for his escape, not that the barricade would have stopped him, but maybe it would have slowed him enough for the guards to catch up.

"Was it Kady?" Coby sat up to look at his sister's face.

She nodded, and Coby pursed his lips together. His brows pushed low over his eyes, and he leaned back into Asheel's hug, wrapping his arms tightly around her like his precious, tiny limbs could protect her from more pain, like they could shield her from the memory of Kady's screams now seared into her waking thoughts.

Asheel sniffed to keep her nose from dripping but tensed as a new scent hit her nose.

"You smell like smoke," Coby said into her shirt.

Still stiff with her arms holding Coby, she bent her head down to his soft curls and sniffed again, lightly so that he wouldn't notice. A whiff of dead leaves. The hint of a corpse. She held Coby tighter. It couldn't be happening, but the stench only her magic could sense was unmistakable.

CHAPTER 5

The scent of Coby's heart, newly touched by anger and pain, had saturated the house by the time Asheel woke up. His bed was empty, but it reeked. His covers lay in a pile, and his pillow was lumpy from his tossing and turning. She straightened the sheets, trying to conceal the stench, but it was so strong that her parents surely could smell it. No. No one ever did. Asheel was alone in her curse, and her mom wasn't aware of the new danger.

Willa looked up from where she sat on the couch with her mortar and a pile of lavender sprigs. "I was about to wake you. You still have some time before the meeting." She nodded to the kitchen then turned back to her incense making. "Grab some lunch."

Asheel stood in the doorway about to ask if her mom could smell the fumes from Coby, but she snapped her mouth shut. She'd decided she was done with everything to do with the reaper, and this could be the first step. She could ignore the smell and save her family from worrying. And the stench was fresh enough on Coby that it could fade. The newer the odor, the less permanent it was. So determined not to say anything, she retrieved dried fruits and a slice of leftover lamb and joined her mother on the couch.

Willa, breathing heavy from grinding the lavender, glanced up from the bowl of ground powder. "When you're done, start on the orange rinds. They're dried enough now."

Asheel chewed the fruit and shook her head. The second step in leaving it all behind. No more incense. "Not today. Dad will say I've blessed it again." Her resolution wavered when her mom raised her eyebrows. Asheel slouched, motioned in front of her with the fruit, and mimicked his squeaky voice. "Look at this citrus blend blessed by my daughter with the reaper's nose. This batch promises to protect your family on reaping night." She shook her head quickly, still impersonating him. "Oh, the triple cost? That's just to compensate her for the energy she expended infusing her blessing in it."

Willa smacked her with a lavender sprig, and a few of the dried blossoms fell to the cushion between them. "Stop it."

Asheel shied away and chewed on the lamb. "I don't want to be a part of it anymore. It's lying."

"It encourages people to buy it."

"So earning an extra coin makes lying okay?"

Willa didn't respond. The stones, grinding together, crushing the lavender, filled the silence.

"It's using me," Asheel said when the lying part didn't disturb her mom. "It's no better than the council making me sniff the townspeople." She let her hands fall to her lap with the last bite of lamb. That was all anyone ever saw in her, a tool, a link to the reaper and nothing else. Even Novoshna officials had sought out her magic. "All I'm good for is being used."

"That's not true." Willa looked down at her grinding and her black waves blocked her face, hiding her expression. "Help me with this and quit being dramatic about it."

Asheel shoved the last of the lamb in her mouth and stood. "No. I'm done being used." She went to the door. She didn't know what other career she could possibly do—all she knew was incense and her magic—but she knew she wanted a say in it.

"Wait," Willa said and stood to follow her.

"No, I need a break." Asheel jerked the door open and left the house.

People milled through the streets again, everyone getting on with their lives and happy their families were safe. A few people greeted Asheel, habitual pleasantries that didn't require a response, which she ignored. Laughter erupted from children, relieved to live another month. They wove through the people, chasing after each other and running errands for their parents.

People gossiped, bartered, and joked, relief making even the most mundane tasks jovial. Asheel watched her feet and scuffed them across the pebbles while she walked. She didn't deserve to join in their relief.

"You!" a lady yelled from the door of the glass shop, startling Asheel. The Farson mother charged toward her. "This is your fault! You chose Kady to be taken." She stomped to a halt in front of Asheel. "What did my family ever do to you?"

Asheel held her hands up, palms forward, instantly defensive. "It's not like that. I don't pick them."

"Tell the truth." The Farson mother stepped forward, too close, her noxious fumes more bitter than they'd been the day before. She was at risk too. Another damaged heart because of Asheel. The mother sneered at her. "You have a deal with that monster, don't you?"

Asheel gritted her teeth, remembering what Lana said about this being the way the Farson mother grieved. She took a deep breath and spoke to the ground. "If I had a deal with the reaper, it'd be not to have my magic."

While the Farson mother sputtered, Asheel stepped back to continue her trudge through town, but before she could retreat, the mother reared back and slapped Asheel hard on the cheek. Asheel skirted to the side, heat building up her neck and down her limbs.

"I didn't choose her. I don't control it," Asheel repeated. "What do you want from me?"

"I want my daughter back." The woman shook with anger or sadness, probably both, maybe frustration. "You cursed my family somehow, and I want her back."

A crowd gathered around them. Heads peeked out of windows and a few parents ushered the kids away from the scene, and over the Farson mother's shoulder, barely recognizable through the many faces surrounding them, the two Novoshna officials stared at the interaction, their eyes wide. Maleen had her hand reached out as if to push through the crowd, but Vimi had her hand on her shoulder, holding her back.

The Farson father came out of the glass shop and grabbed his wife's arm. "Margy, this isn't right." He glanced at Asheel with a hint of hatred in his eyes and continued speaking to his wife. "Leave the girl alone. She's just a child, too."

A child? Asheel clenched her fists. If they thought she was a child, they had even less of an excuse to treat her this way, but she turned without another word and charged through the crowd.

Down another street, people jumped out of her way while she stomped by, and Asheel marched straight into the council's complex and to the meeting room. It still smelled of smoke, just a few doors down from where the records had burned.

Some of the council members sat around a table and wore an array of gold-rimmed spectacles, high-collared shirts, and expressions ranging from perpetually frustrated to unconcerned acceptance. Four stood and chatted along the sides, Stevart, two women whose names she couldn't remember, and the youngest council member who everyone called Uncle. YoAne side-eyed her as she entered. One member, Kayn, the eccentric career advisor, paced at the far end of the room, talking to himself while braiding his long brown beard.

Asheel slid low in the chair farthest away from the head council members, near where Kayn paced, and crossed her arms. She wanted away from this, but her only clear escape, Novoshna's palace, was out of the question. She wanted away from it all, the expectations, the hateful people, being forced to use her magic when all she wanted was to turn it off. She wanted a different role, a job that she could learn and be good at, something that didn't make her hated. Her anger at everything pooled as frustrated tears in the corners of her eyes, but she blinked them away and stared at painted motifs on the stone walls to stop thinking about it. Long-gone elderly stared back at her with flat gazes, never changing, stuck in retired fashions. Stenciled names below their faces held no meaning to her with their legacies forgotten to time.

Eventually, the room quieted, and the members took their seats. Kayn sat beside her while combing out his beard, and Stevart sat near the head of the table by Uncle. He gave her a slight wave then turned his attention to the chairman.

"We only have a few items to discuss for this week," the chairman said and listed off the town projects. His voice, monotone and gravelly, lulled the room, and only a few of the higher members had any input.

Asheel chewed on the edge of a fingernail and stared at a knot in the table in front of her, then traced it while considering what she could do to make her life better. Nothing sounded appealing. Every time she considered leaving, either as a traveling merchant or as a "royal advisor" using her ability for the queen, her heart would ache for her family and Lana. She didn't want to leave the place she called home. Even with the town's hatred, she knew what to expect with them. It was a comfortable familiarity. Barely comfortable, but comfortable enough.

But something had to change. The Farson mother's rage had broken her. Frustrated tears burned her eyes again, and she blinked them back to submission.

But what other choice did she have if she didn't want to leave Seshnia? Was her destiny to be the Seshnians' outlet for their own pain? Why couldn't it be something more fulfilling? Lana was destined to care for those nearing the end of their lives, and she was good at it. What was Asheel destined for if not to use her magic? Selling incense with false promises of safety and blessings? She chewed her lip. She didn't want to trade her certain promises of who'd be taken for false promises of who could be safe.

The chairman tapped his paper, sighed, and looked over his spectacles at the room. "Last night was another tragedy. Despite our best efforts, another one of us was stolen from our grasp, this time a child too young." A choked silence fell over the room. No one shifted in their seats. "We have to find a way to stop that monster," the chairman continued, "and I need everyone's help to figure out our next plan. What went wrong and what can we try next time?"

Asheel slid lower in her seat. She'd helped the reaper escape by opening the door. If Asheel and the volunteer had waited on the roof, they would have been fine. The fire wasn't as big as she'd thought, but she couldn't have known that if they didn't leave their posts.

"We'd had him in the cage," Stevart said, "but he bent and broke the wires like they were straw. We can't use hardwood planks because he'd just light them on fire and would still be able to break through them regardless."

"And as usual," Uncle added, "a spear in his back and an arrow to his skull didn't even slow him down."

"I don't know how else we can catch him, and we can't kill him." Stevart scratched his jaw in thought. "Maybe if we douse him . . . no, he appears from the ocean at one of the islands. Or could we maybe smother him, bury him alive with a landslide or in a pit?"

The council discussed if either of those plans were plausible, but Asheel stayed silent.

Kayn, usually silent as well, even added to the talk. "The reaper moves like smoke," he said. "We cannot smother smoke unless we smother the source."

"The Reaper Gate?" the chairman asked. "You're saying we somehow destroy the Gate he lives in?"

"No." Kayn leaned onto his elbows. "That'd be impossible, and who knows what else lives in there that we might unleash. If it truly removed all the monsters from our world, how do we know destroying it won't bring them back? I'm saying stopping him isn't what we should focus on. We should focus on cleansing the town of the stench that calls him to us."

Asheel sat up a little. Could they really cleanse the stained? People's smells shifted with their hearts, but when the rotten scents signaled their fate as the reaper's victim, not just in danger, that never vanished. If they could cleanse the stained, why hadn't they figured it out already? She wanted to ask Kayn what he meant, but the council members were arguing about how that was impossible and why it wouldn't work.

Uncle slapped his palm on the table, startling the growing discussion into silence. "We slow him down enough and get close enough to slice off his head. Nothing can survive decapitation!"

That drew a few laughs, but a lot of the members agreed it could work until one of the elders, the devastated records keeper, mentioned a previous generation had tried that with no success. The reaper could survive it. They'd moved on from Kayn's suggestion so quickly, but Kayn slumped in his seat instead of bringing it up again.

The chairman nodded along with the back-and-forth until he put his hand up to silence them. "Did we discover any new weaknesses?" he asked. "Any at all that could slow him down?"

The council members looked at each other, shrugged, shook their heads.

YoAne pointed her thumb over her shoulder at Asheel's end of the table. "Asheel had a moment alone with him last night." She didn't have the dignity to look Asheel's way. "Maybe she saw something."

The chairman turned to her and stared over his spectacles. "Asheel? You were face-to-face with the reaper?"

Asheel gulped. This was it. This was when they would find out she opened the door for him to escape. But she couldn't speak. She couldn't face their judgment. She dropped her eyes from their expectant gazes.

"Please don't involve me," she whispered, head down.

"I'm sorry?" the chairman said. "Speak up. You have to tell us what you saw."

"I saw nothing new, okay?" Her hair slid over her face to hide her from their stares, a movement she realized she got from her mother when she didn't like the subject. The reaper's coal eyes somehow showing expressions and his glowing bones with Kady over his shoulder, it was something she didn't want to relive. "The same as all of you. I stabbed him, and he kept running as if nothing happened."

The conversation passed her while guilt at letting the reaper free and anger at YoAne for bringing it up flitted from her body in invisible fumes. Kayn was right; finding a cure for the stench that touched everyone was the best option.

When they couldn't come to an agreement on what to do next, the chairman finally flipped to the last page of his stack. "We have a new item to vote on this week. The economy team proposes using Asheel's magic as an export to bring in more income for the town," he read from the paper. "Kemnuk would be a good trial location to see how interested other cities might be."

Asheel's head shot up, and Kayn jumped beside her, startled. They wanted to sell her ability for the town? Would she see a single coin of what income that brought in? That was a worse option than living as a prisoner in Novoshna's palace.

"I'm not doing that," she said. "I don't want to be exploited."

The chairmen frowned at her. "If the council votes to approve, you have to."

She had to? She didn't have to do anything. She didn't have to tell any of them how much they reeked, even if that meant the reaper would come for her for her selfishness. The council, the queen, everyone always expecting everything from her and planning her life for her, it was too much.

She shoved her chair back and stood with her fists clenched at her sides. "I can't!" she shouted, broken by the weight of expectation, broken from dealing with her mom, the Farson mother, and now the council without reprieve. "You already make me sniff the disgusting town every month, and it only makes everyone involved miserable. It doesn't help! It doesn't stop him. Exploiting me will make me a curse to another town." She'd never spoken out like this in the council meetings, and the relief of finally releasing it energized her. She jabbed a finger at the table to emphasize her words and kept going while she had their attention. "I'm twenty and I can decide what life I want to live. That life doesn't include the Reaper Guard or sniffing people or even the council. I'm done!"

Asheel turned her back on them, strode out of the room, and charged out of the council's complex without her coat. She fled past the glass shop where she'd been slapped earlier and followed the curves of the streets, passing the eateries, the shops, the residences. The buildings became blurs of browns and faded yellows, and the painted awnings streaked into rainbows. Clouds coated the sky, dark and ominous, but Asheel didn't stop until she reached the wheat fields of Seshnia's outer rings where she ducked into a clump of trees and dropped to her knees. She pounded her fists against the dirt and yelled out her rage and anger.

Why was the fate of everyone her responsibility? What did they expect her to do? All she knew was who would be taken next with no way to stop it. She wasn't the solution to their impossible demands. She didn't want to be involved with it. She dug her fingers into the dirt and clutched it tightly in her fists.

The sobs changed from tears of rage to the vulnerable cries of a wounded heart. No one cared. No one knew what she was going through. She was alone in this—a slave to her magic.

Even though she felt that way and voiced the words, she knew it wasn't true. Lana knew what she dealt with. Well, as much as anyone could know. But Lana wasn't here with her clenching handfuls of dirt, and the pain still crashed through Asheel like the reaper himself.

She leaned back, tilting her head to the treetops, and took a few deep breaths while the ache settled in her chest. Her running had been childish, and the council members must think so poorly of her now. None of them had really attacked her, and they hadn't even voted yet. Even if they all agreed, she couldn't imagine them forcing her kicking and screaming to Kemnuk. They probably would have let her cry out her frustrations right there—they were all adults. The Farson father was right about her still being a child.

She sighed, and the humid air filled her lungs.

What was she going to do? Her flight from the council meeting was more embarrassment than what she could face.

Realization that she might lose her position with the town hit her hard. She'd basically told them she quit, but she didn't want it to happen like that. She wanted to discuss it with them, see what they thought, figure out what could make the job easier on her. She hadn't wanted to be forced to sniff everyone, but the impact of being forced out of the position rather than leaving it on her own on good terms with the council made the hurt so much worse. She hadn't realized how much the renown meant to her, even when it hurt her. Had she just ruined everything even more?

The breeze shifted, and fat raindrops pattered against the leaves and dripped down to mingle with her tears while she stared into the waving wheat stalks surrounding her spot under the tree. The wheat was tall enough to hide her from view if a farmer were wandering the field, but he was probably in town with everyone else, trading, buying, selling, living a life of certainty knowing his wheat would grow, he would harvest it, and the bakers would buy it.

She let her tears blur her sight, and the dancing wheat became a writhing mass of gold, shimmering where the sun still peeked through the clouds' cracks. It reminded her of the reaper's fire, and she could imagine him in the wheat, waving his hand along with the stalks, inviting her to join him in the sea of burning colors. She kept her eyes unfocused to hold the illusion and stretched her hands in front of her. She could run away from society altogether. Leave. No Seshnia, no palace in Novoshna. A life alone with no expectations. Maybe the other side of the Reaper Gate was a beautiful place for the people he kidnapped. No one knew. It could be a place where people were cured of the stench.

Asheel traced the illusion with her hand then let it fall to her lap. "This is all your fault," she said to the mirage. "If it weren't for you, I could have a normal life."

Maybe if she met the reaper on the mountain next month, he would leave the other people and take her. But that would only delay the inevitable. He'd be back the next month and then the month after. And she'd already sacrificed enough of her life for the people. Or was it even called a sacrifice if they forced her to help?

She stayed hidden in the wheat for a while, but when the dirt around her turned to mud, she stood and wiped off her pants. Her chest still ached with the pain of the town, from being their outlet for blame, but her heart no longer raced with anger. She wouldn't let herself fill with vengeful rage, wouldn't fall into hysterics until she tried everything she could to make her life what she wanted.

With another sigh, she turned back toward the town. The council meeting would be done, but she could see the career advisor, Kayn, and see what he thought about her future, or maybe if he had ideas for how to cure the town. The walk back took ages compared to the short run earlier. Most people were out of the rainy streets, so no one ducked around her while she walked. No one in the shops looked at her, no judgmental stares from her earlier fleeing. It was peaceful with the streets emptier and rain dripping through her hair.

By the time she reached the council building, rain had soaked even her undergarments.

CHAPTER
6

Asheel's clothes dripped on the floorboards while she hid around a corner. When two council members stepped into their offices, she crept down the hall and peered into the career advisor's office.

Kayn sat behind his desk and paused his beard stroking when he saw her.

"Come in," he said and waved her inside, "and shut the door behind you. I've had enough of those old fools today."

His office had floor-to-ceiling shelves along one wall filled with shiny trinkets, tattered books, and items from every shop in town. A large window took up the opposite wall, and behind him, a tapestry of dried flowers drooped from haphazard nails. The floral scent could have been them, Kayn, or both.

"I thought I'd be seeing you soon," Kayn said. He shuffled papers on his desk. "Especially after that outburst earlier." He looked up at Asheel who was still standing awkwardly just inside the door. "Not that I blame you. Take a seat."

"But my clothes." Her shirt had stopped dripping, but her pants were still leaving a trail of puddles and would soak into the chair. "I can stand."

"Nonsense. Chairs are meant for sitting anytime, not just when we're in the perfect condition to sit in them."

Asheel hadn't had many conversations with Kayn, but something about him soothed her tension. She sat in a seat across from him and folded her hands in her lap.

"I'm sorry about earlier," she said. "I was unreasonable and dramatic."

"No, you weren't." Kayn resumed stroking his beard. "I've always told them not to include a teenager in the council meetings. It's been bad enough that they've burdened you as a child."

It was like he could read her mind.

"After you left the room," he continued, "I gave them a bit of an earful about what they've been putting you through." A paper fell off his desk, but he ignored it and looked her in the eye, the bags under his own brown gaze drooping onto his cheeks from age. "You have the power to tell them no. They may have pressured you before, but they'll listen to you now. I guarantee it."

"What did you say to them?"

"I just told them to imagine you as their daughter and to ask themselves if they'd be okay treating their children like how they've been treating you." He leaned back in his seat and knocked a dozen more papers to the floor. "I even used my angry voice."

Kayn's smile was contagious. Why couldn't the rest of the town be as understanding as him?

"Now," Kayn bent in his chair to grab the papers from the floor, "back to why you're here—"

"My career." Asheel wrung her hands.

Kayn set the papers on his desk, but half of them slid back to the floor and he dismissed them with a wave. "Yes, of course. I'm supposed to tell you that you should continue identifying who might be taken each month and that we don't want to waste the years spent training you for the Reaper Guard."

"I don't want to do that anymore." She picked at the darkened water stains on her knees, lifting the damp fabric and letting it fall heavily back to her leg. "I want to have a say."

"Precisely. You don't have experience in much else, but we can find you something. What would you like to do?"

"I don't know." She'd been trying to figure that out with no luck.

"Then let's figure out what you *don't* want to do."

She hunched her shoulders and stared at the flower tapestry behind Kayn to avoid looking at him while she confessed. "I don't want to deal with people." A picture of her alone in a wing of Novoshna's palace flashed through her mind. "But not alone." Then she saw herself selling incense by her dad with a constant cycle of customers and frowned. "I don't want to have to be around people all day."

Kayn scratched an eyelid. "There's not much that doesn't involve other people."

"Please? I'll learn. I'll learn anything."

Kayn stopped scratching his eyelid, but it stayed closed when he lowered his hand. It opened slowly, and he snapped his fingers. "Ah! The shepherds! They disappear into the fields for weeks at a time and barely interact with each other. That's probably the least communal job there is."

Shepherding. Alone on the mountains' plateaus, but close enough to town to see her family and Lana. That was exactly what she asked for, but with the career in front of her, was she making the right choice? She imagined standing in a field surrounded by sheep, a peaceful image, a career where she could protect the creatures she looked after like how she wished she could protect everyone in Seshnia. It was like a dream.

"I'd love to be a shepherd."

"Would you now?" Kayn was braiding his beard again. "It takes strength and daring to protect those sheep from predators," he grinned, "and themselves."

"I'd rather face those wolves than the ones in town." She bit her lips and reminded herself it was how they grieved. In anger. It wasn't their fault.

"Well then, I can see if any of them are willing to take on an older apprentice." Kayn held his half-braided beard in one hand while the other did circles in the air above his desk. His finger landed on the topmost paper, and he spun it to face her. "Ah, here we are. Jean. He's getting a little older and was in here just a few weeks ago asking for help with his flock. You'd have to deal with him for a few years before he's ready to retire, but he's a pleasant fellow."

She glanced at the scrap paper that only had one line: *Jean's apprentice should be Asheel.*

"You already planned for me to apprentice with him?" Asheel asked.

"Only if you want to."

"How did you know I wanted something like that?"

Kayn tapped his temple. "They didn't give me this job for no reason. I'm good at what I do. Do you want the apprenticeship?"

Asheel stared at her name. She'd be away from her family and she'd miss Coby, but she would move out eventually anyway. Even Lana had started spending more time at the care-home and didn't have as much time for Asheel anymore.

"You can think about it for a few days if you want," Kayn said.

"I'll take it."

"You sure?"

Asheel smiled, scared of something new but certain it was the best option for her. "Yes, that's what I want to do."

Kayn nodded and returned to shuffling his papers. "Jean will be in town next week, and you'll go with him back to the mountains when he leaves. Meet him here after the council meeting that," he cleared his throat and winked, "you won't be attending. Have whatever you want to take ready to go, but don't pack too much. You won't need much on the plateau."

"Thank you," Asheel stood. A water stain from her clothes darkened where she'd sat.

Kayn shook his head. "No, Asheel. Thank you for everything you've done for us. I know you've been through a lot, and I hope you can find peace on the plateaus."

She left the office more hopeful and in control than she'd been in years, but her happiness distracted her from her embarrassing moment in the meeting. She forgot to check the halls for anyone who might confront her about it, and just outside Kayn's office, Stevart waited for her.

CHAPTER 7

S tevart paused mid stride and straightened. "Were you seeing Kayn?"

Asheel nodded and hoped he wouldn't ask anything else before she had time to process her decision for herself. She tried to step around him, but he placed a hand on her shoulder.

"Why? About the Kemnuk position? We voted not to send you in the meeting." He rambled. "He told them they were idiots for making it a council item instead of discussing it with you."

"It wasn't about that." Asheel stepped out of his grasp and turned to face him. A still simmering part of her wanted to snap at him, but she'd burned through her rage in the wheat field and her conversation with Kayn, his understanding and kindness, had been surprisingly healing. Everyone would know soon enough that she was leaving.

"Why did you meet with him then?"

"I'm reassigned to the shepherds." That finalized it, ensured that the whole town would know by the end of the day. Stevart wouldn't be able to keep it to himself even if she asked him to.

Stevart's eyes widened. "What?" He looked frantically at Kayn's door then back to Asheel. "Why? How will you check all of us way out there?"

Footsteps along the floorboards down the hall gave her an excuse to look away while some carpenters passed by on their way to the destroyed records room. "I won't," she said, stepping out of the way of the carpenters. She expected his response from most of the town, but familiar guilt made itself at home in her belly anyway, something she'd have to accept or get comfortable with. She turned to walk away.

"You won't . . ." Stevart grabbed her shoulder again before she took another step. "How will we make plans for the reaper if we don't know who he'll take?"

This time Asheel jerked her shoulder from his grasp. "You'll figure it out. What did Seshnia do before me? Or better yet, take Kayn's suggestion and cure the town instead."

She forced herself to walk at a normal pace without stomping down the hall. Controlling her temper was easier now that she held her own life in her hands.

Stevart yelled after her, but his words got lost in the maze of hallways.

He'd start spreading the news immediately. Asheel needed to tell her parents before they heard it from someone else, and she needed to tell Lana, explain why she wasn't abandoning her friend. Lana wouldn't be done with her shift for another hour and Asheel's mom would probably take it the worst, so she'd tell her dad first, mostly because his shop was closest and his customers would get to him sooner.

The streets were still mostly empty from the earlier rain, the townspeople either going home to prepare for dinner or locking themselves in their workshops to replenish their stock. Her dad's incense shop was still open, but thankfully, no one was inside. The day after a reaping night was always the slowest day of the month for him.

The shop engulfed her in an overwhelming menagerie of scents that ranged from musky and woodsy to sweet and mouthwatering. The room was as narrow as she expected, but it went back farther and felt bigger on the inside like he'd explained. Bowls of incense lined the shelves, and a few lopsided tables held his newest concoctions in a row down the center of the room. At the other end, a back door faced the next street, and he had both the front and back doors propped open to let in more light and cooling evening air.

Near the back door, Kee sat at a worktable where he rolled twigs in the sticky incense mixtures. A separate set of deeper shelves lined the wall in front of him where he set the incense to dry before organizing it in the available stock.

"Finally come to see the shop?" Kee asked. He slid the tray onto a drying shelf. "What do you think of the new place?"

"It smells wonderful in here." Asheel picked up a pine-scented stick. "Why don't we have any of this one at home?"

"That's my best seller. It's better for business if we only use the ones I can't sell." He grabbed a new twig and rolled it in sticky scents, then dusted it with dried grounds. "You can take a few if you want."

She put the incense back and wrung her hands, unsure how to tell her dad that she wouldn't be helping with his incense any longer.

"Come over here," he said. "Help me with these last few sticks."

"I'm actually here to tell you I met with the career advisor today." She decided to get it over with fast. "I'm going to be a shepherd."

Kee left a half-covered twig on the worktable and faced her. "You're leaving town?"

"I'll still visit you every month when we come in for the trades."

Kee stuttered over his words. "You can't be a shepherd," he finally said. "You're supposed to help me with the shop."

"And the town expects me to keep sniffing all of them, and the council wanted to sell my magic to Kemnuk," Asheel said, leaving out her invitation to Novoshna's palace and expectations of the queen. Explaining it gave her more confidence, more certainty that she'd decided what was best for her. "Everyone had plans for me except me, and I've finally made my plans."

"You've never even shown interest in shepherding. Don't you want to do something you know?"

"It's what I want."

Kee studied her, thoughts churning behind his eyes, but she'd already made her decision and her own eyes pleaded for him to understand that he didn't have a say in it. He finally shook his head and released a breath that puffed out his cheeks. "I thought I'd have help with the shop soon."

"You could ask for an apprentice like the shepherds did."

"I don't like those shepherds." He turned back to the abandoned incense stick with a frown and nudged it through the grounds. "They're stealing my daughter."

Asheel grinned wryly. "This town stole my childhood. At least I'm going to the fields by choice."

Kee set the flawed incense in the drying rack and stepped around the table with his arms opened to Asheel. "I knew you'd leave our house eventually, just didn't expect for you to leave the entire town behind."

Asheel welcomed the hug and his acceptance, glad at least one of her family members wasn't mad about her leaving.

Kee let her go, and his eyes glistened, only a few inches above her own. "Does Willa know?"

"No. I'm hoping to find Lana first. Then I'll head home."

"Coby won't be happy about it either."

"I know."

"Well," he clapped his dusty hands together and turned back to his worktable, "you get going and let me finish up here. You can wait for me to be home to tell your mother if you want."

"I think I'll plan on that." If only she could keep the gossipers from telling Willa first. "Thanks, Dad."

Asheel left the shop and walked slowly around the three inner rings of the city to pass the time until the end of Lana's shift. The inner rings' paving was the most worn but with the best craftmanship, but as she got to the fourth ring, puddles that had been clear enough on the inner rings became muddy potholes to avoid. The setting sun shimmered across them in ripples from the wind.

The care-home was a part of the fourth ring with more space around it than the stores and workshops to give the elderly areas for outdoor activities. Asheel sat on a fence post with her legs straddled over the worn wood, in view of the door but out of the way if anyone needed to rush by.

The fence encased a small garden for the wards, some retired farmers who couldn't bear being away from crops after a lifetime of growing food. The patch where their spindly cornstalks had grown was now stripped bare, ready for a fall vegetable to take its place, but a short tree still had unripe fruit clustered in its branches.

She reached for a leaf and tugged it, jostling the branch and sending a shower of raindrops to the mud, then dropped the leaf to the ground for the critters in the soil to find.

After a while, the care-home door swung open, and Asheel spun to greet Lana. But in front of her friend, the two Novoshna officials stepped out.

"What are you doing here?" Asheel asked, clutching the fencepost beneath her. "You haven't gone back to the city yet?"

"We were just . . ." Vimi chewed her lip.

Lana prodded the officials away from the care-home and shooed them into the street. "You were just going back to the inn for a good night of sleep before heading out in the morning, right?"

Vimi scoffed and rolled her eyes at Lana while Maleen chuckled.

"We were asking your friend what would convince you to return to Novoshna with us," Maleen said.

"I'm not going." Asheel's knuckles turned white as she tightened her grip on the post. "I told you that."

"Yes, but we thought we might convince you otherwise with the right amenities." Maleen held her hands up in peace like when they'd first met. "If we weren't clear before, you can have basically anything you want as long as you prove useful."

Anything except freedom, Asheel reminded herself, *with no guarantee of not being feared like here.*

Lana shoved the officials again. "Remember what I said?"

"Yes," Vimi grabbed Maleen's arm and pulled her down the street. "We're going." Their arguing vanished with them as they disappeared into the darkness.

Nothing Asheel could think of would convince her to live the rest of her life in a single wing of the palace, not in her current state, but her friend sometimes knew her better than she knew herself. "What did you tell them?" Asheel asked while sliding off the fence.

"After making them help change sheets and deliver meals, I gave them a stern talking to." Lana's giggle puffed out in a single cloudy breath that disappeared quickly into the cool evening air. "They said I made valid points about letting you tell them what you needed for yourself. And I told them that's what would convince you to go. Allowing you to say no and respecting that decision. I said, 'let her decline.' And Vimi threw a pillow at me and accused me of being an evil genius."

Wind swirled through the trees' leaves and whipped Asheel's hair across her face. Having the ability to decline without feeling like she let down their queen did make the idea of going to Novoshna sound a little better, but when there, she had no guarantee to continue to have a say in anything. And her confidence in her decision to become a shepherd reaffirmed her decision to decline the palace.

Lana pulled her cloak tighter, and they started walking toward their homes. "Vimi really wasn't thrilled to have spent the evening doing chores, but I told them information has a cost and refused their money."

"Seems like she'd rather fight the reaper than clean," Asheel said. "Thanks for what you said to them." She kicked a pebble which skittered to the side into a clump of weeds peeking through the cobblestone.

"Does that make you consider it?"

"Maybe a little." Maybe in the future if being a shepherd didn't work out. "At the Gate Feast, they said they'd come back in a few months to see if I changed my mind."

Lana stayed silent for a few steps. "I'd heard that part."

"I don't know if going there would be any different than what I deal with here," Asheel said. "At least for me."

"I don't want you to go," sadness laced Lana's voice in a tight whisper, "but I won't pretend it doesn't sound a little exciting to live in the palace."

Asheel halted, pulling Lana to a stop. "You could go with me." Maleen had said the queen welcomed anyone with magic.

"I can?"

"You'd have to tell them about your magic, but they'd let you come too. Their royal advisors can show us new ways to use our magic."

Lana shook her head, and her tight spirals flopped across her eye patch.

"We can both think about it." Now Asheel sounded like the officials, trying to convince Lana on an adventure with her.

Lana looked behind them, back the way they came, as if she could see the care-home, and the scent of rain pattering on dirt drifted from her, a smell of disappointment. She looked to the cobblestones between them and closed her eye.

"I'm needed here, at the care-home."

"They might have people to take care of at the palace." The smell of disappointment drifted from Asheel too, but hers was laced with selfishness.

Lana raised her eye but didn't meet Asheel's gaze. "I can't. Telling people their auras? That's nothing like helping my wards be comfortable and fed." Her face brightened, and she finally met Asheel's eyes. "But don't let that stop you from going to Novoshna if that's what you want. I know you're miserable stuck in your job here."

"Well," Asheel looked away this time, "I came here to tell you about that."

Lana's shoulders slumped. "You've decided to go to the palace?"

Asheel pulled Lana's arm back through hers and started walking again, avoiding a puddle stretching across most of the street. Guilt already weighed on her about leaving her friend, a different guilt than abandoning the town.

"I'm going to the plateaus with the shepherds."

Lana smiled wide and jostled Asheel's arm. "You're changing your career? That's so exciting!" But her smile faltered and turned into a grimace. "Right? The council isn't exiling you, are they?"

"No, no. I chose it."

"I guess the palace decision isn't appealing at all now, is it? Is everyone okay with it? With you leaving to be a shepherd?" Lana asked.

"Not many people know yet." She thought about how Stevart

reacted. "I can guess they won't be thrilled about it. I'm abandoning them."

Lana tripped over a cobblestone but regained her footing. "Don't worry about them. You'll never be able to satisfy everyone."

"I want to, though. I want them to be pleased with me and tell me I've done a good job." Without her warnings every month, fear would shake the town even more than it already did, the mothers cowering protectively over their children, the fathers ripped from their families, the shopkeepers vanishing in the night. She didn't want to leave them unprotected, but why did it have to be her? Why was her gift so rare? She glanced at Lana who was watching her feet for more uneven cobblestones. The only other person who had any sense of a person's heart. "You could do it." Then the townspeople might not see Asheel as a deserter. "Can't you let the town know who's in danger by pointing out whose aura has faded?"

Lana shook her head. "It doesn't work like that."

Words Asheel had spoken so many times herself. "I still don't understand." Asheel sighed. "If someone feels too . . . negative, they stink. Even if I couldn't smell sweet hearts too, I'd be able to know who's not in danger."

"It's not really like that," Lana said. "The . . . rotten desires and kind thoughts that you smell . . . It's like they're two different, unrelated things. Like hands and feet. They're both a part of you but are different. Some people can run really fast and some can't, and that ability doesn't affect what they can do with their hands." She shrugged. "I can see when someone doesn't have a blinding aura, but that doesn't mean they have feelings that make them stink. I can't see it, so I can't know how in danger they are."

Lana was more closed off about her ability than Asheel was. Hers was visual, auras hovering around everyone. The brighter the aura, the kinder the heart, but from what Lana explained, that brightness didn't always correlate with someone's actions. Other factors affected decisions beyond just a willingness to be good. It was the same with Asheel's ability, but Asheel had a harder time separating the stench of someone's negative feelings from their actions, had a harder time smelling the sweet when rot was so potent. When their odors had soured too much, it eclipsed any of the sweet notes that everyone carried, even the worst offenders. Not that any of it mattered to the reaper. He only went after the foulest.

"But it's more likely, right?" Asheel asked. "If someone's aura fades, they're more likely to be taken."

Lana shook her head again. "Kady's was still really bright. Besides, you know I don't like to tell people about their aura."

Asheel squinted at Lana, trying to picture a glow around her. "Because you don't want to influence it." Only occasionally would Lana whisper to Asheel that someone's aura was shining especially bright that day. Had Asheel's aura vanished when she decided to ditch the town for the shepherds? Did she still have any kindness or caring left in her, or was she as selfish as she felt? She looked back to Lana. "Can I ask you about mine?"

She didn't look up. "What about it?"

"Is it still there?"

Lana furrowed her brow at the question. "Why do you ask? Are you feeling extra vengeful?"

"I'm wondering if I made a bad decision to be a shepherd."

"Someone's decision doesn't always reflect the type of heart they have," Lana repeated. "A bad decision doesn't make a bad person, and a good decision doesn't make a good person."

Asheel rolled her eyes. "Can you tell me? Just this once? I need a little encouragement."

Lana sighed but smiled. "Fine. It's the same as always. Faded but clear. A pretty light purple." She squeezed Asheel's arm. "You're not a monster yet."

The reassurance was a relief, but something still twinged at the back of Asheel's mind. She'd either have to get over or get used to the guilt. "Are you mad?" she asked.

"Why would I be?"

"Because I won't be around as much."

"No way." Lana squeezed Asheel's arm again. "I'm happy for you. I'll miss you of course, but I'm so happy for you."

"Thanks." Asheel grinned and squeezed back. "Will you be okay?"

Lana shrugged. "I'll survive. But if you decide to go to the palace when the officials come back, you have to come let me know right away."

"And you'd consider it too, right?"

"Asheel." Lana rolled her eye.

"Okay, okay. I won't pester you about it."

They walked in silence until they reached their residential ring of Seshnia.

"When do you leave?"

"Next week," Asheel said, "after the council meeting, which I don't have to attend."

"You're already so much happier." Lana's eye was tight, but she'd never be so selfish as to ask Asheel to stay.

But Asheel was selfish enough to ask Lana to go to the palace with her. If they both went, seclusion in the palace might not be so bad, but Lana would hate being locked up in there even more than Asheel. Novoshna still wasn't an option. Asheel would get by on the outskirts of Seshnia, out in the fields with the shepherds.

CHAPTER 8

"How could you decide to leave us like this?" Willa asked while she shuffled around the kitchen. Pans clattered when she tossed them onto the counter, and she spun with her hands on her hips to face her "ungrateful daughter."

The gossip had already reached Willa by the time Asheel got home. A neighbor had frantically pestered her about who would check if their family was in danger of the reaper, and Willa had been clueless as to what the neighbor was weeping about. Coby hunched in a far corner of the room, just as unhappy but much more subdued, his fumes stifling in the cramped house.

"You went too far," Willa continued berating, "running out of here this morning and getting assigned to the shepherds just to spite me."

"I hadn't planned on shepherding," Asheel said. She hadn't put away her cloak yet in case she needed to flee the house, and she twisted it in her arms. "I just wanted a choice."

"You're not going." Willa returned to her cooking. "I won't allow it!"

Kee finally got home and shut the door just as Willa started a new round of reasons why Asheel couldn't go. He grasped her shoulders and made her face him.

"Stop that. We can't control what she does anymore. She's grown now."

Willa leaned into his arms and fell into a fit of tears. "But we'll never see her again," she sobbed.

"That's not true," Kee patted her shoulders, "but we'll never see her again if you try to force her to be what she doesn't want to be."

Asheel finally relaxed a little with her dad home to guide the situation.

"You don't even care," Willa whimpered.

"I do, but it's her life and her decision." He patted her back. "We're all going to be fine. It's just a change is all."

"What if Coby leaves for some other career, too?"

Kee leaned back from her and smiled. "Love, that's years away. There's no need to worry about that now, but we'll figure it out when the time comes."

Willa quieted, and Kee helped her finish the cooking. Coby still tinkered sadly with a toy in the corner, avoiding Asheel's gaze when she sat on the floor beside him. The smell of decaying leaves and rot had strengthened, twisting her gut while she denied what she knew.

"I'll come back and visit you every month," she said, ignoring her gut screaming the reaper would come for him. He had a month for the stench to fade. He could do it. He was a sweet boy.

"Like the reaper?" He didn't look up.

"Well, no. Not like him at all. They'll be happy visits when I come. I'm sure Mom will cook lots of delicious food, and we'll have little family feasts each time."

He pouted harder and thought for a few seconds before he spoke. "I'd rather starve and you stay here."

Asheel's chest ached. How could she make him understand this was best for her? She'd just turned twenty, had a decade more practice than him, and she still had trouble getting out of her own head long enough to see situations from another's perspective.

"Why won't you stay with me?" He finally looked at her with tearstained cheeks.

"Oh, curly." She pushed his curls back from his forehead. "I can't. I have to do this for me."

"But what about me? Don't you care about me? I'm losing everyone all at once!" He sniveled. "Please, stay!" Tears slid down his cheeks and slipped into the corner of his mouth before he wiped them with his sleeve.

Asheel shook her head, unable to think of a way to explain why she had to go that he could understand. "I'm sorry."

Coby stood and pushed Asheel away, then ran to their room and slammed the door. The stench of rot that oozed from him grew stronger and trailed after him, and worry slammed in Asheel's chest. He smelled beyond foul, and the reaper would find him with ease. But someone else would surely smell worse than him by the next reaping night. Occasionally someone could cleanse their stains, or maybe the council might find the cure quickly.

And if he was doomed . . . She didn't want to witness the moment. Seeing Kady's fate come true was hard, but to see Coby taken . . . Asheel could live in the fields with the shepherds in denial of what happened to him.

She knew she should tell their parents that he was in danger, but it wouldn't change anything. The warnings never did. Better to let them have their last moments together without the fear spoiling it. She wouldn't sever their fraying happiness.

She shook her head. No, all of that was wrong. Coby was

good, and his stench wasn't as bad as she thought. She was just distraught. He'd be fine.

He wouldn't be taken.

CHAPTER 9

Asheel sat in Kayn's office with one satchel of clothes, waiting for Jean, the shepherd, to take her to her new life on the plateaus. She'd discussed the palace option with Lana a few times, but after the initial excitement of an adventure together passed, Asheel was more certain she didn't want to leave Seshnia. Lana was already dedicated to her career in the care-home and didn't think using her gift for the queen would be as satisfying. Plus, Lana had never been to Novoshna, and no matter how tempting a life of luxury was, Asheel wouldn't go without her.

Kayn shuffled through some papers, grunted, then grabbed a decorative metal bird from his shelf and set it on his desk atop the haphazard stack. Asheel watched him while he stared at the metal bird with his hands on his hips. He didn't move until Asheel shifted, breaking the silence. With a sigh, he looked up at her and shook his head.

"I'm trying to get it to hatch an idea for me," he said, straight-faced.

Asheel bit her lips to hold back her smile.

"What?" Kayn frowned.

"I can't tell if you're being serious or silly."

He raised his eyebrows and ran a hand through his beard. "No reason I can't be both. Who's to say serious things can't also be silly and silly can't be serious?"

The bird sitting on the stack of papers faced out the window in a perpetual cold glare while she considered the combination.

"I'm sorry." She apologized when the silence became awkward. "I really don't know what I'm supposed to say to that."

"Ignore me. I'm just being silly," he said with a wink.

A knock at the door interrupted them, and a weatherworn man in a frayed cloak stepped into the office with a hooked staff taller than him.

"Jean!" Kayn stepped around his desk with his arms raised. "Just the shepherd we were waiting for."

Jean embraced the career advisor with bone jarring pats then turned to face Asheel. He had the same hooked nose as Kayn, but his face was craggier and his greyer beard, braided to a point at his collarbone, was half the length of the career advisor's. His scraggly brows raised at recognizing Asheel, but only with surprise, not fear.

"This scrawny thing is supposed to be my apprentice?" Jean's lip quivered as he spoke. "She's not much taller than the rams. I'll lose her in the flock."

"I can do it." Asheel grasped her bag in her lap, creasing the coarse leather. "Please, let me try."

Jean's pitted cheeks twitched into a slight smile. "Oh, I'm sure you can. I'm just teasing my brother here."

Kayn clasped Jean's shoulder and gave it a little shake before returning to the other side of his desk to plop down and reposition the metal bird. "I know what I'm doing, and Asheel will do just fine."

If they were brothers, Jean could be as eccentric as Kayn,

which Asheel would have to get comfortable with if she was about to spend the next few years with him in seclusion. Considering what Kayn said earlier, she might never know when Jean was being serious or not.

The craggy brother rummaged through his leather satchel, stuffed with pink-tinted papers and slung across his body, and pulled out a few rumpled sheets. After flipping through them, he handed the roughly cut papers to Kayn who took them with a child-like grin and slid them into a locked drawer of his desk where he removed a few other pink-tinted pages and handed them back. They stood out from the other documents scattered around Kayn's office, all a cream or brown-toned hue.

"Good to burn?" Jean asked.

"Yep." Kayn pressed a finger to his lips and winked at Asheel, a request not to ask about them. She'd never understand what went through the man's head.

"Ready to get going?" Jean twisted the clasp on his satchel and turned to Asheel.

This was it. No backing out now. She was going to be a shepherd. With a resolution to hide her nerves, she stood and slung her bag across her shoulders. "Ready."

CHAPTER 10

A recently shorn sheep bumped against Asheel's leg, and she nudged it back to its family and sat on the opposite stone from Jean. They'd set up their tents behind them, a barrier to keep the sheep from wandering too close to the cliffside, and a fire flickered between them, making the night seem even darker.

Jean scraped the rest of his vegetable mush into his mouth and set his bowl on the ground beside him. "They always smell better right after being shorn," he said and gestured to the sheep.

"I don't mind the smell too much." It was better than the stench that permeated the town. Asheel ate slower, still getting used to the difference between her mom's cooking and the easier, meager portions the shepherds ate.

Jean nodded. "That's the spirit." A lamb wandered up to him, and he scratched its ears. "I'm still so surprised Kayn found someone to apprentice with me. Not many people want to live way out here, but I guess this is just what you were looking for."

After spending the past few weeks with Jean, Asheel felt a little more confident in being forward. She set her remaining vegetable mush to the side. "Why did you choose this life? Why did the others?" She'd met two other shepherds, both seemingly just as content to live in solitude. "I mean, my circumstances for coming out here were a little different."

Jean prodded the fire with his staff. "I can't speak for the others, but I was much like you."

Asheel jerked at the comparison. Did he deal with smelling everyone's magical odors? Could he smell her stained heart?

"I didn't want to be around people who thought I needed catering."

Asheel slouched again, slightly disappointed that their similarities weren't as literal as she hoped. She rested her elbows on her knees. Of course, he wasn't like her.

"I wanted to be alone in my grief," he continued, "and this is just about as secluded as it gets without disappearing into the mountains." He chuckled. "I'm not a full recluse though. I still want a little of the convenience of society." Jean pointed his walking stick to their stack of firewood. "Set that big branch on the fire for this rickety old man, would you?"

Asheel obliged, and sparks floated upward, disturbed by the firepit's newcomer. "What grief were you running from," she asked, "if that's not too personal?"

Jean puffed out a breath. "It is, but it's been long enough I don't mind talking about it." He glared teasingly over the fire at her. "Although, that's why I came out here, you know, like I just said, to get away from it."

"Sorry." She ducked, hiding behind the flames.

Jean flapped his hand in the air, waving off the apology. "It's fine. My wife and I only had one son. She died a few years after he was born from an illness. She fought it, but she wasn't strong enough.

I was getting along fine raising him." A gust of wind whipped around them, and Jean pulled his cloak tighter under his chin. "He was the brightest thing and had his mother's sharp chin. He'd just started dating, then the reaper had to take him from me." He looked down at his gnarled fingers.

Silence fell between them, and Asheel wrung her hands, unsure of what to say. "I'm sorry you had to go through all of that. I can't imagine." She tried to recall the faces of the parents who'd brought their kids to her in the past, but the faded ones she could remember weren't Jean. "Did . . . did I . . ."

Jean raised an eyebrow. "What?"

"You know . . . uh . . ." She cringed then tapped her nose.

Jean's eyes widened. "Oh, did you check him for reaping night? No, that was all before you were born. He'd be forty this year."

Asheel slouched even further in relief. "I'm sorry. It must be hard not knowing what happened to him. Sorry," she apologized again. "You probably don't want to think about it."

"Oh, I like to think he's out there somewhere living a decent life in a strange, exotic land." He glanced up and smiled at her.

Denial was how she dealt with her grief too, hiding from what would happen to Coby. She imagined Jean's son making electric lanterns across the ocean and put a growing version of Coby beside him. Too far away to stay in touch, but still enjoying life.

"You gave us all a little hope when your gift was discovered, but that reaper's one sly fellow."

Asheel scuffed her foot in the sparse grass at her feet. Hope was worthless. Hoping for something that might not happen, like catching the reaper or killing him or stopping him somehow, would just end in disappointment. She thought about Coby and the stench that had grown around him daily. Had he gotten any better since she left? Worse? She couldn't hope for that though. If she did and he was taken, that would hurt worse than accepting his fate.

"Look over there." Jean pointed his cane at the mountains opposite them across the valley. Asheel's eyes took a moment to adjust to the darkness away from the fire, then she spotted the glowing footprints of the reaper.

"It's reaping night?"

"Hard to keep track of time out here," Jean said. He sighed as if the weight of his concerns traveled down the mountain with the reaper. "I know they'll miss you warning them about their loved ones. A few months ago, the innkeeper admitted to me he was glad he got the chance to say goodbye."

Thoughts of Coby circled back to Asheel. She hadn't told anyone about the danger he was in. Her parents didn't know. He didn't know. He could be taken and no one had any warning. Her own worsening, rotten smell stirred from her selfishness, and she closed her eyes and forced herself to stop denying it. He was next. She knew he'd be taken next. She'd never been wrong, and now she was denying it just as much as the other families always did. She knew he wouldn't be with Jean's son far away.

She opened her eyes and tried to still the shaking in her limbs. The reaper was halfway down the mountain.

"Do you think I made the wrong choice coming out here?"

Jean shrugged. "Maybe for them, but if that life wasn't for you, then they'll have to get used to it. It's not like you'd be around forever to do that." Then as an afterthought, almost too quiet for Asheel to hear, he whispered, "I know I would have liked a chance to say goodbye to my son."

His words drove into Asheel's heart, and she leapt from her seat. "I'm sorry. I need to go."

"Go." Jean shooed her with his staff, a shaky wave that quivered like her own nerves.

In a few quick strides she reached the cliffside and jogged down the slope. Her eyes darted between her feet and the reaper's fiery steps on the opposite end of the valley until trees blocked her view. A race between them, but her house was on this side of the town, and she was closer. She could beat him.

But even if she beat him to Coby, how could she stop him?

Corn whipped at her cheeks while she charged through the fields. She burst out of the stalks, her sides heaving, several streets down from her house. The call was strong. Coby was there, and he reeked. She forced her legs to keep moving despite the burning, but one of her calves cramped and she stumbled into the side of her family's house.

And at the end of the street, around the corner, the reaper's form glowed.

Asheel threw open the door and shrieked for her parents. "He's here!" She slammed the door behind her and skidded into the room. "He's here for Coby!"

They jumped from the table, but Asheel ran past them and into Coby's room. Almost burned-out incense smoked on a ledge at his door. It was strong but not even close to covering his stench.

"Huh?" He rubbed his eyes and sat up, and he grinned when he recognized Asheel. "You're back!" Then his scowl returned, the one he'd had since she said she was leaving for the plateau. "For how long?"

She paused at the edge of his bed. Not even the trained guards had been able to stop the reaper in the past. How was her frail family supposed to do it?

The front door flew open again, a direct sightline to Coby's bed, and sent wood shards flying into the house. Their dad lunged at the reaper, swinging his chair and shattering it across the reaper's front, but the reaper barely flinched and threw Kee across the room where he crashed against the counter by their mom. She shrieked, and Coby yelled.

The reaper strode across the room with his gaze focused on

little Coby, and when he reached the door to their bedroom, Asheel shoved Coby behind her. He fell onto the bed and scurried across it to press himself against the far wall.

"You can't have him!" Asheel shouted. "You've already ruined my life enough."

The reaper paused and tilted his head.

With a scream, their mom charged at the reaper's back and shoved a large cooking knife into his spine. He fell to his knees and coughed through the smoke lacing his mouth shut, then reached behind him to pull the blade from his back. He stood and tossed the blade over Willa's shoulder, across the room. It *thunk*ed into the wall by the entryway and stuck in the wood at eye height.

Their mom whimpered and collapsed to her knees, begging. "Please, not my son."

The reaper ignored her and faced Asheel and Coby again. Asheel kneeled on Coby's bed, facing the reaper, blocking him from her little brother. What could she do? The beast was impervious to weapons and ignored a mother's tears. Coby was a sweet boy. He didn't deserve to be taken.

The reaper grasped Asheel's arm. His fingers, uncomfortably warm, bit through her thick cloak. She couldn't let him pull her off Coby. She had to stay between the two.

"Wait!" Asheel cried, the reaper's hand tight around her upper arm. "Take me instead. I'll go."

The reaper loosened his grip and tilted his head again, listening.

"I'll go with you," she whispered. Coby whimpered behind her, and she lifted her arms higher to protect him. "If you leave him, I'll go with you without a fight."

The reaper's gaze, glowing coals set deep into his skull, shifted between Asheel and Coby. He breathed out slowly, a stream of smoke grazing across her cheeks and consuming her in a haze. Was he exasperated? Was he debating? Was he smelling her stained heart to see if it stank enough?

Asheel gulped then whispered harshly through her teeth, hoping Coby couldn't hear. "My heart is adequately wretched, and you know it."

Finally, the reaper nodded, let go of her arm, and jerked his head over his shoulder to get her to follow him.

She'd finally made a deal with the reaper like what the town always suspected. At least the deal was to help someone else instead of herself.

She spun to face her brother and spoke quickly before the reaper could drag her from the house. "Don't blame yourself for this. I'm giving you a second chance. Forgive me, please. Forgive yourself. Remember you still have lots of people around you who care about you. Don't block them out because of this. They can help you."

The reaper grunted, impatient.

Asheel glanced over her shoulder then turned back to Coby and kissed his forehead. "Be a good boy," she said then slid off the bed while Coby clung to her sleeves.

"No." Coby blubbered and tugged at her. "You just got back."

Asheel pulled her sleeves from his grasp and shook her head, but Coby sobbed and grabbed the back of her cloak. She couldn't face him. She wouldn't come back this time and couldn't change her mind, especially if the reaper's choices were only her or him.

The reaper sighed and rolled his head, definitely exasperated, then reached for her.

"Wait." Asheel held up her hands. "I'm coming. I promise. He's just a kid and doesn't understand. Just give me a second."

The reaper paused with his fingers inches from her and held up one finger then crossed his arms and turned to glare at her parents cowering in the doorway.

With a deep breath, she turned and pried Coby's fingers from her cloak. "Let me go, curly. I'm doing this to keep you safe. You have to let me go now."

His bottom lip quivered and snot dribbled to his upper lip. "No . . ." He curled his fingers around her wrists. "Please . . . Please don't go."

"I have to. We don't have a choice." But this was her choice, and she wouldn't make the wrong one this time.

She squeezed his hands, let go, and slipped off the bed. The reaper and her parents all stared at her, but she dropped her gaze to the floorboards and ran past all of them before anyone could stop her and before she could change her mind.

Her mom's pleas not to take her daughter muted when Asheel charged onto the street, and she didn't turn back. If she changed her mind, if she fought, the reaper could change his and go back for Coby. Though, he could change his mind anyway. She had no reason to trust him to keep his end of their bargain.

She slowed at the end of their curved street and bent over with her hands on her knees, and the reaper jogged up behind her. The expression on his face was impossible to read through the fiery scorched skin, more bone exposed than flesh remaining, but he placed a hand on her shoulder and stared into her eyes.

Asheel let her tears fall freely now that she was far enough that she couldn't back out. She'd finally escaped the town's burdens, finally had a say in her life, finally had something that felt like happiness, but she'd just lost it all. Ugly sobs ripped through her chest, but it was worth it. Saving her little brother was worth it.

The reaper squeezed her shoulder, but she shook her head. "Don't . . ." Another heaving sob ripped itself from her throat. "Don't make me think you have pity."

His hand fell to his side, and he nodded and took a few tentative steps.

"I'm coming." Asheel straightened and pulled in a shaky

breath. She'd made her decision and crying about it wouldn't make it any easier. She wiped the tears from her face. "Just go."

He gave her another unreadable look, his scorched flesh pulling sickeningly across exposed bone, before leading her through the town. The tenuous trust in the deal between them peaked, and Asheel took purposeful, deep breaths each step to keep her panic away.

The reaper kept his pace slow for her, and the quiet night followed them to the other edge of town while the townspeople either cowered behind their closed doors or slept if confident the reaper wouldn't visit them. Were any of them watching through peepholes in their shuttered windows? What a strange sight their procession would have been, a human willingly following the monster. Asheel wiped her eyes again and held her head higher. If they watched, they'd see her bravery and confidence. Or maybe they'd conjure new rumors about her relationship with the reaper. She bit her lips. She wouldn't be concerned with their petty gossip anymore.

The walking got harder just out of the town. The road sloped upward and vanished within trees along the mountainside. Flowers that bloomed in the chill night glittered sporadically through the forest, and the plants that thrived in the day's heat had curled in on themselves to protect their delicate blooms.

Asheel slipped on a thick root, and the reaper glanced over his shoulder. He moved forward again when she regained her footing, his own steps sure, unhindered by the rough terrain. Each step he took sizzled in puffs of steam and scorched the plants in short bursts of fire that extinguished before spreading beyond their trail. The fronds that he brushed against wilted at his touch, blazing a path through the undergrowth along a trail of previously scorched plants. She placed her feet where his had been to avoid the hidden obstacles, which made the going a little easier.

As they got closer to the Reaper Gate, a whirring hum whispered through the trees. She'd never been this close to it and hadn't known what to expect, and the sound reminded her of hovering bugs, how their wings beat obnoxious rhythms. And even closer, it modulated to voices, groans of the lost. Hundreds, thousands of them that tore through Asheel and creeped under her skin. Would her voice mix with theirs?

The Reaper Gate appeared through the trees in a wide, barren patch of grey rock, like it had absorbed all life around it. The floating Gate itself reminded Asheel of a giant flower with dozens of thin, translucent petals, each larger than Asheel, branching from a central, heaving mass of glistening rainbows, like oil on water. The central portion ebbed slowly from the size of a large man to the size of Asheel's palm and then back to the gaping opening.

The reaper paused at the edge of the barren circle and looked between Asheel and the Gate. He scratched at his jaw, then held out his hand to her as an offering to help her through. Asheel glanced at his cracked fingerbones, the flesh having burned away from his hand, and considered it but couldn't take it. She had to do this on her own to remember this had been her decision. Otherwise, she'd feel more like he'd forced the choice on her.

"I don't need your help," she said and glared at his coal eyes.

He changed his offering to a gesture toward the Gate. She wanted to run while she watched it grow and shrink again. Doubts crept through her mind. Did she make the right choice? Would Coby be able to cure himself in the upcoming months? How bad would this hurt? What was death like?

She'd never imagined how her life would end, but climbing into the Reaper Gate never entered the picture. Alone in a field maybe, where she gave up and let herself waste away, or starving in the wilderness having run away, but not at the hands of an embodied nightmare. She changed her mind. She'd run home, grab Coby and her parents, and they'd go somewhere so far away that the reaper wouldn't be able to find them.

She pivoted and ran back down the path, but she only got a few steps before the reaper's burning grasp caught her arm. She punched blindly at him and, after spinning in his grasp, kicked at his crotch. He jumped out of the way, grasped her shoulders, and slung her over his own, then entered the dead area around the Gate. Instantly, the sounds of the night forest vanished, leaving only the groans from the shimmering opening.

Asheel pounded against the reaper's back and kicked her legs wildly in the air, but the reaper tightened his grip across her thighs.

"No!" she screamed, but the reaper didn't pause. He stepped into the wide opening and the oily surface engulfed her.

The forest disappeared, replaced by a sickly yellow haze hindering her vision, and the silence crushed her like a physical weight. It pressed and pulled at her bones, sapping her energy, and she stopped fighting from the extreme exhaustion that consumed her. The thick haze left a slime down her throat that she couldn't cough up.

Pale green ribbons, like materializing and dissipating hands, stroked her arms, legs, and back, as if she wasn't wearing a cloak or trousers. One of the hands mixed with the haze in front of her face then looped under her, between her chest and the reaper's shoulder, and dove through her clothes and skin. With a frenetic energy, it writhed inside her ribs, inside her lungs, weighing her down even more. If the reaper weren't carrying her, she would have collapsed.

She coughed and tried to dislodge the hand, but it grasped hold of her insides and clenched tight. Her coughing turned into panicked hacking, and she clawed at her front, opening the cloak, and gagged at the thought of some ghostly thing inside of her. When it crawled beyond her lungs, she pounded against the reaper's back and screamed. "Something's inside me! I c—I can feel it." She gagged again and sobbed while the hand grasped hold of her spine. "I can feel it moving!"

How it was so physically inside her and writhing around like it was, Asheel had no idea. Her meal from earlier rose up, and she puked into the abyss, possibly a little on the reaper, but still, she couldn't dislodge the hand. It squirmed more, and with a jolt like electricity it grabbed her heart and squeezed.

Asheel's scream choked off, and she fell into a fit of wheezing. She couldn't breathe through the pain. Her muscles locked, and the haze grew thicker.

At her stiffening, the reaper paused and pulled her around in front of him where he cradled her before setting her on the ground still folded from being thrown over his shoulder. Between the hacking, Asheel took short breaths, rapid and shallow, wheezed, then fell into another bout of weak coughs. The hand squeezed her heart tighter, which struggled to beat, and the air grew even hazier. She found the glow of the reaper's coal eyes, barely visible through the fog of her dimming consciousness and blur of her tears, and she anchored herself to those eyes. In that dark place, he was the only light for her to hold on to.

Her vision tunneled, but the reaper knelt over her so that she could still see him. With slow motions, he placed his hands on either side of her face, which filled her cheeks with warmth rather than scalding her. Her rapid breaths turned to more chest-wracking sobs. What was happening to her? The reaper released her face and gently grasped her hands. His coal eyes darkened even blacker, and behind the seams that sealed his lips, he groaned. A thin stream of thick, glowing red liquid rolled from one of his eyes and slid down his cheek.

It fascinated Asheel through her own torment.

After a final squeeze from the ghostly hand inside her, the force of her own awful desires exploded from her heart unhindered. Bitterness, pettiness, selfishness, seeping from her in a stench like she'd never smelled on anyone. The desires shred through her muscles with sharp pain and filled her body and limbs like they'd burst with hatred for the reaper and what fate he'd brought her to. The ghostly hand finally released her and pulled itself back up through her lungs, up her throat, and streamed from her mouth and nose to dissipate into the yellow haze like it never existed. Her muscles unlocked, and she curled into a limp heap with tears still streaming onto the slick, cold surface beneath her.

The reaper grasped her shoulder and grunted, and his eyes pleaded with her. She closed her eyes tight, waiting for death, but instead the reaper sighed and lifted her from the ground, one arm around her shoulders and the other under her knees. Despite his grotesque appearance and her hatred for him, his gentleness gave her the slightest bit of comfort, the knowledge that she wasn't in this place alone.

She kept her eyes closed to focus on his heat that seeped through her clothes while the voices started their groans and chants again. Whispers in languages she couldn't understand. Distant shrieks of agony. Asheel coughed from the haze and opened her eyes. The reaper looked straight ahead like he could see through it, but Asheel couldn't see more than the floating ghost hands and yellow air.

The hands descended on them again, quickly brushing from behind them to in front of them over and over. Asheel screamed; she wouldn't survive another experience like the one earlier, but the reaper held her tightly to his chest. They moved faster and faster, pushed forward by the hands, until a light glowed through the yellow from somewhere ahead of them. It flared brighter until Asheel had to close her eyes, and then the air lightened and the mist dissipated. And when Asheel squinted into the clean air, a new world greeted her.

CHAPTER 11

Out of the Gate, the air cleared without the weight of the haze, and Asheel didn't recognize the broad, flat leaves brushing by them, all decorated with thin pink veins. Dry, warm air replaced the night's chill. It was like a different world.

The reaper carried her down a narrow path, and behind them, a mirror image of the oily Gate grew and shrunk just like it had on the other side. It slipped behind the trees while the reaper carried her farther into the forest.

"You can put me down now," Asheel said, though her heart still pounded, sending shakes through her limbs. "I think I can walk."

The reaper nodded and lowered her legs but held her shoulders until she found her balance. Though the ghostly hands had drained her energy, a mixture of fear and excitement spiked her muscles and gave her more strength. When the reaper started walking downhill, Asheel stayed several feet behind him, tempted to turn back to the Gate but knowing he would easily catch her again. And she remembered her deal was to go along quietly for Coby. The reaper didn't seem to consider her earlier attempt to run back as breaking the deal, but she couldn't take another chance.

The reaper's head swiveled to keep an eye on the trees, and more than once he paused to glare into the forest then pass a pitying glance her way. A few times she thought she saw the glint of eyes in the darkness, but the reaper would start walking again before she could get a good look. Despite the danger, she was alive, which was more than she expected. Maybe the reaper didn't take humans to kill them. Maybe a paradise waited through the unfamiliar trees.

But when they eventually broke through the forest and onto a muddy street lined with decrepit buildings and trashed alleys, Asheel halted. A few steps ahead of her, the reaper stumbled to a stop, then returned to her and followed her gaze.

Monsters of her wildest nightmares paraded in the street like a grotesque circus. The costumes the children had worn during the Gate Feast didn't begin to compare to the beasts in front of her. Beside Asheel, a scream erupted from a mildew-covered shack, and a beaked, feathered beast crashed out of the window and onto a barrel, sending shards of glass across the street and shattering the barrel into large fragments of rotted wood. The bird-beast stood, stumbled back to the window, and climbed back through.

The reaper jerked at Asheel's elbow toward the monsters, but she shook her head.

"I can't," she whispered and gagged from the fumes wafting from every surface. She looked into the reaper's eyes. Surely there was some kindness there she could reach. "Please, take me back. I'll hide in the woods forever with you if that's what you want." A monster growled through the shattered window, and Asheel flinched. "Please. I don't want to die like this."

The reaper shook his head, gently grabbed her hand, and pulled her through the mob. Monsters leered at her, shouted and growled. Some spoke words she understood but would never repeat while others spoke in lyrical, cadenced patterns she didn't recognize. But all of them stepped back when the reaper approached, and Asheel stayed close behind him. Despite fearing him, he was the one thing she knew in this world, and she clung to that slight familiarity.

They followed the potholed street, weaving between the mismatched buildings of wood and stone, some with doors, others missing walls, and all seemingly built without a town layout in mind. Horned and fanged beasts watched hungrily, examining Asheel and licking their lips. When the reaper and Asheel reached the other side of the town where the road turned to black rock and the monsters had become sparse, the reaper dropped Asheel's hand and led her toward a single, narrow mountain sticking out of the ground like a jagged, craggy pillar. A monolith. Lengthy sludge pools encircled it, reflecting her widened eyes and wind-frizzed hair back at her. Noxious fumes rose from their depths, mixing with the odor seeping from the monolith like a tangible thing.

Her feet ached to run away, but to where? Back into the monster town? Into the unfamiliar forest?

At the foot of the monolith, two hulking monsters, like oxen mixed with humans, stood at a cave entrance. They didn't move when the reaper passed them, and Asheel scurried into the cavern after him. Just inside, glowing pink veins laced the walls, ceiling, and floor where they glittered like sequined ribbons. Their vibrancy pierced the darkness and lit their path into a larger chamber with several branching tunnels.

Monsters that looked like snakes with stubby feet but no arms hissed at Asheel. One red-tinged snake coiled around her, and she dove forward and clung to the reaper's vest. He briefly turned, shooed the snake away, and pulled Asheel around to his side. She hated that his presence comforted her, but she didn't cower when he rested his arm just behind her shoulders to usher her into another tunnel.

Only a few steps in, shrieks echoed to them from deeper in the mountain. Asheel's heart pounded and she took a backwards step to flee the cavern, but the reaper's grasp around her shoulders tightened and he pushed her forward with urgency. He dragged her by the wrist again by the time they reached a wooden door that swung open with a small, fuzzy monster tripping through it. The fuzzy monster clutched a glass vial to its chest and peered at Asheel while it stumbled past.

The reaper shoved Asheel through the door and walked past her into the expansive, messy cavern while waving his hands in exasperated motions towards his face.

More pink veins laced the walls and glowed even brighter than they had in the tunnel. From the ceiling, a narrow trickle of pale pink water fell into a pool a little larger than her old office at the council building. But the water didn't sound right, like a drain instead of splashing. Where the trickle met the pool, the water instead flared and flowed upward, disappearing into the ceiling. The glowing veins consolidated at that opening and disappeared into the hole.

Movement beside the pool pulled Asheel's attention from the reverse waterfall, and she stepped back, pressed against the door, when she caught sight of the monster lolling at the pool's shoreline surrounded by empty vials and bottles. She tried to shove the door open, but it wouldn't budge; the pink veins held it in place, closed, locked against the stone walls.

Snake-like monsters climbed over the large, sprawling monster, picking at its scales and clearing debris from around it. They skittered to the sides of the cavern, kneeling with their faces to the floor, when the monster rose onto its back legs and hefted its bulk to face the reaper and Asheel. Oil-black scales reflected the pink glow from the cavern walls and oozed slime down its sides. The skin across the monster's gut bulged, stretched thin like a membrane, and pulsed with dark red light. At its full height, at least three times taller than Asheel, its massive, clawed hands hung just off the ground. Coughs gurgled from its wrinkled, protruding snout, and a spray of pink coated the cavern floor in front of it. It opened its disproportionately large eyes, shimmering like the Gate in a pulsing rainbow of color, which skipped over the reaper and locked onto Asheel who fell to her knees.

"This one looks especially delicious," the monster said in a growly voice. A lumpy, slime-covered tongue flopped over its mismatched fangs.

The reaper motioned frantically at his face again, and the monster chuckled. It lifted a grotesque hand and dragged a claw over the skeleton's mouth, each seam of smoke dissolving in an array of tiny blue sparks. The sparks swirled around the monster's hand and soaked into its skin.

The reaper tossed his hands over his head and finally spoke for the first time in a young, accented voice. "You couldn't wait a few more minutes for me to get here? I'm not that late."

"I always have room for a snack," the monster said then turned back to Asheel. "But look at this one. Not even bruised! Such a beautiful fruit you've brought me."

The reaper turned his head slightly toward Asheel but paused and shook his head. "She came willingly." His voice was clear, low, but not as raspy as Asheel expected.

"I love a willing feast!" The monster clapped his hands once and rubbed them together.

The reaper kept his coal eyes at the cavern floor while he walked back to Asheel and grabbed her hand roughly to drag her to the pool. Though the pink water was clear and calm as a stream's trickle, she knew whatever its purpose, it wasn't good. She tried to escape, to run back to the door, but slipped on the wet stone, unable to escape the reaper's grasp, which left scuffs across her wrist.

He shoved her into the pool.

The water, cold and heavy, swirled around her waist in frothy bubbles that climbed up her torso and over her shoulders. She swiped at the bubbles and reached for the water's edge, but the bubbles locked her in place like chains. They held her there for only a few seconds before slipping back down her sides and flowing like tadpoles to the waterfall, which flowed faster and grew stronger, from a trickle to a cascade.

The waterfall widened and lit up like it was on fire, and like a window, figures formed through it. The hulking, scaled monster watched the display with drool dripping down his neck. The reaper also ignored her, staring at his feet with his arms crossed. Voices started from the waterfall, speaking faster than Asheel could understand, and she turned back to it to find her own pale face staring back but younger with lowered brows and tears in her eyes.

The scene played quickly, rushing through the memory, but Asheel recalled the day, blurred with age. It had been after the first time a friend told her they hated her. She'd retaliated by stealing the kid's toy and breaking it then burying the pieces in the dirt behind a barn. Shame burned her cheeks where she stood in the pool, but she vividly remembered the feeling of rejection.

The image flickered, and another scene played, a few months after the first. They were at school, and six of her peers were circled together when one glanced her way and whispered "she's coming" before the group ran from the room. Little Asheel had chased after them, and when she finally caught up to them, she shoved the girl closest to her and called them the worst names she knew at the time.

Another moment from her life flickered in the waterfall. Then another and another, faster and faster, her actions worsening with each one, lies about her peers to ruin their reputations, a small fire in a flower bed, until she saw herself carving the reaper's head on the desk in her office.

The scene flickered again, and moments Asheel hadn't yet lived played out before her. She grew older, fine lines outlining her face, eyes growing harder. She didn't recognize the horrible person she'd become. The acts she committed flushed her cheeks deeper, more vandalism, thievery, and ruining the lives around her.

"Is this my future?" she whispered.

"Hush." The monster waved a massive hand, dismissing her.

Steam coiled along the surface of the pool just as the image flickered again, and Asheel lurched back. Her face snarled right at her and lit up in flames to reveal the reaper staring in her place.

The oily, scaled monster gasped beside her. Vials clinked and broke under its steps, then it charged through the water and shoved her out of the pool. It held her to the ground under its hand on the opposite shore while the snake-like creatures hissed and writhed along the edges.

"My dear Reaper," the monster said jovially, its dripping mouth inches from Asheel's face, blasting her with rancid breath, "look at this!"

Asheel squirmed under the monster's hand but couldn't move. She couldn't breathe with the weight of it, but the monster lifted its claws before her lungs could start burning. She jumped up and took a step toward the reaper before realizing he wouldn't protect her. She stood quivering between the two beasts, both hopeless and ready to fight for her life, but she didn't have a chance against a monster of fire and a beast larger than a bear. The snakes could wrap around her and hold her still for whatever they were going to do. She glanced at the door, which remained closed with the reaper between her and it.

The reaper had dropped his arms to his sides and stood rigid with his gaze pinned to her, unreadable as ever. She ran through anything she could say to convince him to save her, but she'd already offered her life for Coby's. What more could she offer?

"You've really brought us a treasure this time," the oily monster said. "Aren't you excited?" Its wrinkled face drooped then it sneered. "Good that I had that snack since I can't feast from her now."

The reaper didn't move or make a sound. He just stared at Asheel.

"What's wrong?" The monster snorted then squinted with its eyes darting between the reaper and Asheel. "It's been so long since we've found another. I began to think maybe you were the last. Maybe I should keep both of you around in case there aren't any more reapers left."

The reaper finally snapped out of whatever spell had frozen him in place, and he crossed his arms again. "But my contract . . ." He clenched his teeth. "I'm done working for you now."

The grotesque monster snarled. "It's my contract, and I can change it if I want." It sat back on its haunches. "Besides, the contract is until another reaper changes. She's not yet changed. And about that," its lumpy tongue slid along its top fangs, "you have a month."

The reaper stuttered over a few words and finally stepped forward to place his hand on Asheel's shoulder, which she flinched under, but he didn't look away from the huge monster.

"One? The previous reaper had three months, and it took all three for me to change. Give me at least that long."

"Don't question me." The oily monster flicked a clawed hand, shooing them away.

The reaper screamed and collapsed, leaving Asheel wavering on her feet beside him. "Please!" he shouted between pained grunts. "Why would the previous guy get three and I only get one?" He gasped again and shivered from whatever pain racked his body.

The oily scaled monster licked his snout and rose from his throne, towering over the reaper. "Fine. I'll give you *two* months. But a bargain, if she doesn't change, I'll kill her regardless of if she survives the Stream of Judgment, and her death will be on you." The monster grinned, his fangs reflecting the pink light. "Deal?"

The reaper took a deep breath and clenched his teeth. "Deal."

"Take her. You have two months." The monster turned and

ambled to a large stone throne where he sat while the snake monsters flitted around him. "Go! I need to send for another to finish my meal." He then released a booming roar that had Asheel covering her ears.

The reaper shoved her back through the door and back through the tunnels, and when they reached the first large chamber at the entrance, she planted her feet.

"What's going on?" If she wouldn't be killed right away, she wanted to be prepared for whatever dangers she was about to face for two months.

"Just keep moving." He glanced over her shoulder and grimaced. "Keeping you safe is going to be a pain."

"I'm not budging until you explain," she demanded, her clothes dripping from the pool that showed her past. "What was that display and why are you dragging me back into . . . whatever world is out there?"

The reaper ground his teeth together, then grabbed her around her waist and tossed her over his shoulder like he had carried her into the Gate. "It was showing your crimes," he muttered. "This is like a jail for people who'd end up torturing the human realm."

"But I haven't done even half the things the waterfall showed." Asheel grunted from the reaper's bony shoulder jabbing into her stomach.

"You would have."

Would she? One of the scenes of her cackling while the reaper carried off a Seshnian flitted through her mind. A memory not yet happened. She flushed, knowing it could have happened. If it had been someone who'd been mean to her, spat on her, called her cruel things, she could see herself wanting to laugh while the townsperson got what they deserved, but she wouldn't have blatantly laughed in their face. Would she? Would she get to that point?

The waterfall had also shown her face catching on fire and

turning into the reaper's, and she held back the tears from what she thought it might mean. "I'm supposed to be like you? A . . . reaper?"

"Yes." He didn't hesitate in his answer.

Asheel huffed and squirmed, but the reaper tightened his grip across her thighs. She hated him. She completely, unwaveringly hated him, and she beat his back to ensure he knew.

CHAPTER 12

Asheel kept her eyes on the backs of the reaper's feet while he carried her down a winding path and into a pine forest. At a stone cabin, tucked into a small meadow of wildflowers, he set her on her feet. An expansive pile of pebbles covered the ground around the cabin except for a narrow path that led to a cracked, barely connected wood door with scorch marks around the handle. No other monsters wandered around, and the peace of the setting on top of her exhaustion almost lulled Asheel to sleep where she stood with sunlight dancing through the trees.

The reaper shoved the door open and stepped into the small, one-room cabin. "I know this may look pathetic," he said, "but it's home."

"At least it seems more pleasant than the monolith."

"And safer," the reaper said, "as long as I'm around. Except maybe against Doyen."

"Doyen? The scaly big guy?"

"Yeah, him."

The cabin door creaked closed behind Asheel, and when her eyes adjusted to the dim light from a single window, she met the reaper's coal eyes.

He looked away and left her standing at the door while he scurried around, picking up blankets, vests, and empty vials. His shoulders relaxed, and he moved as if he could finally stop looking over his shoulder. One corner was a kitchen area. Opposite that was an unmade bed. Across from the bed was an open bathroom with a dusty divider folded and leaned against the wall, and the last corner had a simple, lightly cushioned couch. A worn table with dusty chairs sat in the middle of the room, and stacked near a wall, a tower of weapons lay haphazardly. At the bottom, as if it had been tossed into the disarray and skidded down to the floor, her knife, unmistakably hers, glinted at her. The one she'd stabbed into the reaper's ribs.

"I wasn't prepared for a visitor," he said and motioned to the table, "and definitely not the next reaper."

"The next reaper," Asheel repeated, hating the sound of it and tearing her eyes from her knife to sit on a chair hesitantly. She'd seen her face change to his, heard him say as much in the monolith, but she hoped he'd say otherwise. "And if I refuse?"

"You die. Your choice." He retrieved two cups from his kitchen and set one filled with water in front of her, which she peered at, not touching it. "Though, I'd rather you not die, please." He sat across from her with his own cup full of thick, pink liquid and nodded at her cup. "It's fine to drink."

"What's in yours?" she asked.

He frowned at the pink liquid. "Something like medicine. Not for you yet."

She was parched, and the water was tempting. What was the worst that could happen? He'd just admitted he didn't want her dead, so she sipped the water then chugged the entire cupful.

"See?" Reaper smirked. "Fine."

"I expected it to turn me into you."

"A drink won't do that. You have to do that on your own." He looked away and tapped his fingers on the table.

"Tell me what's going on before I lose my mind," she demanded, clutching the empty cup.

"Don't go blaming me for all of this. I can't control any of it." He held up a hand in defense, his words echoing Asheel's own from her past. "You're a reaper like me," he confirmed again, "and believe it or not, that's a good thing. If Doyen hadn't shoved you out of the pool, you would likely be dead. Most don't survive." He dropped his gaze from hers and sipped his pink drink.

Dozens of questions streamed through Asheel. When would she become a reaper? How would it happen? Could she prevent it? Most don't survive? So that massive monster, Doyen, didn't kill all of his victims?

"There are other humans here?"

The reaper looked confused.

"You said most don't survive. So there are other survivors, right?"

"Oh, no. I mean most don't survive the Stream of Judgment, but those who do aren't human after. The stream strips away everything you are. It pulls your humanity from you, which Doyen consumes, and then it crashes back down," he splayed his hand flat on the table, "with everything that's left of you, which is only the inner monster, your most consuming feeling that already exists. Everyone you saw in the city, they're the survivors."

While the reaper rambled on about how he could usually guess by now what monster someone would turn into while watching the Stream of Judgment, Asheel shivered. The monsters had all been human once. She tried to imagine it, the stream stripping away who she was. Would becoming a monster be better or worse than dying?

The reaper continued. "If he hadn't pushed you out and if you survived the stream, you'd look like me right now, but we're the only type of monster he lets keep their humanity. Speaking of."

He sighed and tilted his head back. The tendrils of smoke that danced around him fell along his charred bones, and the scraps of burnt flesh wove together to form muscle and skin. The tendrils from his scalp became shaggy brown hair with fried tips. His skin had a grey pallor to it, decorated by scorched lines where his veins would be. Deep black semicircles arched under his clear, human eyes, and fire-orange irises stared back at Asheel.

The new face that sat across the table from her couldn't have been much older than a teen, and his smile exposed a youthful joy.

"What do you think?" He gestured to himself and winked.

Asheel squinted and reminded herself that he was still the reaper. He was still the monster that ravaged her home every month. "I liked you better before," she said. "A new face won't hide who you really are from me."

The reaper sipped his drink. "This is the real me."

"Is this what you mean that you got to keep your humanity?" Asheel asked. She eyed the black veins crawling up his neck and shifting when he swallowed. "Because you're not exactly human."

He frowned at his grey arms. "This is as good as it gets here."

Asheel fingered the lip of her cup and tried to imagine him without the weird marks. Tried to imagine his skin flushed with color, his hair healthy instead of scorched, his orange eyes a normal hue. Maybe brown. But all she saw in front of her was the reaper she'd always known. Was he really someone more than a reaper?

"What's your name?" she asked.

His frown deepened, but he looked up. "Reaper."

"You don't get to keep your name?"

His shrug jostled his mottled leather vest. "It's what everyone calls me. No one's asked if I had another one in a long time."

"So you do have a name?"

"Just call me Reaper." He gulped the rest of his drink and stared out the window at the lightening sky. "You must be tired. I know I am." He rubbed the dark streaks under his eyes, stood, and fiddled with the blankets on the bed. "I'll take the couch."

"Not a chance." Asheel stood, her chair scraping against the stone floor. He'd been answering her questions, at least somewhat, but how could she trust anything that he'd said? What would stop him from doing whatever he wanted to her when she fell asleep? Her eyes burned and a dull headache pulsed at the back of her head, but she'd only sleep in a den of monsters when she'd completely given up.

"It's already early morning, and you're basically dead on your feet." Reaper flopped onto the couch with a blanket and glanced up at her. "You don't have to sleep but don't leave the cabin. It's not safe out there."

"And being with you is?"

"Believe it or not, yes."

"Why should I trust you?"

"Have you not been listening?" He propped himself up on an arm and smiled at her, a genuine thing that dimpled his cheeks. "I've been waiting four hundred years to find you so you can free me. I'd be an idiot to let anything happen to you."

That made sense if it were the truth, but he hadn't given her any reason to trust him yet. He'd taken her from her home and now she was trapped in his cabin. Though he'd kept of his end of their deal so far—he'd left Coby and taken her in his place.

Exhaustion weighed on Asheel, but now that she was alone with Reaper, she wasn't sure she could sleep with such a monster in the same room.

"I'm not sleeping in your bed," Asheel blurted. "I'm not that tired," she added at his startled expression.

"Suit yourself." Reaper lay on the couch and pulled the

blanket to his chin. "I'm tired enough for the both of us. Just don't leave the cabin without me," he repeated the warning. "I can't protect you if I'm not with you."

And with that, he closed his eyes. If she ignored his scorched appearance, he really did look like a kid. His cheeks still had a roundness to them, and his eyebrows relaxed. Did he think she'd just stay in here? The door didn't even have a lock on it.

She watched the reaper while she stepped toward the door, but her shoe scuffed the stone floor.

He cracked an eye open at her. "If you think you can find your way home, those monsters will shred you before you get anywhere close to the Gate. Just go lay down for a while." He flipped over and adjusted the blanket over his shoulders. "And pull the curtains closed."

She leaned over the bed and did as he said, which veiled the room in darkness. Only slivers of light slipped through the cracks in the door. The bed was lumpy and the blanket felt like old, dried cowhide, but she was comfortable enough. So much had happened since she'd been on the plateau with Jean. How long would he wait for her to come back before finding a new apprentice? Surely someone would tell him the reaper got her.

If she hadn't left her post with Jean, would Coby be lying in this bed instead of her? Would he have died at Doyen's hands instead of sent with the reaper? Would being dead be better than whatever was to become of her? What was her family doing while she nestled in Reaper's home? Had they gone to bed? Chased after her? Were they mourning her loss, or had they already gotten used to her being gone on the plateaus?

Would Seshnia think she got what she deserved? A few years back someone had tried to convince the council to sacrifice her at the dead zone around the Gate, but thankfully, they weren't that heartless.

Her family. She couldn't stop thinking about them, couldn't stop imagining Coby going through this if she hadn't gone in his place. He was safe for now, but could she figure out a way to stop the reaper from this side and keep the innocent people like Coby safe forever? She stared into the darkness toward where Reaper snored. If she stabbed him when he was "human," as he'd called himself, would he recover as fast as when he was a skeleton?

An hour passed, ticking away from an old, dusty clock hanging in the kitchen, while her eyes darted between Reaper and the weapons. Dust covered some, but others glinted, shiny and sharp even in the darkened room. Her knife wouldn't be enough to kill him, but one of the swords could. Debates from the council about decapitation echoed through her thoughts, but was she strong enough to do that?

Reaper's snoring stayed steady while Asheel crept out of bed and to the stack. She carefully lifted a sword from the top, and though it was heavy, she thought the weight might help her strike. Sure, without the reaper protecting her from the other monsters, she was doomed to die, but dying to save everyone would be worth it.

Standing over Reaper, his boyish face relaxed and twitching with dreams, she lifted the blade and calculated her strike. Head? Skulls were strong. Torso? His stomach wounds healed so fast; if any magic stayed in his system as a human, that'd be a pointless strike. She might only have one chance, and even if she wasn't strong enough to cut through him completely, it'd have to be the most severe injury she could cause. The neck.

She raised the blade even higher, aimed, closed her eyes, and brought it down as hard and fast as she could, ignoring the squelch and *thunk*. She let go of the blade and jumped back, tripping over a chair and falling onto her rump before opening her eyes.

On the couch, the reaper's head had completely detached from his body, and the sword stuck into the worn cushion then slowly dislodged and slid to the floor with a clatter. Reaper's eyes were open, staring blankly at the ceiling and his mouth hung in a silent scream.

She'd done it. She closed her eyes to hide the carnage, but

she'd done it. She pulled her legs to her chest, wrapped her arms around them, and sobbed with relief. Maybe every moment of her life had led her to this. Maybe she had to suffer back home to make her despicable enough to get to the monster realm and kill the reaper in his human form. She was the only one who could do it, and no one would ever know it was her.

Her tears soaked her knees and her thoughts shifted to getting to the Gate and back home, but only seconds had passed when the couch groaned. Her head snapped up in time to see the last ribbons of blue smoke weaving Reaper's neck back together. He gasped and sat up, rubbing his neck and grimacing.

"Ouch." He coughed and panted, then his glare narrowed to Asheel on the floor. "Don't you think that's a little unfair attacking someone while they sleep."

Asheel scooted away from him, a chair sliding out of her way with a panicked screech.

"Though I guess I've taken sleeping people before, so never mind. That's actually kind of fair." He took a deep breath then spun to face her, planting his feet on the floor and gripping his knees. "I'll reiterate what I thought everyone in both worlds already knew. I can't die. If I could, I would. Trust me. Forget what the monsters and humans have done, I've tried everything myself."

He couldn't die. Asheel shivered. Then how were they supposed to stop him?

"I'll forgive you for this since you've had a rough day or so." He kicked the sword across the floor to her, and it skidded to a halt at her feet. "Keep that if it makes you feel safer but go lay down. If you wake me again, I'll rip off one of your limbs, and it won't reattach like mine." He raised his eyebrows and nodded pointedly at the bed. "Go."

So the *I won't let anything happen to you* he'd said earlier was really *I'll keep you alive*. She was right not to trust him fully.

Asheel left the sword on the floor and scampered back to the bed where she dove under the blanket and covered her head. She'd been so confident, but all hope of stopping the reaper on either side of the Gate shattered. If he could survive decapitation even in his human form, it was hopeless.

The reaper was truly unstoppable.

CHAPTER 13

Asheel woke to a wooden spoon clattering on the floor. She bolted upright and pushed herself to the far corner of the bed while her mind caught up to where she was. Doyen's eyes that pulsed like the Gate had been staring at her in her dreams, sometimes his scaly body forming in the haze of her mind's eye.

"Sleep well?" Reaper asked.

Setting sunlight streamed through the window. She'd slept through him leaning over her to open the curtain, and the thought made her sick.

When she didn't answer, Reaper lifted a pot and tilted his chin toward it. "Want some lunch?"

Her mind wanted to relax after the previous night of terror, but her body was torn between hunger and flight. She had to get out. She shook her head and frowned. She couldn't leave. She wouldn't survive the monsters out there.

"Probably a good thing if you skip a meal." Reaper mistook

her head shake for refusal. He sat at the table with the pot and took a large bite. "Being hungry might make your first transition easier."

Transition? Having her skin burn off and becoming a fiery skeleton? No, dismemberment by monster was a better fate. She would escape as soon as she could, but she needed food or she'd collapse halfway back to the Gate. She slid off the bed and hesitantly joined him at the table. The sword from her failed attack had rejoined its companions in the weapon pile.

"What is that?" She nodded at the pot.

"Maple leaf stew." He held the spoon out to her.

Asheel sniffed the spoon then took it and tasted the watery, leafy concoction. The bitter broth landed in her stomach with a gurgle, and when she asked for more, Reaper retrieved a bowl and split the meal between them. She ate slowly, lost in her thoughts, guilt building with every bite. Guilt that she'd slept so deeply for so long. Guilt about talking to the reaper, about being chosen as one herself. Guilt about eating with the monster who'd terrorized her life, finding out he was something more than a mindless beast. Fear joined the guilt. She'd attacked him, hurt him. Surely he'd want revenge. Though, he'd said it was a fair trade for his own actions.

Reaper chewed and watched her. "You seem a little confused. Anything you want to know?"

"Why do you do it?" The question leapt from her mouth before she could stop it. It had looped back around repeatedly while she'd fought sleep. "Why do you kidnap people?"

"It's part of the cycle. I take stained people out of the human realm before they turn into monsters, Doyen gets his meal of their humanity, and the human realm stays a utopia."

"Utopia?" Asheel scoffed. "We live our lives in fear of who'll be taken next. That's not a utopia. Half the people haven't even done anything wrong yet."

"But they will." Reaper shoveled in another spoonful. "That's part of the deal. I only take those with a monster brewing inside them."

"You mentioned inner monsters before. What is that?"

"It's in their nature. Something happens and thoughts start to set in for revenge, power, thievery, you name it."

She remembered the moment Coby's own stench had burned her nose after Reaper took Kady. It wasn't in his nature. Coby was a sweet kid, just angry about his friend. He would have never reeked if Reaper hadn't caused it himself. He wouldn't have even done anything other than stew in his anger until the stench left him. "Why take them before they act out?" she asked. "You don't know if they'll make that choice."

"They will. Just like you will. Some deny that they would have acted out until the day they die, but it's there."

Asheel wrapped her arms around her knees. "Why not leave them alone and let them commit crimes, then take them? Then you could know for sure they'll become a monster."

"Again, to keep the human realm clean. If we don't take them before their inner monster consumes them, they'll change over there, and it's contagious. If one person gives in, another will mirror them, and so on. It becomes more than just accepted as a part of life. It becomes expected. That's why the Gate exists. A prison for monsters. We force the monster out of them, strip them of their humanity, and they can never go back to infect the world."

Asheel sat up. "I'm stuck over here? Why can *you* go back to the human realm?"

"No, we're the exception. We keep our humanity, and the Gate allows us back through. It only lets humans whose inner monsters have awakened enough through to this side and only monsters who still have enough humanity left back through to the human side. That's why we're the only monsters who have to let our monsters out without being forced by the Stream of Judgment. It removes humanity, and if we didn't have enough left, the Gate would trap us inside it forever."

Her heart stuttered at the thought, the Gate's yellow fog squeezing it and pulling her farther into the mist. She never wanted to deal with those hands again, but she had to face them to get back home, which she had two months to figure out. "Why us? You, me. Why not some other type of monster?"

Reaper shrugged. "The best answer I could get from Doyen when I asked that same question was that we have a little something extra inside, by the inner monster."

Something extra? Like the magic she had that made the world smell so foul? Had Reaper been like her? "How do you know who to take in the human realm?"

He pointed to his eyes. "When in the reaper form, I can see it." He dropped his hands to his lap, palms up with his fingers slightly curled, and he stared at his hands with his brow furrowed. "It pulls me like a magnet, and I can't ignore it."

Asheel's magic didn't pull her like that, especially not visually. It repulsed her, made her want to flee. "Before you became a reaper, did you have something like that reaper sight?"

He tilted his head. "Not that I remember. Nothing like the trails like I can now."

"Could you see auras around people?" Lana's ability sounded more like what he described but not quite the same.

"Like the Okulars? Definitely not." He wrinkled his nose and scrunched up his face. "I expected questions about what's to become of you and how this world works, not such weird questions about my past." He narrowed his eyes at her. "Can you see shadowed trails to people now? As a human?"

"Just curious." She shook her head and ate more of the unsatisfying stew. "What's an Okular?"

"I forget the human realm doesn't know much about sensory

magic yet." He leaned back and stared at the ceiling while ticking off names on his fingers. "Okulars see visual disturbances around people. They can tell who's trustworthy."

Lana. Her magic had a name. She was an Okular.

"Don't ever kiss a Lingual," Reaper continued, "or you'll be begging them for more. It has something to do with their taste. They know exactly what someone wants." He held up a third finger. "Audibles are the most annoying. They can hear what you're thinking about them, but that makes them grumpy rather than dangerous. Aromators smell someone's deepest desires."

Aromator. She had a name too. She dropped her gaze to her bowl, stirring the leaf chunks. The way Reaper was speaking, magic was common or at least well known in the monster realm.

"I'm not sure if Aromators and Linguals are rare or if they don't know they have magic since their gifts are subtler."

Subtle? The waves of putrid manure rolling off Reaper weren't subtle at all, but maybe other *Aromators* weren't as blunt as her.

"Then there's us Physiqals." A fifth finger joined the others, and he examined it like he'd only just noticed it existed. "I'm one of them but didn't realize it for a long time. It's a subtle ability too, so most don't realize they have it until they get over here. We can momentarily influence perceptions through touch. It fades though, so it's kind of pointless."

Asheel's spoon clattered in her bowl as she pushed back from the table. "You have magic?"

"Yeah," he waved off her concern, "but I don't use it much. Like I said, it's pointless to influence someone temporarily if they'll go right back to how they feel about you." When she didn't relax his smirk turned to a frown. "Don't worry. I won't use it on you. You have to change on your own, and my influence won't make that happen." The corners of his mouth dipped lower. "At least I don't think I can influence that."

Asheel leaned away from him.

"No," he said to himself. "Maybe as a last resort."

An ominous silence fell over the room while Asheel considered how to avoid her future altogether. This had to be a dream. She'd wake up from the nightmare and find herself surrounded by sheep on Seshnia's plateaus.

"Does the Stream of Judgment not take sensory magic from them with their humanity?" she asked.

"Nope. If anything, it's why some of them become monsters. Power seems to hasten corruption. A lot of nobles and royalty end up here too."

The Novish king could be here. And the royal advisors, the three with sensory magic, could become targets. Her questions kept spilling out of her. "How common is magic here?"

"There's a few in every community, but it's their fangs and claws you should worry about." Reaper looked at the window and chewed on his bottom lip. "I really need to finish some errands before I go to the human realm, but I can't leave you here unprotected."

Fangs and claws she could see. It was their unseen dangers that worried her more. "Do all the monsters want to kill me?"

He shrugged. "I wouldn't put it past any of them just to get revenge on me, and I'm sure all of them know you're here by now." He stood, opened a deep trunk at the foot of the bed, and dug through a pile of the strange leather he wore. "They may know you're with me, but I'd feel better if we can keep their eyes off you." He offered her a hooded shirt from the pile. "I haven't used this one in a long time."

Asheel pulled it over her head and left the hood up. The sleeves hung several inches too long and the shirt fell halfway down her thighs, but if hiding her appearance was what Reaper wanted, he succeeded.

"It's a little big." Asheel held up her arms to let the sleeves dangle in front of her.

"You're just short." He returned to the kitchen with the pot and her half empty bowl and dumped the rest down the sink. He then shoved some pink-filled vials into a bag along with a few creamy white papers, tossed it over his shoulder, and turned to scrutinize her.

"Can't I just stay here? You said it's safe in here, right?" Going back out among the monsters sounded as appealing as having her flesh burn off. "I promise to behave."

Reaper snorted and shook his head, tossing his hair across his forehead. "It's safe with me, not my cabin. They know where I live, so come on." He pushed open the door. "I'm already late."

"Late for what?" She slid to the edge of her chair but didn't stand.

"You ask a lot of questions, don't you? You're about to experience the intricacies of the black market." He smiled, but tension creased his eyes. When she still didn't move, his shoulders drooped. "Look, I can drag you around all evening tossed over my shoulder, but we'll both be more comfortable if you use your own little dainty feet to get moving."

With no other choice, she followed Reaper out the door, pulling the hood low over her eyes.

If she didn't know any better, the forest surrounding his cabin reminded her of home. Pines stretched above them, but the undergrowth grew sparser with plants she'd never seen, all with the ever-present pink veins. No monsters hid behind the trunks, but Asheel knew better. Monsters were out there, even if not in that forest.

Reaper tried to keep the conversation going, but Asheel ignored him, lost in her own thoughts again. After several ignored questions and a stretch of awkward silence, Reaper sighed.

"I guess you *should* stay quiet," he said. "Best if you don't talk while I'm handling the deals."

After a few more minutes of walking, the path exited the

forest into a field of waving grasses. A few monsters huddled at a crossroad, chortling and grunting in languages Asheel didn't understand, and she trotted up to Reaper, staying close enough behind him to grab the back of his vest if she needed. The monsters eyed her as they passed, but nothing happened.

"I hate this," Asheel muttered.

"You'll get used to it. It'll be easier when you've changed since they won't be able to touch you then. Doyen's magic will heal you from anything they could do."

She shook her head behind Reaper's back. She wouldn't. She refused to be a monster. She'd escape and get home somehow.

They passed more monsters, all staring but keeping their distance. They were calmer than the ones she'd seen in the monster town, and a few feathered children ran past, shoving each other but playing rather than fighting. They'd been humans. They could even be kids she'd recently checked. But then she caught their accented shouts, a different language, nothing like she'd heard before.

"Where are they from?" Asheel whispered.

Reaper glanced at the kids. "The outskirts of Vardi."

The country with electric inventions like the lantern the traveler had brought to Seshnia's Gate Feast. "Did you have to learn everyone's language?"

"No. But you don't need to know a language to understand how they feel. Joy is still joy, fear is still fear, and pain is the same. Humanity is global. Language just provides depth to it." He then waved and shouted a greeting at the kids in their language. He was right. Asheel could understand his intention, but the kids still shrieked and ran away. "But after so many years, you can't help but pick up some words."

Asheel stayed close behind Reaper while they entered the city and during Reaper's trades. He stopped at decaying buildings, slipped into alleyways, called to a bird creature on a rooftop, and even stomped on a sewer hatch, but for a black market, their dealings were public. In the open, in view of the whole city, he traded vials of the pink liquid for food, tools, services, bargained deals for later dates. He traded his white papers for pink-tinted ones with a beast in a darkened alley. Some asked questions about Asheel, which he waved off with a promise to introduce them later when she wasn't in shock. Each of them reeked in a soup of the worst scents. A breeze of feces, a whiff of compost, someone in the mix even smelled like the tanner shop full of animal hides back home. It overwhelmed her so much that she couldn't pin any of the odors to particular creatures.

A long-limbed monster covered in grey-brown fur welcomed Reaper and lowered the front of her small cart to the ground to trade with him. Her biceps bulged with the movement. With bluish, human-like eyes, she examined Reaper's offering over a stubby nose.

"This is all you're giving me?" She held the clinking vials between them. "If you keep giving all of them away, I'm out of a job!"

"Relax. I only traded with my usuals." Reaper jerked his head toward Asheel. "I'm sure you've already heard about the human. Supplies are low today thanks to her."

"Fine. Fine." The grey-brown monster rolled her eyes at his excuse and handed him a large satchel of greens. They left her, the most pleasant creature they'd met so far, while she organized the new stock on her cart.

"That's the, uh . . ." he held up a pink vial and tapped it, "the peddler. There's not many of her kind. She's easy enough to get along with, but don't try to get the better end of a bargain with her."

The monsters who Reaper didn't trade with watched her like an oddity. Some came closer and sniffed or reached toward her but then scurried away when Reaper spun to face them. One hairless creature with a crown of stubby horns motioned at her to leave Reaper's side and join her under an awning, clicking her tongue as if Asheel were an animal. Asheel avoided the crowned creature's gaze and pulled the hood so low she could only see Reaper's feet in front of her.

She hid in the shadows behind Reaper while he exchanged a small vial with a slimy creature with ruffly green fins sticking out of his face.

"This is it?" The creature wrapped webbed fingers around the vial. "I can't get you half the seaweed you want for this."

"That's all that's left." Reaper crossed his arms. "You want it, you pay up."

While the two argued over the trade, Asheel tried imagining the monsters as humans. They'd all been like her before, every one of them, but seeing past the animalistic qualities was difficult. A clawed hand fell onto her shoulder, and she turned to find a bat-like face. The creature put a finger to Asheel's lips, and a wave of calm washed over her.

"Let's go somewhere a little safer for you, shall we?" the monster said, her own lips pulling up to reveal serrated fangs.

Asheel didn't want to go. She knew she didn't want to, knew she should stay by Reaper, but something at the front of her mind pushed what she knew to the deepest crevices of her thoughts where it vanished, all her focus and wants tying to the bat creature.

"Where's safer?" Asheel asked, turning to face the bat. She couldn't look away, and the desires hummed across her skull like a hypnotic rain shower, tingling and calming.

The bat tightened her grip on Asheel's shoulder and guided her away from where Reaper was finishing his last trade. "My place is perfect for you to relax." She leaned close to Asheel's cheek and sniffed. "You can stay there as long as you like."

The words didn't make sense. Asheel didn't like the idea of going home with this strange creature, but her worries slid away until it didn't matter. The bat sniffed at her cheek again and opened her mouth to graze a fang across it. The pain registered briefly before slipping away with the rest of her thoughts while the bat licked a smudge of blood from the cut.

"Leave her alone," a familiar voice called out. It was a voice she hated, but it reached the thoughts that had been lost in the depths of her mind. It was a voice she wanted to hear, and she let her head roll back until she could see Reaper to give him a sloppy smile.

"I found a friend," Asheel mumbled.

The bat hissed at Reaper before letting Asheel go and fleeing down an alley, running from Reaper's presence like everyone else he hadn't traded with. Asheel's legs buckled with the warm buzzing from the bat's touch gone, and she fell into Reaper's open arms with a giggle.

"You okay?" He held her elbow and wiped his thumb across the small wound on her cheek.

Asheel's own thoughts emerged through the murk in her mind, memories of who Reaper was, what she was doing here, quieting the foreign thoughts of wanting to follow the bat monster. Shivers crept up her spine and her limbs shook from the shock.

"What happened?" she asked.

Reaper held her elbow longer, steadying her and guiding her first few steps out of the alley back to the street. "A Physiqal. The feelings pass quickly once contact is broken. Back to yourself again?"

She did but with new feelings of being betrayed. She hadn't been under the monsters influence for more than a minute, and she couldn't imagine how much more morose she'd be if it had been longer. She wanted to go back to Reaper's cabin and hide.

"How much more do you have left?" Asheel's shaking touched her voice.

"That was the last trade."

"Good. Your dingy cabin is better than this city."

"We're not going back there. I have to do my reaping in the human world now."

If she was going back through the Gate, escaping might be easier than she thought.

Reaper turned down another path, exiting the city, heading away from the setting sun. "I have an acquaintance that owes me, so he'll be watching you."

Her few seconds of hope for returning to the human realm slipped away like sand through her fingers. "Is he dangerous?"

He shook his head. "Don't let him lick you, though. He's a Lingual." He side-eyed her with a smirk. "Actually, you might like if he does."

Asheel looked away, not wanting to deal with every person with magic that she'd tried to avoid in the human realm, in Novoshna's palace. The idea of spending time with any of the monsters she'd seen chilled her limbs and pooled like ice in her belly, which gurgled with emptiness and nerves. Adding their magic to make her lose her own senses, how was she supposed to survive?

They walked for a while away from the city before Reaper turned them down a side path and led her to one of the largest and cleanest houses she'd seen in the monster realm. Gaudy, completely naked statues plated in silver lined the path to the entryway, which arched around a brightly colored door. Reaper kicked it a few times, and a translucent, curvy woman opened it. Her short dress hung open halfway down her front, and her organs pulsed, beat, and flexed underneath the blue-tinted skin.

She sneered as soon as she recognized Reaper and ignored Asheel hiding behind him. "Virgil!" she screamed over her shoulder. "The mutt's back! Wait there," she said to Reaper. "I don't want your ashes soiling my home."

She wandered away from the door, leaving it open, and a tall, transparent man with slick, limp hair and a hooked nose peered around the edge of the door. He frowned when he saw Reaper, but his greeting was slightly friendlier than the woman's.

"I heard you have a new apprentice," he said, his accent identical to Asheel's. He had to be from somewhere within Novoshna's borders. Then he spied Asheel behind Reaper, gasped, and covered his mouth and sharp chin with long, pointed fingers. "Is this her? She looks like she's been through Doyen's belly a dozen times. Poor thing."

Reaper interrupted the man's rambling. "I need you to watch her while I'm gone tonight. Make sure no one tries to kill her."

"Tonight? I have customers. I don't have time to babysit."

After some arguing and a little bargaining as if Asheel weren't standing right there, Virgil finally agreed to let her stay with him, but Reaper had to "provide double" on his end of their agreement, something they'd already worked out.

Reaper exchanged a few white papers for pink-tinted ones with Virgil and finally turned to Asheel. His human eyes, fiery orange and kind behind his hard expression, flicked to the cut on her cheek then back to her eyes. "I'll make this as fast as I can, but it'll still be several hours. Don't do anything stupid." He stared into her eyes for a moment longer with one of his unreadable expressions, then turned and ran down the path back toward the city.

The mansion was just as gaudy on the inside, though littered with claw marks, frayed tapestries, and the occasional questionable stain. Stairs wrapped around the sides to a landing that stuck out like an indoor balcony. The room, larger than her whole home, reeked of something that reminded her of the time she had an infection in her nose. She'd had to smell the sour odor for weeks and was thankful no one in Seshnia smelled like that. Standing in a fog of it was like being surrounded by constant infection.

In the center, several chairs and couches formed a loose circle, and Virgil plopped himself into a seat with his feet propped on a curved, short table. He flipped through the papers Reaper had given him with a slight smile before folding them into his pocket while

Asheel hesitated a few steps from the door, unsure of monster etiquette and not wanting to make herself at home as if she'd accepted her circumstances.

The curvy woman walked back into the room and straightened at the sight of Asheel. A sly smile masked the grumpiness from just a few minutes ago. "Do we have a new customer?" she asked and stroked silky dark waves of hair over her shoulder, but her smile slipped to a frown while she studied Asheel. "She's a tiny one."

Asheel tugged at the edge of her hood to hide her face, wishing to vanish.

"She's not exactly a customer," Virgil said. "Reaper's doubling our trade for me to watch her."

"Why's that?"

"Take a look." Virgil stood, pinched the back of the hood, and pulled it from her head. "She's still human."

The woman crept closer and delicately lifted a lock of Asheel's black hair to rub it between her fingers. "What we could sell her essence for . . ."

"Or how much essence Reaper's paying us with."

"We could sell her for more than he'll pay."

Two other translucent creatures entered the room and wandered down another hall, whispering to themselves and ignoring the conversation about Asheel.

Virgil shook his head. "He'd kill us before we could figure out how to get it out of her."

Asheel leaned back, and the woman let the lock of hair fall out of her hand.

"Why?" the woman asked.

"Haven't you heard they found the next reaper?"

The curvy woman's eyes widened as understanding settled, and she took Asheel's hands to lead her to the seats where Virgil had returned. "You have a rough time ahead of you," she said then spoke over her shoulder to Virgil. "It's hard to imagine Reaper as human as this girl. I almost feel sorry for him." She pursed her lips and frowned. "I take that back. I don't. He's vile and even less human than us." She turned back to Asheel and gently pushed her into one of the seats, the bouncy cushion squeaking under her like it'd had too many residents. "I'll get you a drink. You look like you've sweat out everything in you." Her sashay back into the room she'd come from was mesmerizing.

Virgil smirked while watching Asheel, his feet propped between them. "That's Ratel," he said. "She's the spunk in our home, keeps us on our toes." Another trio of translucent monsters and a fuzzy bug-eyed beast wandered through the room. Virgil watched her while stroking his hair and narrowed his eyes at her shaking limbs. "You can relax, you know. I promised Reaper I'd keep an eye on you, and no one here will bother you. We like to pretend that we're civilized. How do you feel?" he asked.

"Awful," she answered honestly. "How can I feel anything other than awful and disgusted?"

Virgil sneered. "Disgusted by us? Come on. We're the best monsters in this place."

"No," Asheel shook her head quickly, trying to take back the unintended insult, "by my circumstance."

"That doesn't make much sense either." He lifted another strand of grey hair and fiddled with it. "As far as this realm goes, you have just about the best deal. Protection." He lifted a finger. "Visiting the human realm. Staying mostly you." He lifted two more fingers. "At least, I think you do. Can't be sure on that last one since I'm not a reaper." He combed through his hair and grabbed another lock.

Asheel dried her sweaty palms on her pants, deciding Virgil might be her best option to get more information. "Aren't you still yourself?" she asked.

"You think I grew up looking like this?"

Greenish-blue shimmers glinted off his translucent skin when the light hit it, and he smiled to reveal tiny, pointed teeth.

"I mean, besides outwardly." Asheel cringed. She hadn't fully experienced the Stream of Judgment, and she wasn't sure if that was personal to ask about. "Are you not who you were before? Like . . ." Did he have the same personality? Did the negative desires of his heart grow stronger? She shrunk into her chair. "Never mind."

Virgil twirled his hair between his fingers and let it brush against his nose like a swishing tail. "I get it. We're not really. We're shells of who we were. No one can be themselves when they have their decisions, identity, and future selected for them."

"What do you mean?"

He dropped his hair again and sighed. "None of us chose this. Most of us are being punished before even committing the foul deeds that supposedly brought us here. That's why I say you have it good. No one else gets any choice in being what they become."

Asheel balked. "I didn't have a choice—" She bit her lip. She did choose this. She sacrificed herself for Coby. But she didn't know what she was choosing. If she'd known what was on the other side of the Gate, what she was willingly joining, would she still have made the same choice? Coby could have been sitting here instead, frightened around the monsters. Even if he'd become one himself—she didn't want to imagine that.

"Well, no, I doubt anyone would follow Reaper willingly, but I mean you'll choose to be one of us."

"A monster? I won't."

"I wasn't around for the last reaper change, but they're tricky guys. You will."

"Was anyone around for it? Anyone I could ask about fighting against it?"

"Just Reaper himself and Doyen." Virgil's nose scrunched at the names.

The answer chilled Asheel, the hair along her neck standing on end. Those were the two monsters who seemed to want her changed the most.

"Do you think I can resist it?" she stumbled over her words in a hurry.

"No. Doyen would never let you stay human."

Ratel returned with two cups of a sludgy drink before Asheel could press for more information.

Ratel handed one to Asheel. "It tastes better than it looks. I promise."

"Where's mine?" Virgil complained.

Ratel glared at him. "You can get your own, you lazy bum."

He harrumphed and elbowed Ratel on his way to what Asheel assumed to be a kitchen.

In the cup Ratel had handed her, foam coated the surface of a maroon mixture which smelled fruity and tantalizing and made Asheel's mouth water, but she hesitated, untrusting and overwhelmed.

"Try it." Ratel nudged the bottom of Asheel's cup then took a sip from her own. The liquid slid down her throat and disappeared behind her open dress.

"Are you sure this is okay for a human to drink?" The foam popped and sizzled, dissipating a little to reveal a syrupy liquid.

"Absolutely. We still eat all the same stuff. Mostly. Some of the more beasty monsters can get a little cannibalistic, but we here at the mansion are more refined than that."

After another sniff, Asheel took a sip and then a gulp and another. The syrup coated her mouth and throat and tasted like every fruit from the orchards back home had been mixed together with an entire sugar stick. It hit her stomach and spread an airiness through her limbs like what she could only describe as contentment and peace, and the calmness soothed all the anxieties, exhaustion, and fear she'd been drowning in.

"Wow," she whispered.

Ratel sipped again and slid into a seat. "It's the perfect cure after a long night of work." She smiled into her cup.

Asheel gulped from the cup and more of the pleasantness washed over her. "Really, this is amazing. What's in it?"

Ratel listed several ingredients that Asheel only recognized parts of—berries, nectar, and tree sap. "Then," she continued, "mix that one for one with human essence and you've got yourself the most tantalizing beverage. Delicious, right? It's my own recipe."

The first part of the drink sounded innocuous enough, but that last part woke Asheel from the drink's stupor. "Human essence?" she asked. Was she drinking juiced humans?

"It's just a phrasing." Ratel stumbled over her words. "It's not real humans or anything." Her fingers tapped against her cup. "So where are you from?"

Asheel ignored her attempt to change the subject. She'd had mentioned wanting to sell Asheel's "essence." Would monsters one day be drinking a part of her? She set the cup down and stared at Ratel with all the confidence she could muster.

"What's human essence?"

Ratel picked at her lip. "It's completely edible. Don't worry about it."

"Am I . . ." Asheel swallowed. "Am I drinking liquified humans?"

"No, no. Of course not." Ratel shook her head aggressively. "It's just the part that gets removed when we become this." She gestured to herself. "It's fine. Everyone drinks it."

Reaper had traded vials of pink liquid throughout the monster town. That was it, human essence. "That's disgusting!"

"No. Yes." Ratel set her cup down, too. "Let me explain. It's like . . . it's like the residue that's left when humanity is stripped away. It's not liquified humans. Just . . . it's just what made them human."

"I drank a human." Asheel gagged again. "I think I'm going to puke."

"I'm sorry. I just—"

"No really, I'm going to be sick." Asheel covered her mouth.

Ratel jumped up, gently pulled Asheel from her seat, and guided her down a hallway with several closed doors, Asheel covering her mouth and gagging the whole way. Halfway down the hall, Ratel shoved a door open.

"I'm sorry," Ratel said. "It's a normal drink here. I didn't consider how you might think of it. Let me get you some water. Are you okay?"

Asheel shook her head and scrambled to the toilet while her stomach roiled. "Can I have a minute?"

"I'll be right back. I'm so sorry." Ratel left and closed the door behind her.

The bathroom was larger than Reaper's whole cabin with two large tubs, what looked like machinery hanging from the walls, and the polished toilet she clung to. One large window stretched from wall to wall across from her, and the moonlight streaming through glinted off crystals that covered every surface.

She squinted at the dazzling display, but the flickering glinting only sickened her more and she heaved up the meager contents of her stomach. Ratel knocked on the door and entered with a cup of water, which she set on the counter beside Asheel, then handed her a wet cloth.

"I'm so sorry," Ratel apologized again while lighting sconces, adding another layer of wavering light.

Asheel kept her eyes closed and wiped her face. "It's okay." It wasn't. "I'll be okay." She heaved again. "Can I be alone for a minute? I'm . . . I just . . . this is a lot."

"Of course." Ratel rewet the rag and handed it back to her. "Virgil's next customer showed up so he'll be busy for a while, but I'll be in the sitting area when you're ready to come out. Straight back down the hall where we were." She patted Asheel's back then left the room again.

The weight of Asheel's situation crashed through her chest, and she collapsed into a ball on the jeweled floor. She was doomed to become the monster Seshnia had always seen her as because she wouldn't survive this realm as a human. She wrapped her arms around her legs and clutched at her filthy shepherd's trousers, the rough fabric a contrast to the gaudy display around her.

"What's all this for?" she whispered and sobbed, great tears streaking into her matted hair. "Why does this exist? Why am I here?" The questions faded to unvoiced, wordless flashes of the unfairness of everything. Reaper's face mocked in her mind, the fiery, skeletal monster who ripped her from her home. She wanted to go home. Reaper had said she could still go through the Gate, but getting back to it, running alone through the realm of monsters, reaching her family and getting them somewhere safe, was impossible.

She was alone for the first time since she arrived in the monster realm, truly alone, and she wanted to keep it that way. She crept to the door, closed it, and twisted the locks, then slid to the floor and wrapped her arms around her legs, burying her face in her knees.

CHAPTER 14

Over the next few hours, Ratel and Virgil took turns knocking on the door to check on her, and each time, they sounded more agitated.

"You're taking up our best bathroom," Virgil whined. "If you want to be alone, we have some vacant rooms you can lock yourself in instead."

But Asheel still couldn't face them, the monsters that surely looked with jealousy at her human appearance. Whose essence had she drank? Did they know? She gagged again and bit her lips to stifle the reflex.

"Leave me alone," she whined back through the closed door.

"Just come out—"

"Leave me alone!" she shouted, and he left her.

Asheel closed her eyes and leaned her head against the door. She wouldn't be able to stay in there forever, especially when punctuated by her stomach growling, but she'd stay as long as she could. Minutes dragged on, and the sky through the window started to lighten as the sconces burned out.

Quiet footsteps approached the door again, and another knock tapped above where she sat while she waited to hear if it was Ratel or Virgil.

"Asheel?" Reaper's voice called to her. Her time alone had come to an end.

"What?"

"They said you'd be in there but wouldn't tell me why." He waited but continued when she didn't say anything. "Can you come out?"

She stared at the sunrise across from her. What did this day hold for her? Was it her last one as human? Couldn't she stay at least until the sun had risen?

"I can burn this door down easily, so either open it on your own or stand back."

"Fine," Asheel said, unlocked the door, and opened it an inch.

Through the crack, she met Reaper's human gaze. His eyebrows raised expectantly. His tousled, fried hair stuck out in several directions, and black veins laced through the whites of his eyes, which asked her voiceless questions.

"What?" she asked.

"Want to tell me why you're hiding in the bathroom?"

"I've lost my home, my family, my life." Asheel paused for a translucent monster to pass behind Reaper. "Can't I have a little time to myself to process all this?"

Reaper tilted his head. "In the bathroom?"

"I could be worse off than hiding in the bathroom." She dropped her eyes to his chest, then down to his feet. "I got sick."

His nose scrunched in disgust. "My cooking's not that bad."

She kept her eyes on the floor. "Not from that. From drinking humans." What had Ratel called it?

"You drank humans?" Reaper's brow furrowed then he flinched. "They gave you human essence?"

Asheel didn't stop her tears from sliding down her cheeks. "I can't do this. I'm not here to be a reaper. The deal was me for Coby. That's it. I held up my end of the bargain. All of this," she motioned wildly, letting the bathroom door creak open farther, "wasn't part of the deal."

Reaper's mouth flapped open and closed a few times before he found his words. "I . . . I know." He looked away while he spoke. "I know what you're going through." He lifted his hand, holding it out to her. "And I promise it gets better. It gets worse first, but it'll get better."

Silence stretched between them, and Reaper lowered his hand.

"I can see about you staying here if you're more comfortable in their mansion."

Asheel nodded. If her only choices were Reaper's barely upright cabin or a mansion, she'd pick that.

"Okay, we can do that." Reaper's face drooped, but he slipped his fingers around her hand and guided her out of the bathroom. "Come on."

Down the hall before entering the main room, Asheel dug her heels into the carpet. "I don't want to go back in there." Asheel tried to pull her hand free of Reaper's, but he tightened his grip.

"If you're going to stay here instead of with me, you'll be around them a lot."

A few sluggish monsters of various shapes passed their hallway and stepped out of the mansion, and Reaper pulled her into the main room. Two translucent monsters whom she hadn't met sat where she'd talked with Ratel and Virgil. One sipped a beverage, and Asheel shivered at the sight of the pink-tinted liquid slipping down his throat.

Reaper dragged Asheel to the sitting area and addressed the two. "Get Virgil."

"He's with his last customer. You'll have to wait."

Reaper grabbed a drink from the table and tossed the cup at the monster who jumped from his chair and flicked his dripping hands.

"Hey! Don't waste it!"

"Get Virgil, now," threat laced Reaper's voice, and he held a hand, palm up, in front of him, "before I scorch the life from you." Smoke rose from his fingertips.

The dripping monster darted from the room, his friend tagging along.

Reaper stayed put with his hand still around Asheel's while they waited. Heat pulsed from him and wisps of smoke rose from his shoulders, but he remained human. Still terrifying, but human.

Finally, Virgil showed with no shirt and his pants hanging open.

Reaper dropped Asheel's hand. "Find her a room. She'll be staying here for a few days."

"No way. You said it was just for tonight." Virgil crossed his arms.

"And plans change. Let her stay here while she gets used to the realm for a few days."

"I have customers!" Virgil reached for his pants sliding down his hips. "I can't babysit her for that long. My biggest clients need me at night, and having to check on her constantly ruined my schedule. I lose them if I can't provide service for them."

"This human is more important than your stupid clients!" Reaper's shout silenced the other monsters rummaging around the room.

"Only to you." Virgil bared his pointed teeth. "We tried to be nice to her, but she only thanked us with a tantrum and locking us out of the bathroom."

Asheel cringed. It was like being back in Seshnia with people arguing over how important or harmful she was to the town. A monster's unconcern for her shouldn't have bothered her so much, but she'd been so used to feeling important, even if while being mistreated, that having someone say otherwise was a blow.

Reaper's shoulders shook. His hand lit up in fire, and he was three steps to Virgil before Asheel yelled at him to stop.

"I don't have to stay here." She darted forward and grabbed his shoulder. Even if the translucent monster didn't like her, he didn't deserve to be hurt because of her. "Your cabin is fine."

The fire dimmed and returned to his normal ashy skin, but he still shook with rage.

"Don't ask me to watch her again," Virgil said through curled lips. "I'm not letting you ruin the life I've worked so hard for here."

Reaper lifted Asheel's hand from his shoulder and led her to the door. "Consider that all you have left. Don't ask me to deliver anymore messages," he said over his shoulder as he stepped outside with her.

Few monsters were out in the early morning, and the ones who were yawned, stretched, and peered at her with half open eyes. Reaper fumed while they walked. She'd gotten almost comfortable with his calmer demeanor, and she wished he'd calm down. It was the translucent monsters' home, and they could decline housing her if they wanted. Virgil had done nothing wrong.

She tried to pull him out of whatever spiraling thoughts kept him angry, but he ignored her mundane questions, the most of a response being a grunt. His fit was no better than her own outbursts.

"Aren't you something like a thousand years old? Shouldn't you have more patience than this by now?"

"Ha. Maybe I'm so old that my patience ran out."

He ignored her pestering again after that, but when they reached the forest that surrounded his cabin, he finally unclenched his fists to organize a few stones at the edge of his rock garden.

"How old are you, anyway?" she asked.

He shoved open the door and rolled his eyes at her. "I told you before."

"When I was distraught and overwhelmed with all of this? I had bigger concerns than your personal history then."

"Why does my age matter?"

"I'm just wondering how much slower your aging is to mine since you still seem so young."

"I don't age."

"At all? Not even extremely slowly?" She stopped just inside the door and faced him. "You're completely immortal?"

"Kind of." He retrieved drinks and set them on the table. "But not really. I just don't age until Doyen releases me from my contract." He patted the table telling her to sit. "Though, if that appeals to you, then yes, as a reaper you get to be immortal, but you have to release your monster first." He smirked at her. "Ready to start trying?"

She sat at the table and peered into her cup. Normal water. A relief. She sipped it while mulling over the idea of immortality, forever staying as she was, twenty years old with no more life to live, a slave to the slimy beast in that wretched monolith. She shook her head. "I can't."

He sipped his drink and licked off a film of pink that coated his upper lip. He was drinking human essence right in front of her. She shivered, but he ignored her and continued. "It's the only way to see your family again. Immortality? Getting to visit your family? No other monster has it as good here. Why not accept your fate?"

Virgil had said the same to her, that she had the best deal in the whole place, and she had to admit seeing her family again was infinitely more tempting than immortality. Getting to see Coby grow up, getting to tell her parents she was fine.

Then she remembered the image of her face bursting into flames. The magic that locked away the reaper's voice. She could try to tell them in writing, but would they hate her as much as they hated Reaper? She tried to imagine what she would think if a tiny reaper handed her a letter that said he was Coby. She'd be just as terrified. She wouldn't believe him, and her family would probably do the same to her. No, they were better off thinking she was dead than finding out she'd become a reaper.

She glared at his cup. "That's not enough to convince me. Seeing them isn't worth my skin burning off and becoming a monster."

Reaper banged his fist on the table, clattering the cups and leaving a crack in the stone. "I should have told Virgil not to tell you about human essence. He's ruined everything."

"It wasn't him—" Asheel started, but Reaper shoved his chair back and stood.

He slammed his fist again. "We don't have time to convince you everything here is butterflies and sunshine." He stomped to the couch and retrieved a messy bundle, which he tossed at Asheel. She caught one piece, but the other fell to the floor.

"What's this?" she asked.

"A gift." He continued his stomping to the door and jerked it open. A glint shimmered in his eye when he turned and slammed the door behind him.

Even though Asheel had only known Reaper as more than a silent skeleton for a few days, his outbursts weren't like him. Or maybe he was letting his guard down and this was the real him. No wonder everyone despised him. If he acted like this all of the time, she'd be tempted to change just to get away from his erratic mood swings.

If she changed, would she have his strength and speed? She could figure out how to change on her own and charge through anyone who tried to stop her from finding the Gate. She'd be on Reaper's level, technically. He had centuries on her, but she had motivation, a need to flee the monster realm and get back home. How was the change supposed to happen?

Asheel held her hand in front of her face and willed it to change, but it remained her own filthy, unbathed flesh. Reaper had said it had to be her decision. She glanced at the door then sighed. "I choose to be a reaper," she whispered to her hand.

Her gut tingled. Was that the change happening or was the tingle only anticipation? She stared at her palm, willing it so she could get to the Gate. Were those heat shimmers? She flexed her fingers, but again, nothing happened.

The door swung open, and Asheel dropped her hand to her lap where it landed on the gift she'd forgotten about.

"Sorry," Reaper said, creeping back in the cabin with his head down. "I've been waiting for you for so long. I want it all to be perfect, to be quick and easy."

Asheel lifted the gift and examined it, a jacket that had the same tough, textured leather that Reaper seemed so fond of, matching the oversized hooded shirt she wore, and the odd leather blanket on his bed, but it was a paler orange, like it hadn't been burned hundreds of times yet.

"What is this?" she asked.

"Clothes."

She rolled her eyes. "Can't I have something more comfortable? Like, I don't know, tree bark?"

"That's firebreather pelt." Reaper returned to the kitchen and rummaged through a few stained pots. "It won't burn up when you change." After placing a pot on the hearth, he glanced over his shoulder at her. "Tree bark would ignite, though I doubt anyone would care if you wanted to run around the realm naked."

"Firebreather?" Asheel had never heard anything like that back home. She pictured an orange creature like a boar. Was it a creature only on the monster side of the Gate? The animals she'd seen were all familiar, a couple of dogs in the town and a flock of birds they'd seen while walking. The only new creatures were . . .

"Is . . . is this a monster skin?" What was once a human . . . a human skin?

Reaper's shoulders hunched, and he turned to face her with a grimace. "Yes, but—"

"Ew!" Asheel tossed the jacket to the floor and tugged at the hooded shirt hanging around her neck. "That's barbaric!"

"No, wait." Reaper hurried to retrieve the clothes from the floor and dusted them. "They're fine. I didn't kill them or anything." With reverence, he laid the clothes on the bed then stroked his own. "These were given willingly. Each firebreather died of old age, their family skinned them, and I bought them for a fair price. They don't mind giving their skin when they die to clothe and shelter their families. And it's the only thing our fire won't disintegrate." He returned to the kitchen without looking at her. "They're expensive, as they should be, and you should treasure them."

Asheel had more questions than she could ask. But foremost, how was he making her feel guilty for not wanting to wear someone's skin as clothes? She held back a gag. "That doesn't make it any less gross."

"It's normal for them. They live in the lava fields where fabrics burn up, so they wear each other's skins, use them in their homes, even decorate with them. They have a whole ritual for each skin, and they're the most peaceful group here."

That didn't make Asheel feel any better about it. But the blanket on the bed . . . she'd slept under it. Her stomach twisted, but she was able to hold back the water that sloshed in the bottom of it.

"I don't think I can handle much more of this place." She dropped her head to the table, the cold stone not as comforting on her forehead as she'd hoped.

"I know you've been rushed into all of this. I'll try to take it slower. I'll . . ." He clanged around his cooking hearth while he thought. "I'll show you around. Show you it's not so bad. I mean, it's not good, but it's not all misery."

Asheel lifted her head. Reaper was back to his calmer self, and his calmness soothed her own tensions, though her head and chest still ached with everything she'd witnessed and experienced. At least she knew she was safe with Reaper since he needed her alive. If Virgil was his most trusted friend in this place, and they were as quarrelsome as they were, she couldn't blame him for his earlier moodiness. She'd been just as moody back home, though she hadn't had centuries to learn patience or rein in her anger.

Reaper set two bowls on the table and filled them with a sludgy mixture that dropped from the pot in unappetizing clumps.

"Don't worry. It's not anything that was once human."

"What is it?"

"Chicken stew."

Asheel sniffed it. "That's not chicken stew."

"Close enough." Reaper was already shoveling it into his mouth. "I'm not the greatest cook."

"You've had centuries to learn how to cook and this is the best you can do?" Asheel tasted it, and her stomach rumbled, pleading to be filled. It tasted better than it looked, not as earthy as the maple leaf soup. At least he'd used spices this time.

"It's good enough for me." Reaper swallowed another bite.

The stew was satisfying enough to fill her, but she missed the flavors from home. The herbs from their forest. The fresh fruit. The meat skewers from the food stands during town celebrations. If she were going to let herself become the reaper, it would be to get back home, not for the monster in front of her.

"I've been thinking of how we can protect you while I'm out reaping tonight since we can't use Virgil," Reaper said and leaned back in his chair. "I think I'll leave you to Mama B."

CHAPTER
15

Asheel slept on top of the blanket during the day while Doyen's blue, green, purple eyes swirled in oily ripples, watching her in her dreams. Using the firebreather blanket like a cushion felt more appropriate than shrouding herself in it. Sleeping under it felt too much like trying to wear it like a second skin.

Reaper had explained he didn't always sleep during the day. His schedule rotated to match whatever time night was for where he'd be going to in the human realm. Sometimes he'd step into the Gate in the middle of the day and come out on the other side surrounded by darkness.

So when he took her to Mama B's house, night was still a few hours away. Her home sat in an open area close to desert lands in the middle of a large community of houses with straw roofs, fabric walls, and plenty of open-air communal areas. The monsters who scurried from house to house were about Asheel's own height and covered in long quills. They avoided Reaper, but rather than giving him glares and snarls like most monsters had, they avoided looking at him as if pretending he didn't exist.

"She'll keep you safe," Reaper told her about Mama B. "She's wise but doesn't listen to me, so you'll have to keep an eye out, too. She doesn't owe me anything like Virgil did, so I don't exactly trust her to want to help me. But she'll help you."

"Why me and not you? I haven't even met her yet."

"She cares for everyone, but only if they haven't wronged her."

"How did you wrong her?"

"I took her from her home," Reaper said with a shrug, "just like everyone else. It'd be hard enough for a human to forgive their kidnapper, much more so for a monster with deeper, personal struggles." He pointed to a house just ahead of them. "That's her."

A creature, slightly rounder than the other quilled monsters, sat on a stool in front of her house with a table of quills woven in flat shapes. She glanced up at their approach and sighed with a shake of her head. But when her gaze drifted to Asheel, a smile lit up her wide face. A slit where her nose should have been stretched from her mouth to her eyebrows, and her eyes were sunken beneath thick lids.

"Have you brought me another child?" she asked in a heavy accent with unusual fluxes and stood to greet them.

"I'm not a child," Asheel muttered.

"Shush." She winked. Despite her disfigured appearance, her smile was kind and the twinkle in her eye reminded Asheel of Jean.

"Can you watch her for me tonight?" Reaper said while Mama B grabbed Asheel's hands and lifted them to her face where she kissed each one with soft, velvety lips. Reaper continued, ignoring the odd greeting. "She needs somewhere to stay with people who don't want to hurt her to get to me."

"Of course, of course." Mama B pulled Asheel away from Reaper. "Though, I'm surprised you didn't ask Virgil."

Reaper frowned at Virgil's name. "I'll be back in a few hours."

"You don't have to." Mama B winked again while gazing at Asheel who tried to pull her hands from the woman's grasp.

Reaper rolled his eyes. "It's probably better if you keep her inside. Just to keep eyes off her."

"Shoo." Mama B finally looked at him. "I'll watch her."

While Reaper trotted away, Mama B pulled Asheel into the house.

"What is your name, sweetheart?" Mama B asked.

Asheel stuttered. This was the first time a monster had asked for it. Would it grant them any power over her? She shook her head. If it did, surely they'd all be asking her for it, and it hadn't given Reaper any extra leverage over her. "Asheel," she finally muttered.

"Pretty name for a pretty girl." Mama B patted her hand. "Everyone calls me Mama B."

Dried mud walls with straw peeking through the cracks circled a home that was divided like a pie with a smaller communal, circular room in the center.

"Welcome to my home." Mama B finally dropped Asheel's hand. "Please, sit." She motioned Asheel toward a stool in the central room then disappeared down a hall.

Asheel wrung her hands in her lap. Walkways with rolled up fabrics for doors branched from the center for each slice of the pie-like house. Last rays of sunlight streamed through tall windows, and woven quills like what Mama B had been making outside hung over them, twisting in the breeze, casting splotchy, dancing shadows throughout the home. Though the walls and floors were mud and dirt, the place didn't feel dirty. It was warm and spacious.

Mama B returned quickly with a tray of large nuts sliced in half with a layer of paste over the top of them, laid with care in a circular pattern. "Eat. Be filled with hospitality and peace."

Asheel lifted a nut from the edge. None of it was pink, but she still hesitated. How often did they consume human essence? With every meal? "What is it?" she asked.

"Ringas." Mama B's heavy accent made the word sound like two words. "Desert tree nut and fish paste. Eat."

Neither were related to human essence, so she ate it. After the garbage Reaper had fed her, the creamy yet crunchy treat was gourmet. She grabbed another and then another while Mama B smiled. She placed the tray on a small table and watched as Asheel stuffed her face.

"Can you teach Reaper to cook?" Asheel asked, swallowing her sixth ringa.

"No." Mama B's smile drooped, but her hooded eyes still twinkled. "You like it?"

"Absolutely." After a few more, Asheel forced herself to stop before she ate the whole tray.

Mama B left and returned again with another tray of ringas just as quick footsteps thudded into the house.

"I got us a vial!" a familiar but hardened voice called.

A small, quilled monster with dots across her face like freckles ran into the room with a pink vial and skidded to a stop to stare at Asheel open-mouthed.

"You," she said flatly then shook her head. "What are you doing here?"

"Greet the guest with kindness." Mama B frowned at the small monster.

"No, not after what she's done."

The small monster's voice finally registered, and Asheel jumped to her feet. "Kady?" she asked. "Is that you?"

"Yes, it's me!" She stomped over to Mama B and handed her the vial while squinting at Asheel, and her thin lip curled. "What kind of monster are you?"

Asheel couldn't believe her eyes. She knew people from

Seshnia had to be in the monster realm—Virgil sounded like he was from somewhere near there—but she didn't expect the first person she knew to be Kady. She was alive. She was a monster, away from her family and home, but she was alive.

"Well . . ." Asheel hesitated. She hadn't had to explain her situation to anyone yet. Reaper had handled that part. "I'm kind of still human."

"What?" Kady's shriek echoed out of the home and into the evening.

"Manners, Kady." Mama B placed the vial in a cabinet and lit a lamp in the darkening room. "She's our guest."

"No," Kady repeated. "She ruins my life then gets to stay human? That's not fair!"

"Explain." Mama B guided Kady to a seat and forced her to sit. "Why are you so angry?"

Kady crossed her arms, and her quills bristled straight out. Other quilled monsters entered the house along with a few non-quilled creatures, but Mama B waved them off toward the ringas while coaxing the cause of Kady's distress from her. Kady pouted then finally gave her version of the night she was taken.

"She marked me somehow with her weird powers," she wiggled her fingers in the air, "and made the reaper take me. He pulled me right out of my mom's arms." Tears fell down her cheeks and clung to the tiny quills lining her chin. "Then she was right there in the doorway, and she didn't even try to save me. She let him walk away with me!"

"I tried," Asheel said. She wanted to reach out to Kady and comfort her, explain what had happened, how lost she'd been herself, but Kady snarled.

"You didn't try very hard! You marked me in the first place."

"That's not—"

Kady jumped up from her stool and stuck a tiny finger against

Asheel's chest. Her quills vibrated, and one fell to the floor. "You're the worst monster here!"

"Calm down." Mama B patted Kady's quills. "Give our guest time to speak."

"No!" Kady shouted and jerked away from Mama B. She turned back to Asheel, shaking with a fresh wave of tears in her eyes. "What about Coby? You're here. Now he's all alone! You left him all alone!"

"Kady . . ." Asheel started, but Kady ran out the door and into the night.

Mama B sighed and ate a ringa. "Please forgive her. She's still young."

"It's okay." Asheel slumped on her stool. She'd thought suffering in the monster realm had hardened her to the pain back at home, but the impact of Kady's anger proved it still had weight over her. "I deserve to have her hate me. I mean, it wasn't my fault, but I guess she has to be angry at someone, right?"

"You don't deserve it." Mama B offered Asheel another ringa, but she shook her head.

Quilled monsters watched as a brave one ventured closer to Asheel, reached out, and squeezed her shoulder. "I don't understand all of that," he said in an accent that sounded Yulgerian, "but it sounds like the kid is confused. She's just that. A kid. Don't take it too hard."

"Thanks." Asheel forced a smile at the man. He didn't understand her life had always been that way, even with the adults, but his sympathy reminded her of Lana and that was enough to remind her not to take it personally.

The quilled creatures seemed kind, though hesitant and skittish. Some meekly smiled at her. Some avoided contact. Though she knew she shouldn't generalize them all. Many had been boisterous and terrifying in the city.

"Why did she become like that?" Asheel asked. "Why are

some monsters like you and some like that?" She gestured to a scaled monster rubbing something over his arms.

Mama B followed Asheel's gesture and nodded as if agreeing to something. "It's because of whatever tempted us the most. No, tempted is the wrong word." She picked up Kady's fallen quill and examined it. "It is our deepest struggles come to the surface."

"But why are there different monsters? Why not just one type?" Asheel cowered as the scaled creature walked by her, its fangs sharp enough to slice off her arm.

"Everyone's struggles are different, and they present differently on the surface." Mama B grasped the hands of a quilled monster passing by and kissed them like she had with Asheel before nudging the monster toward the ringas. "Mine was jealousy and crushing sorrow."

"Sorrow is a struggle?"

"Drowning in it is. Letting it fester so much that it consumes your mind, your waking and sleeping thoughts, needing others to suffer with you. That is a struggle to overcome."

What were Asheel's struggles that made her destined to be a reaper? She had the same struggles that Mama B did, wanting Seshnia to feel the suffering they'd caused her, being selfish. She was bitter about it all, too. And jealous of the normal lives around her.

"Why are there other types of monsters here in your home, not just the quilled ones?"

"Why not?"

"I don't know. Seemed like everyone sticks to their own kinds mostly."

"They are our kind." Mama B's eyes twinkled. "We look different now, but we come from the same."

"Then why do the same types seem to stay together?"

"Most get along with their own kinds better. The un-quilled that you see enjoy us more than their own."

Asheel agreed with them about that. "I like your kind, too."

Mama B left and returned with another tray of food that looked just as delicious as the ringas, but Asheel had lost her appetite. The quilled monsters ate quietly, chatted calmly, and filled the remaining stools and rugs. More trays appeared and the group passed them around, each looking decadent. A tray of pink puffed treats disappeared quickly, and she decided she'd stay away from that one.

Despite trying not to take it personally, the anger from Kady spun through her mind like a tornado, uprooting any sense of peace that she'd started to find in her new fate. The more she thought about it, the more she decided Kady's anger was fair. It wasn't anything new, anyway.

Eventually, Mama B sat by Asheel again and placed a hand on her knee. "You're quiet."

Asheel smiled weakly. "Sorry."

Mama B patted Asheel's knee then pulled her hand back to straighten a few quills along her own arm. "What was home like for you?" Her attempt at conversation with Asheel was obvious but appreciated.

"Not great." But she missed it for some reason. Maybe it wasn't as bad as she thought it was. "I was being trained for something I didn't want to do, and I kind of ran away from it." What was it she missed so badly? The familiarity? Knowing how to use her talents and skills? "I used to help my family make incense. My dad has a shop." She missed the methodical grinding, rolling the twigs in the sticky scents, laying them out to dry. She closed her eyes. She could smell them. The citrus blends. The fresh pine. The floral bouquets of snow lilies. She'd give everything she had to be back home, making incense with her family. She could almost see the supplies laid on the table waiting for her.

"You like making incense?"

The question hit her hard in the gut, and she nodded and

opened her eyes. "I didn't know it at the time, or maybe I just miss it now."

"Can you make incense here?"

She considered that. Did she want to make incense for fun? Would it soothe her like her memory of it? Would she end up surrounded by more incense than she could burn? She turned to Mama B. "Would the monsters here want any if I made it?"

Mama B glanced to the monsters lounging in her home. "Maybe some. We would be interested."

That was something Asheel would have to try. Maybe she could bring a little normalcy, a little of home, back into her life. "If I could go home, I think I'd join my dad in his shop," she confessed but bit back the tears threatening to fall. She either had to get over it or do something about it. Moping wouldn't help her situation.

CHAPTER 16

A fter the monsters visiting Mama B for their meals had left, she showed Asheel to a guest room for her to rest. Shelves lined the walls, and spiraled quill ornaments hung from the ceiling like their own little galaxies, twisting in the breeze. The bed was more comfortable than the one in Reaper's cabin, but she wasn't tired enough to sleep. Through the pulled back curtain, the sky had darkened while she slumped on a chair. Reaper would be back any minute to take her back to his cabin and start her first full day of coaxing out her monster, and she spent the time thinking of ways to get him to postpone it.

Growling outside the home had her bolting upright and rushing to fasten the curtain, but a scaled hand grasped the frame and a fanged face appeared, nudging between the curtain and the wall.

"There you are human," the monster whispered and entered the guest room.

Asheel screamed and stumbled over her chair.

The scaled monster lunged and covered her mouth, adding new gashes to her cheek with his claws. He snickered while raking his claws down her neck, drawing thin trails of blood, and her muffled shrieks slipped around his hand.

Mama B charged into the room, shoving the scaled monster off her. The attacker threw Mama B onto the shelves that shattered and buried her under a pile of debris. His snake-like eyes turned back to Asheel, and he grabbed her foot, dragged her to him, and clamped a hand around her neck.

"We'll see how Reaper enjoys seeing his key to freedom vanish."

Asheel's mouth flapped open and closed. His fangs, shining in the torchlight, stretched around Asheel's arm, but Mama B recovered and charged with her head down, skewering the monster's chest with her quills which broke off, stuck in his scaled flesh. The monster jerked to the side, releasing Asheel's throat, which she grasped at, wheezing and blinking the spots from her vision.

The monster reached back for Asheel, but Mama B was prepared this time and stood between them.

"I'm just as ready to kill you, too," the monster said, the broken quills still jutting from his chest.

Mama B raised her head, and her quills bristled while the monster charged at her with his jaws stretched wide. She ducked and lunged to stab her quills into his mouth, but he dodged and dug his claws into her. She screamed as they dragged across her stomach.

Blood oozed from the wound, and Mama B fell to the ground with a grunt.

"Leave her alone," Asheel shouted and threw a scrap of the shelves which missed and rolled against his feet.

The scaled monster turned and ambled toward Asheel, the quills sticking out of his exposed chest. She braced herself. It was like the night Reaper took Kady. Being practically defenseless with a monster charging at her.

As the monster lunged, Asheel dipped, grabbed a quill sticking out of him, and shoved it deeper. He screeched and swiped his fangs, latching onto her shoulder, drawing a chunk of flesh from it. More heat seared through her body as she arched away from the fangs and stumbled, falling to her back.

Mama B clawed across the floor, too far away, unable to stand.

The scaled monster hissed and reared back, and Asheel crossed her forearms over her face. His claws landed on either side of her and scraped through her clothes, the sharp edges sinking into her flesh, radiating pain as they scraped against her ribs.

Splotches blurred her vision, and though she could see the monster's mouth moving, a ringing in her ears blocked out all sound. The attacker reared back again with his fangs exposed, this time, aiming for Asheel's throat, but Reaper's fiery form flashed across her remaining vision and launched the monster away from her. Despite his wounds, the monster lunged once at Reaper, but he stood over Asheel ready to fight, allowing the beast to flee back through the window where he disappeared in the darkness.

Reaper dropped to his knees beside Asheel who groaned in a puddle of blood. His hands hovered over her wounds, but he floundered for words.

Coughing up phlegm and wheezing through the pain, she could barely see him now through the greying splotches in her vision. The ringing grew louder. He shook his head and mouthed something, but she couldn't focus on what he was saying.

From his vest, he pulled out a pink vial, which he opened and brought to her lips. She twisted away from it, causing shooting pains up her sides. Her heart beat fast and faint, but through the pain and her lucidness she knew she didn't want what was in that vial.

Reaper's bony hand clenched around her jaw, slipping a little from the blood that still spilled from her cheek. He held her face where she had to look at him.

Just leave me alone to die. She couldn't get her mouth to move to say the words.

She tried to shake her head, but his hand held firm and he spoke again, louder. "Save you" were the only words she could understand through the ringing. Most of her body had gone numb, cold, and her eyes rolled as her vision disappeared. Hot glass touched her lips and warm liquid slipped down her throat.

The effect was immediate. Calmness. Contentment. Peace. Her pain remained, but the drink soothed her into a state of such bliss that even her body quit fighting to live. The ringing grew higher, and the grey nothingness eased beyond her vision and took her.

CHAPTER
17

In the emptiness that followed, Doyen's eyes pulsed, greens and blues, watching her. His black, slimy scales shimmered, reflecting light that didn't exist, and his bulging gut bounced with his laughter. Laughter at her failures and suffering. She had to get away from his mockery. Had to escape his ever-watching eyes.

Faintly, she registered the hideous blanket in Reaper's cabin draped over her before pain overtook her again, pulling her back into sleep. It happened several times, ripping screams from her before she vanished inside the nothingness again to meet Doyen in her mind.

She could fight the unconsciousness a little longer each time she woke. No more than a few seconds, but sometimes in and out quickly and she could pick up snippets of what was going on in the room. At some point, Mama B came to visit her.

". . . for her, not you," Mama B said.

Asheel faded out and missed some of the conversation, but Mama B was alive, which was a relief.

Reaper was across the room when he spoke. "I'm worried about her." His voice was hushed and frustrated. Asheel fought harder to stay alert. Reaper worried. Why?

"And don't want to wait another four hundred years to . . ." Mama B's voice faded away.

Four hundred years. That's right. He'd waited four hundred years for her. That's why he worried. He didn't want to wait four hundred more.

Then Reaper's voice faded back in. ". . . different with her," he said. "She's real, not just another number, and I feel bad for her."

Then she was gone again and couldn't learn why he said that.

In her short bouts of consciousness, he'd trickle sweet human essence into her mouth. It poured into her stomach, danced along her sides, soothed her wounds. And eventually she woke up enough to open her eyes.

CHAPTER 18

Though the pink drink healed her mind and fueled her body to accelerate her recovery, it didn't fully mask the pain, and as soon as she could sit up without fainting, days after the attack, she refused to drink it.

Reaper fussed over her, feeding her snacks from Mama B, cleaning her wounds, helping her to his pitiful bathroom. He watched her like she could vanish. It seemed odd, his attentiveness, like he cared for her rather than just for what she could do for him.

Both Mama B and Virgil guarded her while Reaper was away in the human realm. Virgil pretended he was only doing it to get Reaper to keep their previous deal, but the tightness around his eyes hinted at guilt and concern for her.

Before another week had passed, Asheel was moving around the cabin on her own, and the worry that sat like a fog over Reaper disappeared. But his smiles were different, happier, and his attentiveness didn't fade.

The conversations with Mama B and whispered concerns when he thought he was alone when she'd been unconscious nagged at the back of her mind, and she finally got the nerve to ask about them while he watched her eat with a giddy smile that made him look even younger.

"I don't understand why I'm so important to you," she said between bites. "And don't say it's because I can free you from the contract. You're different now."

He finally looked away and down at his lap where he folded his hands.

"Reaper?"

"It's Hud."

"What?"

"My name. It's Hud."

Of course he had a name other than Reaper. She chewed slowly. "Okay, Hud. What's gotten into you?"

He picked at his lip while he studied her, his eyes darting between hers. "I'll tell you the truth," he finally said, "but you can't tell a soul. I have a reputation that I'd like to keep. Otherwise, I'd be mauled every time I stepped out this door with them thinking I'm not as tough as I am."

"Deal." She leaned back in her chair and massaged her aching sides where only scabs remained of her wounds.

"I don't want to kidnap people from their homes." He stared at his lap while he spoke, like he was ashamed of his confession. "I know what it's like to be ripped from your family, and I don't want that for anyone, but it has to be done." He scratched at his forehead, hesitating. "If I'm honest, I'm lonely. I interact with people every day. I trade them vials of essence. I get to watch the children grow up, some becoming almost decent, like Mama B, and others becoming exactly what the Stream of Judgment showed them to be, like the lizard who attacked you. But I'm an outcast here." He glanced up to see her reaction. "No one wants to get too friendly with the worst of the worst who ruined their life."

Asheel frowned. Surely someone in the entire monster realm wanted to befriend Hud. "You mean to tell me in this entire place of horrible creatures, there's not a single one that wants to buddy up to you just to be friends with the 'worst of the worst'? Even just for the notoriety?"

He shrugged. "There might be, but I don't want to be around those kinds of people. They want to cause chaos and destruction while I want to make this place as comfortable as I can for everyone. Friendship is a two-way deal, even if the worst monsters want to buddy up with me, I don't want to be a part of that. I mean, I've tried it before, but it was just as miserable. The friendships were shallow. I might be lonely, but I have standards. Then anyone I get along with dies off eventually. They don't have Doyen's magic in them to make them immortal." He dropped his gaze back to his lap. "It's been a little different with you around." She knew what he meant. The past few weeks with him caring for her had been almost pleasant. "We're not friends, obviously—I couldn't ask that of you—but we have conversations. We have meals together." He motioned to the scraps of their meal on the table. "It's close enough."

Asheel's heart broke for him. She knew the feeling. She understood what he meant to be surrounded by an entire town and feel like an outsider. To know the faces, the names, the cliques and to be pushed to the side because they saw a curse instead of a person. Even with Lana. She couldn't be around all the time, and even when she was, Asheel had felt guilty for having anything to do with their peers rejecting her, too. Solitude with another wasn't as bad, but feeling like the cause of their mutual solitude was worse.

And Reaper—Hud had felt that pain for four hundred years. He had a chance out through her, and yet, he hadn't made her feel pressured or rushed even though he only had a month and a half left.

What would it be like to be the reaper? Would she immediately be bound by magical contract to do Doyen's bidding? If she changed, she would free Hud. Then could she break the contract herself and stop the cycle? Would she have the strength to resist the contract at all?

"Why don't you just kill Doyen?" she asked, considering the council discussions of stopping the torment at its source. "Wouldn't getting rid of him release you?"

"I tried, but his magic, the contract, stops me before I can do more than scrape off a few of his scales. It didn't even hurt him, and then he said something about the world not surviving without him. He's tied to it or something."

"The contract stops you?"

Hud nodded. "You can still do whatever you want under it, but if you try to fight it, it'll make you wish you hadn't thought about disobeying."

If she had the reaper's strength without being restrained by the contract, maybe she could do it, but she'd been a hopeless mess against the lizard monster. She didn't know how to fight, but maybe having the strength could be enough. "Does it hurt?" she asked.

Hud screwed up his face. "The contract? Not when he sets the spell."

"No, I mean," she rubbed her arm and pointed to him, "the fire. Changing all the time."

"Oh. Not really. The first change was excruciating, breaking down the barrier inside to let the monster out and letting it burn away your human skin, but after that, it's just like putting on a scalding jacket. Though, I can't imagine it'd hurt much more than what you just went through. The change lasts maybe a minute then it's over."

Her sides and shoulder ached where the scabs were still healing, and she brought a hand to her face to trace the gashes already scarred. "How does it happen?" She wasn't saying she'd do it. She was just curious.

"You have to let the most pained part of you consume you." Hud pulled a foot onto his seat and rested his chin on his knee. "The part you've always fought. You know what I'm talking about."

She knew it. The heat of rage at her circumstances and the things beyond her control, letting it color every aspect of her life. Everything she tried to stifle with excuses about why she deserved all of it. The need for revenge begging to overflow.

"You have to let go of your inhibitions, forget the part of you that wants to care, and release the monster boiling inside you."

Her rage was easy to find. She felt it, or at least she thought she felt it. Heat pulsed in her stomach and warmth flowed down her arms, but she silenced it. She wasn't changing. Hud had it rough, and she was somewhat thankful to him for saving her, but she wouldn't have needed saving if he'd never brought her here. She still wanted to go home. Not be tied as an immortal to the monster realm.

Hud interrupted her thoughts by jolting straight like something had jabbed his back, then standing and glancing at the door. "He's late, but I have to go."

Asheel glanced at the door too. This was Virgil's turn to guard her, and he'd been reliable since her attack. "I'm sure he'll be here soon," Asheel said. "You can go on." Hud frowned at her, and she held up her hands in innocence. "I know being out by myself isn't safe, and I'm still too hurt to find the Gate on my own. Plus, everyone will assume you have someone guarding me."

He hesitated but retrieved her knife from the weapon pile and set it on the table. "Please don't do anything stupid."

"No promises."

"Just don't."

He gave her a stern look that had lost its effect on her after she'd seen his softer side, then left. She was alone. No captor. No guard. But she couldn't imagine leaving the cabin. Monsters were out there hunting her.

She fiddled with the knife and poked the tip of it into a small crack in the stone table. Was Hud's face still carved in the desk back at her office? Had they smoothed it out or replaced the furniture? She let go of the knife, giving it the option to balance on its tip, but it fell with a clatter.

Where was Virgil? He'd been punctual the other times he watched her alone. Had a vicious monster attacked him? With a sigh, she stood and peeked out the cabin door. No sign of him. Or anyone else. Just pine trees, pebbles and a trickle of water just out of view.

The pine needles scattered across the ground reminded her of the fresh-scented incense her dad had said was his best seller. She should have taken a stick of it like he offered when she went shepherding. If she had, she could have had a piece of home with her on this side of the Gate.

She glanced around the sparse forest and all was calm in the daylight, so she wandered to the tree line and gathered what she needed to give herself a piece of home. She found a couple of stones that could pass as a mortar and pestle, grabbed dried pine needles and scraps of bark, and carried it back into the cabin where she set it on the table and sunk into her seat.

Gathering the supplies hadn't taken much effort, but it winded her recovering body. The scabs itched and ached, and she held her sides to soothe the residual pain. When she could sit up, she got to work.

The motions came right back to her, meticulous and methodical. It soothed her like she knew it would, and she closed her eyes to focus on the memories. The nights she helped her mother grind the powders. The races with Coby to see who could grind the most. Rolling sticks in the scents with her dad. She could see their faces, their smiles.

The happy memories meant so much more now than they had back then. Even when she complained about helping, even those got re-sorted in her mind as happy.

Pretending she was back home was easy while the scent of pine permeated through the cabin. Until she opened her eyes. She wanted to hold onto those moments, wasn't ready to stop, so she retrieved water and oil from the kitchen and made a paste to roll the thinnest twigs she could find.

She hadn't done this part as much, and the first twig came out lumpy, but by the third, she'd found the rhythm. She mimicked her dad's dry, cracked hands from years of incense making. And the peace that consumed her, fueled by the memories and feeling of tradition, soothed her more than even the human essence had.

When she'd rolled a dozen sticks, she set them on the windowsill to dry in the sun. Surely Hud wouldn't mind that his house smelled like pine. She'd say it was an improvement herself. The flickering light of the sun through the trees mesmerized her while she knelt on the bed and dreamed of home.

A knock on the door broke the spell she'd cocooned herself in, and Virgil peeked inside.

"Is he very mad?" he asked.

"Furious." Asheel lounged on the bed, tired from her efforts and feeling oddly drained in her chest, while Virgil sat at the table.

"He'll get over it." Virgil flapped a hand to dismiss it. "Sorry. I slept in."

"It's the evening." Asheel glanced at the lowering sun. "You might as well have slept until tomorrow."

"When most of your clients like their appointments at night, you sleep during the day. I thought you'd figure that out by now."

"Get a day job." Asheel teased him.

"Get a night job." Virgil teased back and winked.

Asheel stuck out her tongue at him.

"You know, I was thinking," he traced the design of the cracks in the table, "if you stayed at the mansion, we wouldn't have to worry about me coming over here every other day."

"I thought you didn't want me there." Asheel propped herself on her arm.

"That was before I knew I'd be spending so much time walking between the mansion and here. If I have to watch you anyway, no reason you can't stay at the mansion." His translucent cheeks pulled up in a sly smile. "And we could put you to work with that night job."

"I'm not sure he'd be okay with that now. He'd only offered to let me stay away from the cabin because I was having such a hard time with everything in the realm. He doesn't really scare me anymore."

"But I'm more fun to be around, right? I'm less scary, right?"

Asheel rolled her eyes at Virgil's need for reassurance and flipped over to look at her incense on the windowsill, still reveling in the calmness her craft had given her. Virgil was fun to tease and joke with, and Mama B was so loving and motherly. Asheel could have friends in the monster realm like she'd wanted in Seshnia, at least for the time being.

"Is that incense?" Virgil asked and pointed to the sticks.

Asheel nodded.

"My dad would never let me buy that back home. He said it was a pointless novelty for the superstitious."

Asheel fingered a twig, rolling it along the sill. "Where was home for you?"

"A growing town called Seshnia. Mostly farmland. But my dad had a furniture store."

"Wait, really?" Asheel sat up.

Virgil raised an eyebrow. "It wasn't that neat. He made cushions and stuff like that and bought the frames from carpenters."

"No, I mean, you're from Seshnia? I thought you might be from Novoshna. I'm from Seshnia, too."

His other eyebrow raised, and his eyes widened. "The human world is a small place. I should have realized . . . your name . . ." His brows lowered and he shook his head slightly. "I mean, you do sound like home." He looked back down at the cracks in the table and traced the design again. "I've heard it's changed a lot."

"Sorry, I didn't know the furniture maker."

Virgil shrugged off her apology. "He changed careers a while back from what I heard. Not many people know him anymore." He nodded to her incense and pointed the knife at it. "That really smells great. Can I have some?"

"Sure, but it's the first batch I've done by myself. And it needs to finish drying first."

Virgil stood, grabbed a stick, then went to the couch to lounge and sniff the thing like it was a new delicacy.

Asheel passed her attention between reminiscing of home and watching Virgil fiddle with the stick he'd taken. She smiled despite everything she'd been through, being stuck in the monster realm, being told she had to become the next reaper. It wasn't so bad. She even enjoyed the time she'd been spending with her archnemesis, the reaper, who wasn't as bad as she'd grown up believing.

She considered her original frustrations and anger toward Hud and how they'd changed. What deeds had he shown her to make her anger valid? The only wrong she could see in him was kidnapping humans, and even that Doyen force him to do. She could just as easily end up in the same contract. How was her anger fair to him?

She hadn't noticed her determination to stop him from hunting Seshnia and the other cities had frayed, but now, as she put words to what she was feeling, she realized she didn't care about stopping him anymore; it all shifted to Doyen. Hud was lonely, he was hurting, and he was ready to move on. She could repay him for saving her. She could give him what he wanted. And she could use the reaper strength to stop Doyen.

Hud returned after sunset, and Virgil rushed out of the cabin to get to his appointments.

"What took you so long?" Asheel asked.

"Rough capture and the human didn't handle his change well." Hud retrieved a drink and plopped onto the couch. "Then transferring him to his community took forever because it's on the other side of the realm."

"How does that work?"

"Simple. After the Stream of Judgment changes them, we take them to where their kind lives."

"Do I need to learn where everyone lives?"

"Eventually. Worry about becoming a reaper first. Then I'll teach you the intricacies."

Asheel stared at the ceiling and chewed her lip. She'd decided. It was time. "I'll try to become a reaper," she said.

Hud froze and whipped around to face her. "What? Why? I mean, what changed your mind? You've been so against it."

She pictured it, becoming the fiery skeleton and learning the secret of being the monster. She pictured attacking Doyen and freeing everyone. And if that didn't work, escaping to the human realm and having them lock her up, bury her miles underground, whatever would stop her from abducting more humans.

"I'll become the reaper," she repeated. *To free you and end this cycle for good.*

CHAPTER 19

In Asheel's dreams, Doyen's eyes watched her again, prowling, pulsing, waiting for her to become a reaper. She dreamed of Seshnia, her parents' house, and Doyen's eyes watched from the window. In the fields, the eyes of the sheep became blue, green, and purple, rippling like Doyen's. She yelled at them to go away, but they all turned to stare at her, walking slowly, their feet moving in sync. She couldn't run. Even the smallest lambs approached until their oily eyes reflected her scorched expression back at her, and when she raised her hands to her face, they glowed with fire, the bones peeking through charred flesh.

She screamed herself awake.

Hud jumped up from the couch, arms ablaze ready to fight whatever monster had come to attack her, and Asheel buried her flushed cheeks under the firebreather blanket.

"What happened?" Hud asked through a yawn.

"Nightmare." She lowered the blanket and pressed her palm

to her forehead. "I keep dreaming about Doyen. His eyes. Always watching me."

"Oh." Hud stretched and slumped back onto the couch. "Yeah, everyone dreams of him here. You get used to it."

"Is he watching our dreams?" The hairs along her arms twitched to attention. Was he watching everyone now somehow?

"Maybe."

They went through their morning routine, and when the sun had fully set, Hud dragged her outside to try to provoke her change, which he described would be like a volcano boiling over that he didn't want in his house.

"What gets your inner monster clawing to get out? What boils your blood?" He rocked onto his heels.

But fire wasn't in her veins. New grief was. She'd spent the night saying goodbye to her humanity and accepting her impending demise, and all that remained were the memories that had changed from bitter to fond nostalgia and a knowledge that she was finally doing what she'd been meant for all along. And consequently, the monster inside had fizzled out. Only calm acceptance was left.

She nudged a few stones from Hud's rock garden while she tried to find her fire.

"Stop that and focus," he said and gently placed the rocks back with the others. "What stained your heart so much that it got you here?"

Asheel tried to recall it. She tried to remember her need for revenge and to prove herself as better than what Seshnia thought of her, but she only felt comfort in knowing that by becoming the reaper, she was keeping her promise to Coby.

They'd been at it a few hours when Virgil jogged up the path with Ratel and a winged, jagged-eared monster.

"It's not your turn to watch her," Hud said with his eyebrows drawn in confusion.

Virgil gave him a crazed smile, and his eyes kept darting to Asheel. "I can't visit for the fun of it?" he asked.

Hud tilted his head and motioned to the other monsters. "And I'm to believe these two are here because . . . why?"

Virgil turned to Asheel and grasped his hands together, ringing them, nervous. "I burned that incense last night."

"Was it dry enough?" Asheel asked. "You should have given it a full day."

Virgil nodded. "Darling, we need more of it. That was amazing."

It was just incense, and poorly made at that. Amazing wasn't exactly the term she'd use for it. But her dad had said the pine scent was his best seller. She'd have to burn a stick to see if it was really that good. "There's more on the windowsill. You can have that, I guess." She could make more for herself, and it'd be better the next round.

Virgil knelt his tall frame in front of her and grasped her shoulders while staring at her wide-eyed, close enough for her to see the fine lines in the creases of his translucent face. "You don't understand. It was amazing. I felt . . ." he glanced over his shoulder then back to her and whispered, "I felt myself again."

She knew what he meant. Human. Who he was before the Stream of Judgment ripped his humanity from him.

"I need you to make more," Virgil continued while Hud glared at them with his arms crossed. "They want some too, and they're willing to buy it from you."

"It's just a hobby." Asheel shook her head. "I don't want to sell it." That hadn't been her plan. If she could go home, she'd be happy to work in her dad's incense shop and have a simple life selling the twigs, but having to do the same thing in the monster realm where simple had long since passed, that was infinitely less appealing.

"Please." Ratel walked toward her, stepping into Hud's rock garden.

His orange eyes widened, and he waved his arms at Ratel, hurrying to where she stood. "Get out of there." He tugged on her arm until she stumbled over the pebbles, kicking a few rocks out of the pile, which Hud gently placed back with the others.

Ratel spoke to Asheel while watching Hud tend the rocks. "Please, consider selling it to us. We need it."

"You two sound like she gave you the best tasting human essence you've ever had." Hud straightened, his garden back in order.

Ratel tossed her dark hair over her shoulder and adjusted her corset. "It was more than that. It wasn't like a bandage over a wound. It was like we were actually human again. I mean, not with human bodies, but we were so calm, like our monstrous sides were soothed."

"Careful," Hud said. "You'll end up Doyen's snack with feelings like those."

"We'll trade off guard duties," the winged creature pleaded. His accent was light, with the *T*s sounding more like *D*s. "We'll do whatever you want."

Asheel and Hud exchanged confused glances, and Hud shrugged. "I don't know what you did to them."

"Fine," Asheel gently removed Virgil's hands from her shoulders. "I'll make more, but I really don't understand. It's only some dried plants."

"Trust me," Virgil said. "If you share it with everyone in this realm, no monster could ever imagine harming you."

Virgil left after that for a midday appointment, and Ratel and the winged monster, Ziyiel, stayed, watching Asheel struggle to find her inner reaper. She had an even harder time with the extra eyes. It felt too intimate a task to figure out while they watched.

Mama B eventually showed up, and Hud left for his reaping duties, thankful that he didn't have to leave Asheel with monsters he didn't trust.

And Asheel got to work. She picked some wildflowers to dry

for a future batch—obviously the trio would keep asking for more—
and gathered more of the dried pine.

The guests watched her work and almost looked disappointed
when the pestle didn't glow like she was brewing a potion in a
fairytale. But she ignored them and let the process soothe her like it
had the day before.

She remembered the joy. She felt the warmth of the memories.
And then her mind started drawing from her current state. She smiled
at her new purpose. Someone, several people, wanted the incense she
made. They wanted her skills for enjoyment rather than through fear
like her duties back home. She'd never felt wanted like that.

"It does smell good," Mama B interrupted. They'd explained
to her why she wasn't guarding Asheel alone. Her shallow wounds
had healed before Asheel's, her quills already grown back and scars
fading, but she was thankful for the help.

"Back home we used these for focus and protection, to mask
odors." She didn't want to explain what kind of odors, didn't want the
judgment and weird looks from back home. She definitely didn't want
to explain how each of them reeked like vomit, spoiled fruit, and
rotting flesh. "We're supposed to hold on to pleasant, happy thoughts
while we make it so that when it burns, it releases only positive
energy. I'm remembering my family and how we'd do this together."
She smiled again at the memories. "Some people burned it to keep
the reaper away from their homes. Others just liked the smell; it didn't
mean anything to them."

Mama B stuck her finger in the powder and sniffed while
Asheel rolled out the sticks. She finished twice as many as the
previous day while answering more questions and telling them about
her home. Ratel stayed quiet on the farthest corner of the couch,
awkward and uncomfortable in the reaper's home, but Ziyiel joined
Asheel and Mama B at the table.

The sun was rising by the time Hud returned, scowling at the floor and shooing the guests from the cabin. Asheel sent the drier sticks with them and saved a well-made one for herself. He collapsed on the couch, still scowling and silent.

"You can have one, too," she said and brought him a stick. "You don't have to pout about it."

He took the stick, barely glancing at it before closing his eyes and returning to his silence.

"Are you okay?"

"Yeah, just a rough day," he opened an eye and studied her. "You look like you had fun."

Fun. She was in the monster realm, surrounded by terrifying creatures, and she had fun. What did that say about her? Had she always been meant for life on this side?

"I guess I did. It's not so bad over here, you know?" Asheel walked to the bed and sat cross-legged on it.

Hud ignored her and closed his eye.

"Why was today rough?"

He didn't respond.

"If I'm supposed to do this, I'd like to be prepared for whatever went wrong."

"The guy didn't make it." Hud clenched his eyes closed tighter. "He died. I killed another."

"You killed someone?" She was under the impression that he had to bring his captures to Doyen alive.

"Technically, it was the Stream of Judgment, but I shoved him in, so I killed him."

How could he have been doing this for so long and still feel remorse when people died? There was no way. After so many years, he'd have become numb to it.

"Sorry." He leaned forward, his elbows on his knees, and rested his forehead in his palms. "I should have gotten over this before coming back."

Asheel chewed on her lip. He'd been such a strong, terrifying force for her entire life, but over the past few days, he'd really changed. He opened up to her. He showed this softer side. He truly was more than a monster and still had just as much humanity in him as she did.

"Is there anything I can do to help?" she asked.

"I'm just so tired of it!" He lowered his voice. "And ready for it to be over."

So she *could* help, but their attempts at getting her to change earlier hadn't created so much as a wisp of smoke. If he was still hurting after years of this job, was it really something she wanted to do? She could barely handle fifteen years of a thankless job in Seshnia, hated it so much that she declined moving to Novoshna's palace. Could she handle four hundred years of worse suffering? She wanted to free Hud who'd proved he still had a heart. But was she really ready to lose her own humanity in his place?

CHAPTER 20

O ver the next few days, Asheel's grieving for the life she'd agreed to give up was balanced by the purpose she found in making incense. Virgil and Ratel shared it with their clients, their clients shared it with their communities, and within a week, Asheel had a thriving business that she couldn't keep up with. The only monster who refused to give her incense a chance was Yory, the furry humanity peddler. Hud had tried to trade incense with her instead of the humanity vials, but she'd already lost so much business from her customers preferring incense to human essence that she refused to give the sticks a chance out of spite.

The new customers pleaded for turns to guard Asheel, waiting for hours before Hud's time to leave, resulting in a constant rotation of guests at his cabin. Some even worked on the dingy cabin, replacing broken stones in the walls and floors, patching the roof. Hud's whole countenance changed after he accepted his privacy would no longer be the same. He smiled more, even laughed sometimes, and the monsters who'd held grudges against him for so long put those aside to meet the small human girl with magical incense.

Asheel made more tentative friendships, none of which were as genuine as her bonds with Mama B, Virgil, and Hud, but she appreciated the attention all the same. It was like what she'd always wanted back in Seshnia.

Only when Hud returned from his reapings did the crowd of monsters leave them in peace at his cabin. He'd shoo away the guards, sometimes angrily depending on how the reaping went.

But during his angrier episodes, after sitting at the table with Asheel, he would finally calm down and offer her smiles and the occasional chuckle.

"Seems like you have every monster in this entire realm at your fingertips." He sipped some water. He hadn't needed the pink drink in weeks, and his trades of humanity vials had changed to trades of incense. The humanity peddler got almost all his vials now. "How do you do it?"

"I don't know. I was never good with people back home." If she'd chosen to work with her dad in his shop instead of the shepherds, maybe she would have eventually grown closer to the townspeople, been less of an outcast. Or maybe if she'd gone to Novoshna's palace where she hadn't already ruined people's perception of her, she could have found a group she fit in with.

"No, I mean the incense. Where does that magic come from?"

She'd been trying to figure that out herself. She couldn't remember the incense back home ever doing anything even close to magical, but she'd never done the process all the way through by herself, never ground the powder and rolled the sticks for the same batch. The incense her father made could have magic to it, but because the users were still human, no one noticed. Maybe she would have learned how to do it eventually at the palace with the other people with sensory magic in Novoshna. The officials had said they could teach her how to use her magic. Maybe she could do even more with it.

"I don't know," she admitted. "The closest I can guess is maybe it has something to do with being able to sense rising monstrous sides while human."

Hud lowered his cup and narrowed his eyes. "You can sense it?"

She forgot she hadn't told him about that yet. "Yeah. It stinks. I thought that was why the Stream of Judgment showed me as a reaper, but you said you didn't have anything like it before you changed."

"You're an Aromator?" His eyes flicked from his hands to her face. "I shouldn't be surprised you have sensory magic. Well, if it helps you make the incense, I'm glad you have it. You'll have an easier time than I have here."

"Will I?" She couldn't imagine incense, even if magical, being enough for anyone she kidnapped to forgive her. One day, all the current monsters who had no reason to hate her yet would be gone, replaced by those who did. She'd asked about that, why the monsters didn't have their own children. Apparently losing their humanity made them barren, something Cay had implemented when he made the realm, another way to prevent their influence from spreading.

"You will. Have you seen how badly they need it? They can't live without it now." He leaned forward and placed a hand over hers, ignoring a stick of incense burning on his own table. "Which means they'll need you."

She wrapped her fingers around his. "Thanks, but isn't that just like your 'friendship is two-sided' thing and not wanting to be friends with the ones who wanted to use you?"

"Nope. Sure, some of them won't be willing to forgive you, ever, but some will. They'll want to befriend you, and you'll want to befriend them, too." He let go of her hand and leaned back in his chair. "It's not the best friendship, but you'll still have it better than me."

He looked away with a furrowed brow, and Asheel wanted to grab his hand again, to comfort the pain that tightened his eyes. Even with frequent guests at his cabin, he was still lonely, and she hated that for him. She wanted to give him the friendship he desired. She wanted him to be happy with her.

Her eyes widened, and she busied herself with finishing her meal before Hud could notice her shock.

Being around him had made her more content than she'd ever been. Thanks to him, she had a life with purpose and meaning, had fulfillment, and the trust she had toward him through their mutual circumstances rivaled what she had with Lana.

Her heart ached. Maybe she should have been disgusted, but instead, contentment pooled in her like cool shade on a sweltering day.

And that made trying to let her inner monster out that much harder. She wanted to stay in that moment forever with the monsters needing her and spending her days with Hud. She tried, she really did, but in her contentment and happiness, she'd forgiven Seshnia for hating her because of their fear. She couldn't blame them for that. It hadn't been pleasant, but she'd been an outlet for their mourning and grief.

A few more weeks passed like that, struggling day and night to release her reaper, but her inner monster slipped farther from her grasp.

"You're not trying!" Hud shouted. The crowd around them hushed.

"I am!" Asheel shouted back. Her fingernails dug grooves into her palms, and a speck of blood dripped from the top of her arm where they thought physical pain might trigger her. "Why can't you just force it out of me somehow? You're supposed to be making me change right? Force me with your magic."

"Only the Stream of Judgment can force someone to become their monster side by stripping out everything that makes them human, and without your human side, you wouldn't be able to get back through the Gate. It has to be your decision." Hud shoved his hands into his hair and tugged at the roots. "We have less than a week left. You've been getting too comfortable." He glared at the audience and waved them off, jerking his head toward the path that lead out of his forest. "Get out of here! All of you!"

The monsters stood motionless, stunned and confused by Hud's sudden disapproval of their presence.

"Don't take it out on them," Asheel said.

Hud shifted to his skeletal form, and his bones glowed with unspoken threats. "Leave!"

Monsters took off, running or flying in the direction of their homes, but Virgil took a step toward Hud. "It's my turn to get more incense," he said, but Hud punched his arm, leaving scorched blisters across his bicep.

Virgil flinched and stepped back, clutching his burn, and the remaining monsters jogged away in whispers. Whispers and glances over their shoulders that felt so familiar to Asheel. Virgil turned to her.

"Let me get Virgil his stuff." Asheel started toward the cabin, but Hud grabbed her arm. She yanked out of his grasp and turned to him. He didn't scare her anymore. She understood her importance to him, and she wouldn't let him bully her out of the happiness she'd found. "Let me get his stuff," she repeated flatly, her own threat lacing her voice.

Hud stepped out of her way, and she ran in the cabin to gather the dried sticks, a floral batch and what was dry of the latest herb mixture. She gave them to Virgil with a grimace and a mouthed apology.

When Virgil was gone, she turned to Hud with her hands on her hips. "Why'd you have to chase them away?"

"You were getting too comfortable." He picked a fleck of ash from his wrist. "I need you to be enraged, want revenge, spew hate. Where's the venomous girl I took from her home?" The remainder of the charred flesh on his face turned up in a sickly smirk. "Are you enraged *now*?"

She was frustrated at him for driving off the companionship that she'd craved for so long, but he was right. They had only days to get her inner monster out or Hud might be stuck for another few centuries in the endless cycle. She couldn't be angry at him for wanting his freedom.

"I'm not," she answered honestly.

"And why not?"

"I'm . . . happy."

"Happy? I just chased off all your friends. You're stuck in a realm full of beasts, away from your family and home, and you're *happy* here?"

"Well, compared to before, I have a purpose now with the incense." She motioned toward him. "I have someone who understands what I've been going through without giving me blind sympathy. I have you. I'm content." She shrugged again. "Even with them gone, I'm comfortable."

"Happy," Hud repeated with a blank stare, his arms hanging loosely at his sides. "With me." The scorched flesh of his mouth turned up slightly, and he stared at Asheel with an expression she'd never seen on his face before, like he was looking straight through her to the inner monster they'd been trying to find, blazing a trail of heat through her. His smile drooped, and he shook his head with a scowl. "You can't be comfortable with me."

She crossed her arms and buried her chin in the firebreather's shirt. She'd never meant to admit that. He was vile. He was a monster, and admitting that she was comfortable around him, happy around him, was a betrayal to her family and the entire town of Seshnia.

Hud's scowl changed to a frown. "Don't. Don't be happy. I'm not on your side." He trudged into his house and returned with the few undried sticks of incense she hadn't given Virgil. He ignited them in his palm, the sticks sizzling and shriveling in a blaze. While Asheel gawked at him, he turned to the tree line. "Try to figure it out on your own today," he said over his shoulder. "Alone. And don't make any more incense." Without a second look, he sauntered into the trees and disappeared, leaving Asheel standing alone with no protection on the path outside the cabin.

He'd come back. He wouldn't leave her unprotected where monsters still wanting revenge could find her. Would he? He was coming back, right?

He was right. She'd gotten too comfortable around him. She should have kept all of that happy feel-good stuff to herself and not have admitted how much he meant to her.

The creaking branches of the swaying pines changed from peaceful to ominous, but surely Hud was watching her somewhere out there, probably waiting to see if she'd do as she was told and try to change herself.

She sat on the dirt path, crossed her legs, and closed her eyes to try to summon the monster hiding inside her. The anger and disappointment, the misery she'd been looking for had returned, just below the surface, and the monster bubbled deep in her center with it, but instead of boiling over in rage, it sunk like a rock, weighed down by sadness. After a few more minutes of trying to pull the monster to the surface, she finally admitted to herself what she felt was rejection. He'd rejected her, but she knew why, which let her pain exist without turning into anger or resentment. It still hurt, her eyes stung as proof of that, but she couldn't expect a different outcome. She knew that.

Asheel waited on the path for hours for Hud to return, half-heartedly tugging at her monster, but he didn't come back and she didn't make any progress. He'd be in the human realm by now, reaping another human from it to feed Doyen. She fell onto her back with her arms and hair splayed around her and stared at the stars. She wouldn't be able to change and would fail Hud, fail with protecting her home from the reaper, and he'd forbade her from making incense. What would he do if she made more? Burn it all before she could give it to anyone? What was left on the monster side of the Gate for her except disappointment? She traced designs in the stars with her eyes. They could have been the same ones from back home, but she'd never taken the time to memorize them. She wished she had.

She wanted to go home.

She sat up. What was she doing? Why was she trying to become a monster? She'd gotten too caught up in trying to fix Hud's life, she'd forgotten to take care of herself and do what was best for her. She wanted to go home, and maybe she could. Maybe this was her chance. She knew the Gate was on the other side of their central city, and she had a decent idea of how to get to it. Cutting through the city wouldn't be as dangerous now that she knew some of the monsters who wandered the streets. Though, they could drag her back to Hud's cabin if they realized she was escaping the realm and taking her incense with her. Or maybe drag her back if they thought Hud might give them a reward.

Asheel retrieved the oversized firebreather shirt from inside the cabin and pulled the hood over her eyes. She'd been wearing her own, more fitted set for the past month and hadn't touched the hooded shirt, not since before she'd started making incense, so maybe the monsters wouldn't realize the tattered hood concealed her.

Her feet couldn't move fast enough while anxiousness to be past the city drove her onward, and when she reached it, she slowed to a stroll to prevent unwanted attention.

She passed the city's buildings—homes, shops, lounges, and various questionably smelly eateries—and stayed close to the rotting walls while keeping the hood pulled lower over her head. She slipped through the shadows, willing herself to go unnoticed, to be one of the crowd. The monsters were out in hordes, though, and she had to shimmy around them.

The same fights she'd seen when she first arrived in the realm clashed mere feet from her, but she saw them with new eyes. Sure, some were brawling, but now she recognized some as introductions like a handshake, some as friendly competition, some simply a sign of camaraderie.

Hud had kidnapped every one of them and knew most of them by name. A cat-like creature stretched lazily across her path, and Asheel sidestepped around him. If she stayed in this realm, the monstrous inhabitants would one day be because of her.

A few antlered monsters with shifty eyes in an alley passed something between each other. Winged monsters perched on the roofs and called into the night, their faces raised to the stars. What kind of monster did they think hid under her cloak? She might have recognized a few beasts, but away from the cabin, she couldn't be sure. She hadn't yet figured out the nuances in some of the similar faces and bodies.

So far no one had looked at her long enough to question who she was, and she continued to slip by unnoticed. As far as she could tell, she walked in the right direction, but when the top of Doyen's monolith crept over a rooftop, she knew she'd taken a wrong turn. That was fine. It gave her a reference for which direction to go.

She turned down an alley to find the next road over, and continued her search, trying to look inconspicuous and as if she belonged there just as much as the other monsters. She held her cloak's hood tightly and passed a lizard-faced creature who eyed her quick steps.

Maybe with her small size they'd think she was a quilled monster. She hunched her shoulders more and scuffed her feet. A white monster that dripped puddles onto the dirt studied Asheel's progress.

She was doing too much. She relaxed back into her casual stroll and thankfully no one followed. The road curved at odd times, and some of the alleys were too dark for her to consider turning down. She continued wandering for a while away from the monolith, but when the road curved back around and headed the way she came, she had to slip into an alley to cut over to the next road.

A translucent creature leaned against a stack of junk and stared at her as she passed, but she hadn't met that one, at least she didn't recognize him, and he didn't stop her. She slipped further into the darkness of the alley and hurried through to the other side where she smacked into a pearly beast.

"Hello there," a slender bug-like creature clicked through her pincers. A scar stretched from the side of her face and down her body.

Asheel didn't recognize the creature and tried to back away, but the bug monster crouched and peered under her hood, her eyes widening in recognition of the human in front of her, odorous fumes leeching off her in a sharp warning. Asheel didn't wait to see what would happen. She ran.

Monsters scattered from her as she darted toward them, surprised by the tiny, cloaked creature charging at them. Two deer-like beasts clashed together, their horns connecting with an ear-splitting crash, and she ducked under their entangled antlers. She let go of her shirt's collar to maneuver, and the hood fell from her head. Her name whispered past her, but she fled, ducking, diving, not looking back. Some of the monsters wouldn't hesitate to kill her, fueled with their undying need for revenge. She could smell it on them.

She lost track of where she was running, but she still ran,

charging down another alley, not caring who might be hiding there. On the other side, she stumbled over a thick tail. Its owner squawked at her and tried to grab her around the middle, but she jerked the other way and tripped over an empty barrel. Large, speckled hands grasped her arms before she crashed to the ground. She struggled to free herself to keep running, but they held her firm.

"Why are you running, little thing?" the cat-like monster asked. His claws jabbed her biceps through her shirt.

The giant bug slithered out of the alley and opened her pincers wide. "Hold her while I take care of this nuisance."

The cat, giddy at the promise of violence and gore, turned her around to face the bug while Asheel struggled helplessly. She hadn't put up with almost two months of the monster realm to die because of a bug's need for revenge, but the cat's claws dug deeper the more she squirmed and the bug's pincers approached quickly.

"Asheel!" Her name echoed through the street, more faces turning toward her.

While a horned monster jumped between her and the bug, a translucent monster ran to her and pried her from the cat's grasp. Some winged creatures joined the horned one, fluttering their wings to push back the bug, and with more crowd forming around Asheel like a shield, the bug finally slithered away with the cat.

The monsters chattered at Asheel, asking her why she was in the monster city, begging for incense for protecting her, requesting her to come home with them. They grasped her arms and shoulders, tugging her like she belonged to them, until Ziyiel's accented voice boomed through the street, and he dropped from the sky with a spear of crackling light that he pointed at each of the monsters until they gave Asheel enough space to breathe.

Ziyiel's eyes glowed brilliant yellow while he spoke. "I'll take her from here. Disperse. You can get your incense from her as you've been, at Reaper's cabin."

The monsters muttered but didn't leave. Ziyiel, his eyes glowing brighter shoved his spear toward them.

"I'm not afraid to steal all of your remaining years. Leave!" He shouted, and they began to wander away. When most had disappeared down alleys, Ziyiel's eyes dimmed and he turned to Asheel, spreading his wings to block them from prying eyes.

She rubbed her arms where they throbbed from the claws. They had to be bleeding a little, but thanks to her thick shirt, the wounds felt more like pricks than gashes.

"Thanks for that. They were getting ready to divide me into parts."

Ziyiel rolled his shoulders and stretched. "I heard Reaper sent your guards away. I didn't realize you'd be wandering the streets alone." A passing monster eyed them, and Ziyiel raised his wings higher. "So why are you out here all alone instead of at his cabin?"

What could she say? What excuse could make her dangerous venture plausible? What was she even thinking, that she could get through the city and find the Gate before anyone found her?

"I just want to go home," she whispered and dropped her eyes to the stone street.

"You can't do that." Ziyiel raised his wings along with his eyebrows. "We need your incense."

"I can't do it." Something wedged between her frail determination and shattered it. Hopelessness. "I can't do it anymore."

"What do you mean? Your magic is gone?"

Asheel shook her head, her black hair swinging across her cheeks. "There's no more incense! I can't be what I need to be here. I need to go home. I can do better there now." She swept her hair back and pleaded with her eyes. The two of them weren't close, but she was comfortable around him. He seemed about as honest as a monster could get. "Can you show me where the Gate is?"

Ziyiel shook his head reflexively, glancing around as if

someone would overhear them and stop them. "I don't understand. What's wrong?"

"Everything! This whole place is wrong." She had to convince him. "Please, Ziyiel. I want to go home."

Ziyiel's bottom lip stuck out and his eyebrows raised in the middle, creasing his forehead with worry lines.

She almost had him and nudged a little more. "If you could go home, wouldn't you do everything possible to get there?"

"Fine." Ziyiel glanced around them again then led her through the streets in silence until they reached the opposite edge of the city. He pointed down an alley and looked back to her with tight eyes. "Go through here, then follow the edge of the forest until you see a break in the trees. The path disappears a little, but the trees lean away from the Gate. If you lose the path, just go against the trees." He reached around her and pulled the hood back over her head, giving it a slight tug at the front above her eyes before dropping his hand to his side. "Reaper is going to kill me for telling you."

"Thank you." Asheel brushed his arm with her fingertips. His yellow eyes would have scared her when she first arrived, but now she saw him for who he was, another individual cursed with a life they didn't deserve.

"I'm sad to see you go, but I hope you find your way home." He flapped his great wings and disappeared over the rooftops.

CHAPTER 21

Asheel followed the path like Ziyiel said. She hadn't noticed the trees when Hud brought her through the Gate almost two months ago, but like Ziyiel had said, they leaned slightly toward the city, away from the Gate, as if a constant gust of wind pushed them. She couldn't remember the ones outside Hud's cabin leaning like that.

She followed them, keeping an eye on the ground and ducking behind trunks when twigs snapped. The hike was longer than she remembered, but the path opened to a dead zone with the Gate pulsing in the middle, rippling blues, greens, and purples like Doyen watching her. Its translucent petals rippled from it in a rainbow display, the voices of the lost groaning their wordless warnings to stay away. She wanted to cover her ears, but she had to face them. Would the hands test her for her humanity? Would that hurt as much as when they checked for her inner monster? What if they paralyzed her again without Hud there to drag her out? What if they didn't let her through, trapped in the fracture between the world of the living and free and the world of the broken and imprisoned?

She hesitated. But surely the hands would guide her through. She wasn't even monstrous enough to become the reaper. Her humanity was as strong as ever, and with that reverberating through her, she stepped into the dead zone and up to the Gate where it grew and shrunk in a slow pulse like it was breathing. After two months, she'd finally made it. She was going home.

Reminding herself again that she was still human, she touched a finger to the center of the oily surface like a toe to cold water. It rippled painlessly around her hand, then something grasped her wrist, hot and searing. Her feet skidded across the stone below the gate, and she tried to yank her arm back to her, but it stuck. She'd been wrong. She'd been too long in the monster realm and the Gate was going to consume her.

She tugged and skidded more, then she finally pulled her hand out with bony fingers encircling her wrist, followed by Hud's skeletal face. He stepped out of the Gate with a large man tossed over his shoulder, his fingers still holding her wrist and his eyes glowing with rage.

But instead of guilt or anger back at him, waves of relief washed over her. It hadn't been the Gate dragging her into its depths. It had been Hud. Of course it had been Hud.

Ribbons of smoke laced through his mouth, but his eyes said everything he needed to say. They darted between her and the Gate, then dropped to where he held her wrist, but he didn't let go. Instead, he dragged her back down the path and through the town, the monsters who'd just seen her watching them curiously.

"You're hurting me," she muttered and tried to pull her arm from his grasp.

He didn't let go, but his grip loosened. His fingers slid down and looped through hers, tight but less painful than they'd been around her wrist, warming hers in familiar and comforting ways. She wanted to let go.

The human over his shoulder groaned and Hud shifted the bulk, but the man stayed unconscious.

"Did you do that to him?" Asheel asked. Or was it the Gate?

Hud shook his head. The Gate.

He continued past the city and up the rock path to Doyen's monolith. Would Doyen kill her if she returned before she changed? He had to know she hadn't become a reaper yet. How many days did they have left? Four? Would he cut the deal short?

"Hud," Asheel whispered, eyeing the ox-man that guarded the entrance, "please don't . . . please don't make me go back in there."

He glanced back at her, shook his head, and pulled her into the monolith. The pink veins that lined the walls, floor, and ceiling pulsed, triggering nightmares of Doyen.

Tremors shook her legs and arms and shivered into her fingertips where Hud gently squeezed. He hurried his steps. Snake monsters moved out of their way as they passed, and faster than seemed possible, they were at the door for Doyen's chamber.

"Please," Asheel pleaded again and pulled at his hand, trying to free her fingers.

He faced her and finally let go, then brought a finger to his lips and pointed at the ground. He held his palm out towards her. She nodded. She'd stay. Deal. As long as he wouldn't drag her into Doyen's chamber, she'd stay.

Hud entered the chamber with the man over his shoulder, and the door sealed behind him. Their muffled voices sounded almost casual. It sickened Asheel. This was a man's life they'd just upheaved, and they sounded as if it was an everyday thing for them. Though truthfully, it *was* an everyday thing. That sickened Asheel more.

The room silenced for a few seconds, then agonized shrieks pierced through the door. The shrieks mixed with panicked splashes, and she could imagine him trying to escape the Stream of Judgment.

She covered her ears. He'd be changed soon, and it'd all be over.

But the shrieks slipped around her fingers and changed to guttural roars and coughs, then cut off. He was done. Another monster for the realm of broken lives.

More muffled voices were followed by another splash, then the door opened and Hud emerged alone with hurried steps, not stopping. Asheel had to jog to keep up.

"What happened?" Asheel asked. "Where's the guy?"

"He didn't make it." Hud led them through the main chamber.

Asheel glanced over her shoulder. Snake monsters eyed her, and a couple followed at a distance. "And you're just going to walk away? What about his body? Does it get buried?"

Hud spun to face her, and she bounced off his chest before he grabbed her shoulders in one smooth movement. "The snakes eat it while Doyen eats the humanity."

"They eat the ones who die? That's awful!" Asheel leaned away from him. "Why don't you take them for a proper burial since you take them from their homes? You owe them that much."

"Do you think I like seeing people go through that?" His coal eyes darted over her shoulders. Over his own, more snake monsters watched them. "Stop talking about things you don't understand."

She clenched her jaw while he turned back around to lead them out of the cavern. Near the entrance, he picked up a small rock. They walked in silence past the sludge pool with their reflections taunting them and followed the winding trail back into the pine forests. The scents had become so familiar to Asheel, and she hated that the sight of the cabin felt like coming home, though she needed to accept it if she was the next reaper.

Hud paused at the edge of his rock garden, glanced at the pebble in his hand, closed his eyes, then tossed it among the others where it clattered to a stop.

"What was that for?" Asheel asked.

Hud stared at the expanse of rocks. "Everyone who didn't make it."

The rocks surrounding the outside of his cabin were mostly like the black rock walls of Doyen's monolith, some with flecks of faded pink. Some were brown and smooth and even fewer were reddish. Most were around the size of a hand. Thousands of them scattered the ground with only an occasional blade of grass peeking through the gaps that Hud hadn't weeded yet.

It was a graveyard.

Asheel spun to face Hud, but he'd already turned to enter the cabin with his shoulders slumped forward, leaving her out with the rocks. She looked back across the graveyard and stepped back from the edge where her toes had bumped a stone from its home. These were his memories of each person he'd brought to their death. She imagined each rock turning into a tiny person. Men, women, children of every age, shape, and color. Lives cut short. People who probably hadn't even done anything wrong yet.

Thousands of them.

Asheel entered the cabin to find Hud curled on the couch. He didn't cry, didn't yell, but the grumpiness and silence he sometimes came home with finally revealed itself as internal pain, screaming inside him in a never-ending cycle.

"I thought this was going to be over soon," he muttered into the couch.

Asheel walked over to him and placed a hand on his shoulder. "We have four days left. There's still a chance."

"Really?" He flipped to look at her and flung his arm toward the door. "You just tried to escape the realm. I thought you'd accepted all of this." He narrowed his eyes at her. "I thought you'd been trying."

"I have!" She backed away from him. "But you seemed so mad that I couldn't do it and took away my incense making, so what else was I supposed to do? Let Doyen kill me to become one of your rocks?" She hated that she said it as it passed her lips.

"No." Hud rolled over to face the back of the couch. "Of course not."

Asheel left him to his pouting and climbed into the bed. She'd tried to comfort him. She was the one struggling. She was the one in a new world. So what if he had to keep doing what he'd been doing for centuries? That was nothing new to him.

But the graveyard of rocks plunked itself in the center of her mind. He'd suffered like this for every one of them. Mourned them and gave them as good a memorial as he could in the monster realm. He was kind, and none of the monsters saw that. He worked hard to make up for his crimes against them every day, eating scraps and living in a cabin that was falling apart so they could afford vials of human essence. And he'd done all of that for centuries. Alone.

Asheel had been in a thankless job, and she didn't even last two decades before fleeing it. Hud was on his fourth century of it.

He'd worked so hard for his freedom. To be able to move on. He'd earned it.

Why couldn't she give it to him? Why couldn't she find the monster inside her to free him?

Why did the two parts of her have to be so selfish and so caring at the same time?

CHAPTER 22

Asheel lost count of the hours she spent fighting her thoughts yet again about becoming a reaper. Once she changed, she could still have her incense, have those bought friendships, and she could figure out how to break free of the contract with Doyen.

She could give Hud his freedom.

She'd stayed up so late tossing and turning that she'd slept almost to the next sunset. Hud sat outside by the rock garden, rolling the stone she'd knocked out of the graveyard in his hand.

Asheel stood back, keeping a distance between them. She knew he was four hundred years old, and yet sitting there with tears in his eyes, accepting another however many centuries of reaping, he looked like a young man who'd lost the love of his life.

"I'll try harder," Asheel said while wringing her hands together.

"Forget it." He threw the rock back in with the others. "I'm trying to figure out what to do with you. I don't want to add a rock for . . ." He eyed where the stone had landed. "Doyen might accept leaving you as you are if I bring him two people each night. Maybe three."

"How will you handle two grown men on your own?" The one the previous night would have been more of a handful if he'd been conscious. She couldn't imagine how difficult dragging two victims to the monolith would be.

"I'll figure it out. Don't worry about it."

Asheel dropped her hands to her sides. "Why are you saying that?"

"You." Hud tilted his head over his shoulder to look at her sideways. "Because I'm tired of all of this. I'm tired." He lay back and stretched his arms above his head. "But . . . it's not . . . as bad with you around, and when I imagine you doing this, getting to this point . . . I'm horrible, but I can't put this on you." His chest rose and fell slowly with a long sigh.

He sounded just as defeated as Asheel felt. They'd both been trying hard, but it hadn't been enough. Not yet. "I'll try harder," Asheel repeated.

"We only have three days left now."

"I'll try harder."

"Why?" He sat up and glared at her. "Why would you ever choose this life?"

She wrung her hands again and looked away. She couldn't tell him it was all for him because it wasn't. Part of it was to make up for the mistakes she'd made back home, but when she didn't respond, his eyes grew wide. He stood and closed the distance between them, raising his hand slowly through the last few steps to slip a lock of her hair behind her ear.

His orange gaze slid from one eye to the other, his fingertips grazing her scarred cheek. "You're doing this for me. That's why you can't change. It's too selfless."

She closed her eyes. "I don't know."

He stepped even closer, their bodies only inches apart, and he wrapped his arms around her, pulling her to his chest. "And that's why I'm saying to forget about it. You're not meant for this life."

Soft puffs of air tickled the top of her head. The foul bits of his inner monster sullied his breath, but the faint, sweet aroma of his remaining humanity fought for its own attention. Like he said, he was horrible, but he was good, too. Both sides existed in him. She lifted her arms and wrapped them around his waist.

"You can't go back home—Doyen would never allow it—but I'll convince him to let you stay as a human here."

"But you won't be able to move on."

"It won't be so bad with you around, having a friend." He squeezed her tighter, his inhuman strength holding her in place against his chest. "It's been so long since I've had someone want to do something for me without making a trade, let alone to make such a big sacrifice for me."

"It's not just for y—"

"Let me have this moment." He cut her off.

"But it's really not just for you." She didn't want to mislead him. It was for everyone, the humans, the monsters. She wanted all of them to be free of Doyen, and she didn't have enough time left to figure out how to free them. Her only choice was to become a reaper and hope that strength could stop him.

"But I'm a part of the reason, and that's enough for me." He dropped his arms and stepped back from her. "I'll make a new deal with Doyen." With a sad smile, he turned and darted into the trees faster than Asheel could follow.

Her stomach clenched. Even though her decision to become a reaper wasn't just for him, being included in what she cared for had been enough for him to accept however many more centuries of reaping. But her staying human wasn't supposed to be their fate. He was meant to move on as soon as she changed, and as a human, she'd only be a reminder of what she couldn't do for him. She twisted the edge of the firebreather's shirt and kicked at the fresh layer of fallen pine needles.

They were supposed to have a few more days, but if Hud was headed straight to Doyen to change the deal, she was out of time.

She could do it. She clenched her teeth and kicked pebbles out of the makeshift graveyard. "Come on monster!" she shouted to the dead that rolled across the dirt. "You've wanted to come out for years, and now I'm letting that wall down. Show yourself!" Anger rose inside her for neither of them being able to have what they wanted. A need for revenge for the stolen lives they could have had. The unfairness of it all. Asheel would stop Hud from making another deal with Doyen, even if it meant diving into the Stream of Judgment and securing her fate in the monster realm. She'd face Doyen and fight for Hud's freedom even if it meant losing what little remained of her life. She wanted to kill, maul, torture Doyen for the suffering he'd inflicted on those monsters. Mama B, Kady, Virgil, Ratel, and Ziyiel flashed through her thoughts. Even the monsters who'd attacked her might have been different if they'd never been judged before their crimes.

It wasn't fair. Being punished for uncommitted crimes was worse than the misplaced blame she'd dealt with. Heat boiled in her stomach and roiled up her throat, and she darted away from the cabin, remembering Hud's warning about the fire. Her footsteps pounded down the walkway while the heat kept building, her feet stumbling over each other as she ran into the forest.

Coughs spurted from her chest out of control, tasting of ash and soot. Her lungs wheezed into strenuous hacking while rage and vengefulness grew inside her. Her knees gave out, and before she could brace herself, she crashed into the base of a tree. Something new ignited inside her chest, something that she hadn't felt in months. Determination flared like bile from her throat, sending a stream of

fire into the air that cascaded back down around her, burning away
her skin. It bubbled and ruptured, ripping a scream from her scalded
throat, a sound that she didn't know she was capable of, that she'd
never forget, searing into her memory.

Asheel tried to stop it, tried to change her mind, but her
resolve still boiled to the surface.

Sizzling flames ate into her skin and peeled back the layers of
flesh which flaked off and fell to the muddy ground like dried leaves
from a campfire. She shrieked and sobbed and tried to beat out the
flames that covered her body while her humanity burned away.

Her hair shriveled to her scalp, leaving behind tendrils of
smoke that draped down her back and danced along the mud at her
feet. The tree she crashed into popped from the heat, and Asheel
tried to move away from it but instead released another shriek and
coughed up more fire.

Lava poured from her eyes and evaporated her tears, and her
eyes turned to coals. Her blurred vision cleared, but black, sparkling
flecks swirled at the edges of her sight. She collapsed to the ground in
a ball with her hands wrapped around her head, waiting for the agony
to stop.

After seconds that felt like hours, the raging fires retreated,
and Asheel curled tighter in the mud with the continuous hiss and
occasional pop where smoldering embers flowed between the cracks
in her exposed bones. The firebreather's leather that Hud had said
she'd be thankful to have remained hanging from her shoulders,
unaffected by the flames of Asheel's pain.

She braced her hands in the mud and lifted herself onto her
knees to test her movements. Her bones ached, but her skeleton lifted
easily, buoyed by her drive, her determination for revenge. She didn't
question how it still moved as long as it would get her to Doyen's
monolith.

With the pain passed, she now felt like she could topple

buildings, uproot trees, destroy towns. This power, it was more than what Hud had described. What had once been blind rage driving her to assault Doyen now was a new, tangible strength. She truly could do it now. But first she had to stop Hud from making the new deal with Doyen. She'd changed. There was no need for him to make it now.

Asheel threw her head back to breathe in the night, and the scents of monsters throughout the realm filled the pits where her nose had been. She had no eyelids to close to focus on the smells, but the sparkling black flecks on the edge of her vision swirled tighter like dancing stars until they filled her sight. She breathed in and found the noxious odor of Doyen. The fumes swirled visibly over the path to the monolith, and she took a step to face her chosen fate.

CHAPTER 23

Asheel ran down the path until she broke through the tree line. Beyond the sludge pits, the monolith stuck out like a beacon. She pulled her blackened, charred mouth into a grimace. If Hud had already made a new deal, how would her being a reaper fit into it? She could still free him, right?

She darted past the last sludge pool and into the cavern, hoping anyone who saw her might mistake her for Hud. The snake monsters slithered up to her, curious like they'd been the first time Hud had brought her into the realm, but with her new strength, the powerful fire coursing through her limbs, they didn't scare her like they had before. She could burn any of them to ash if they tried to hurt her.

She passed a quilled monster crumpled against a wall, and the shimmering flecks in Asheel's vision hovered over her. The flecks glowed, shimmering as if reflecting the life that remained in her. The quilled monster had fainted, tears still staining her cheeks. Doyen was insatiable.

Asheel hurried down the tunnel to the door for Doyen's chamber then paused. Ripples of odor came to her but nothing that seemed like Hud. He must have already made the deal and left to complete his first night of reaping two humans. But Doyen would be in there, lounging by the Stream of Judgment, unsuspecting of another reaper at his door, a reaper not yet bound to the realm's ruler. She'd planned to stop Hud and release him from his duties, but with her unhindered by Doyen's magic, this could be her best chance to free everyone.

New questions spun through her. Was her new strength enough to end him? Would the surprise give her enough leverage? If the snake-like attendants protected him, was she willing to kill them too? She'd let reflexes decide that if it happened.

What was Doyen's weakness? His neck was well plated and his limbs armored. The eyes that taunted her in her sleep could be a target. She could blind him. Then what? Maybe she could attack his engorged underbelly. That was her best option. What would be her punishment if she failed?

How fast did the contract activate? Did Hud have to be there to transfer his, or would he be released as soon as hers activated? Too many questions, and she was risking her last moments of freedom by—

The door flung open, and several snake monsters lunged through it at her, wrapping themselves around her limbs and dragging her inside. The fire in her bones flared, scorching the snakes, but the ones that peeled away in painful shrieks were replaced, winding themselves around her again.

Between the pool and his throne, Doyen sat back on his haunches with his tongue lolling over his mismatched fangs. "You've decided to join us at last!"

Asheel kept fighting the snakes, scorching them, clawing at them, until Doyen motioned for them to let her go. They slithered away, blocking the door and leaving Asheel standing alone in the center of the room.

Doyen reached for her, but Asheel sidestepped his grasp and dove between his forearms. A chuckle heaved his sides as if she were a puppy running around his legs. Grazing her fiery hand across his bulging gut, she tore the taut flesh there. His claws slipped by her then snatched the back of her jacket. With an easy tug, he slammed her to the cave floor, crushing her under is weight, her bones crunching against the pink-veined stone.

Doyen's laugh gurgled. "Did you think you could kill me, foolish girl. What? You don't think a reaper's ever tried to kill me to get out of his contract?" While he spoke, the shredded flesh of his stomach knit back together like a grotesque doll. "No wound can destroy me." The snake monsters along the edges of the room hissed as if applauding the statement.

Asheel squirmed under his hand and tried to flare her fire, but even though it scorched and charred Doyen's scales, he didn't even flinch. She'd failed. "Just kill me," she screamed. She didn't want to care about it anymore.

"Every reaper has tried what you've attempted, and all of them lived and fulfilled their contracts." He sat beside her but continued to pin her to the floor. His belly had flattened a little where some of the pink humanity he'd consumed had leaked out, and a faint glow emitted from where the flesh had woven together.

She spat ash onto the claw closest to her face.

His lips curled at her action. "Stop struggling. Reaper will be here momentarily, and we'll get everything sorted out."

She couldn't move much, but for the next several minutes, she spat, bit, and writhed with no success. When she was about to give up on her struggle, Doyen spoke again.

"Ah, my feast."

Beyond the decayed scent of his hand, Asheel sensed the

mixed, soured smell of a human not yet stripped of their humanity, still dredges of sweet lacing through the human's stains, sweet scents that she'd have ignored in the past when checking the humans in Seshnia. The humanity that would soon be stolen to leave behind only what rotted them from the inside. What would Hud say when he saw she'd finally released her inner monster? Probably be happy he could move on. Or maybe even proud if she was lucky.

A piercing cry echoed off the cavern's walls. A younger human? Wait, which city had he gone to that night? Asheel clenched her teeth. It had been almost two months since she'd come to the monster realm. Had he been back to her city twice already? Who had he taken last month? Did he even know? She hadn't considered asking.

The cry turned to sobs, and Asheel tilted her head back to peer at them upside down.

In the doorway, Hud met her gaze and motioned wildly for Doyen to release his lips, but Doyen left his mouth sealed.

"Look at this!" He bounced, still pinning Asheel, his movements freer with the loss of his bulk. "The little human has decided to join us, finally."

CHAPTER 24

H ud shoved the teen into the pool and motioned again at his mouth. The teen shrieked a stream of profanities with a Yulgerian accent, and spasmed while his future crimes flared brightly in the waterfall, private desires exposed in flashes.

Doyen stopped bouncing. His eyes danced while he watched the scenes, his glee fully focused on the display.

Asheel tried to squirm again, but Doyen's hand wouldn't budge.

The last scene played, and the waterfall paused, folded over on itself, and crashed onto the teen. His back arched, and he screamed and writhed from the pain as he vanished in the vortex of water around him, the Stream of Judgment stripping him of his humanity. The vortex slowed, and finally, Doyen lifted his hand to toss Asheel across the room where she crashed into Hud. He barely caught her. Their bones clinked together unpleasantly, and as soon as she got her feet under her, he let her go except for a hand firmly grasping her shoulder to keep her in place. She kept her mouth shut. He would finally get what he'd been wanting. At least she could free one person.

Doyen raked his claws across the top of the water where a sludgy pink film floated in a thin sheet that bunched with each claw. It draped from his claws like algae, which he slurped in several gulps to refill his belly of what Asheel had sliced from him. When he stepped back, the water returned to its normal upward flow. Near the bank of the pool, washed up by a small wave, a new, feathered monster floated. Asheel tore her eyes away from the limp teen. Had he survived, or were the snakes about to devour him?

"Now, where were we?" Doyen wiped his mouth on the back of his hand and patted his stomach. "I think we have some contracts to transfer."

Hud grunted and pointed to his mouth.

"Oh, right." Doyen reached toward him and traced a claw across Hud's mouth to draw the blue flecked smoke back to him.

"What have you done?" Hud asked before the last of the smoke had settled back under Doyen's scales.

"Me?" Doyen placed a hand to his chest. "Why do you assume I did something?"

Hud tilted his head, gripped Asheel's shoulder tighter, and faced her. "Did he force you into the pool?"

Asheel didn't move. Didn't say anything. This wasn't happening. Denial flooded through her. She hadn't let her pain consume her, hadn't chosen destruction. She wasn't standing in Doyen's cavern about to receive the contract. Hud wasn't about to disappear, free of his contract, and leave her alone in a world that hated her. She hadn't failed again.

But denial didn't change the truth, and lava leaked down her cheekbones.

"Asheel!" He shook her.

Doyen stalked behind them, and his voice boomed out. "She

pranced into my mountain all on her own, all aglow with her newfound power, and I had my worshipers invite her into my throne room. I didn't even touch her." He paused in his circling. "Wait. No, I did touch her." He crawled back in front of them and arched over Asheel. "But only after she ripped me open and strewn my guts to the ground. Look at this." He lifted his hand and wiped a single, massive claw on Asheel's shirt. "It hasn't had time to dry."

Hud opened, shut, and reopened his mouth. "You . . ." His smile was more of a grimace, and his grip on her shoulder loosened. "You did it."

Asheel dipped her head. What could she say?

"Now," Doyen rubbed a smear of humanity between his claws, "all that's left is the contract."

Hud dropped his hand and spun to face Doyen. "No. She wouldn't be any use to you yet. I haven't taught her what she needs to do out there."

Doyen clenched his fists and leaned forward. "What have you been doing all this time? Wooing her?"

Hud's shoulders dropped. "I've been trying to convince her this job was worth doing to get her to accept it. Explaining how it all goes would have made the process harder."

Doyen laid a hand on his forehead with his wrist angled dramatically. "Fine. Use the remaining days of our deal to train her." His gaze shifted to Asheel, and he licked his lips. "But no reason we can't already set her agreement."

Asheel stepped backward, but Doyen placed his hand behind her where it covered her entire back. His eyes glowed and blue dust with yellow sparks drifted from his other hand, which hovered in front of her face. She glanced to Hud who was wringing his hands, his eyes shifting between her and Doyen, but he shook his head and turned to the pool. He moved quickly to avoid the bubbles starting to gather at his fingertips, and when he bent over the child, a drop of lava fell into the pool, turning to rock with a sizzle. He cradled the teen whose arms had turned to blackened wings.

Doyen's voice brought her attention back to him though she wanted to watch Hud with the boy.

"Every day when the world on the other side is dark," Doyen said while blue dust drifted through the air to circle her head, "I will seal your lips and lock you in your reaper form while you enter the human realm. Reap from them someone with an awakened monster to feed and sustain this realm." The blue dust thickened, blocking out the cavern, and the only thing she could see was Doyen's grotesque head full of elongated teeth and his hand hovering between them, covered in oozing scales. His pulsing eyes mocked her like they did in her dreams. "You will do this task, immortal and unageing, until you find another reaper to take your place, whether that be days or millennia. If you disobey my orders, my magic will become agonizing pain through your every limb until I die." He smirked. "And I never die."

The blue dust circling them shot toward her face and entered her eyes, nose, and mouth to lock every ember, every hope of escaping, in magical chains. The magic twisted around her heart like the hands in the Gate had and tightened until her heartbeats slowed and weakened to barely a quiver. She was still alive, but her movements, her internal workings had paused, like life couldn't move on until she finished her task.

Her sight cleared of the blue dust, and she coughed while the stream from Doyen's hand cut off. Hud had returned beside her with the teen cradled in his arms. Thick, brown fronds replaced the boy's hair, and feathers stuck out of his shirt and layered over his scalp. His head lolled to the side, revealing a long, fanged beak that started at his forehead and ended at his chin, and his ears had turned to stubs. His eyes had completely vanished.

Anger crackled through Asheel's bones, which glowed with

her rage. She would never do this for Doyen—no one deserved to be forced to change like this—but Doyen's magic awakened, sending excruciating pain shooting through her skull like a metal rod shoved through the top of her head and into her spine. Even the thought of resisting his spell activated the torture.

She glared at the grotesque beast still hunched over them, putting as much venom into her gaze as she could. With a deep breath, he turned to his throne where he retrieved a large pot, coughed a few times, and vomited thick pink liquid into it. Before the sight could make her sick, Asheel dropped her gaze to the vials on the ground at his feet. She needed to leave. Each thought of hate and disobedience toward Doyen jabbed new pain through her, and she needed to get away from him to stop thinking about how much she despised him.

After dipping a few vials into the pot and sealing them, Doyen handed them to Hud and returned to his throne to lounge with his eyes closed. Asheel eyed the familiar pink liquid, not believing what she saw. Surely not. Surely that wasn't what she'd seen all the monsters consuming, but when Hud shoved them in his pocket, she couldn't deny it. She'd drank monster vomit.

Another searing pain jabbed between her eyes. She hated Doyen more than she'd ever hated anything.

Doyen flicked a hand at them, shooing them. "Leave. I can't deal with that exhausting little thing anymore tonight."

Hud nudged her with his elbow and jerked his head to the door, and Asheel followed him out of the lair, sulking through the cavern with the whispers of the worshipers haunting her.

"Two reapers?"

"Was Reaper not released? Is he stuck?"

"Get ready for double the monsters in this place."

The bird-teen stirred in Hud's arms, and Hud rushed out of the monolith with the whispers still following them. He didn't slow until they reached the opposite edge of the sludge pit then set the bird-teen on the ground and changed back to his human form, smoke settling as flesh along his limbs, and the boy stirred again, releasing something between a shriek and a squawk from his beak.

"Shh." Hud soothed the boy, stroking the thickened fronds protruding above the beak. "You're safer now. Can you stand?"

The boy flailed his wings around him and tossed his head backwards, trying to cough out words.

Hud grabbed his wings at the elbow. "Slowly. You'll hurt yourself. Limit your neck movements while you get used to the weight of your beak."

At that, the bird-teen put both his wingtips to his face and squawked again. His bulky jaw opened and closed rapidly and clamped down on his wing. He screamed, tearing agony through Asheel.

"Do something!" She grabbed Hud's shoulder to keep herself from collapsing, too. "He'll hurt himself."

"I'm trying. They're usually unconscious longer than that, but he's been a fighter the whole trip." Hud pulled the boy's wing out of multiple rows of fangs. "You need to calm down, kid. I'll explain everything if you calm down and show you can listen to me."

The boy flung his head back again about to cry out, but Hud tugged him forward to face him and grabbed his beak. "Stop it. If you keep crying like a wounded animal, you'll get killed. You're safer now, but some people here like to kill for sport."

The boy shivered but paused in his thrashing.

"That's better." Hud released the boy's beak. "I know this is hard. We've all gone through it, and if it helps, you're more than welcome to hate me. Everyone else does. But right now, I need to get you to your own kind. I can't teach you how to live in this new body, but the others like you can help you out. They'll teach you how to see again with the features of your kind."

The boy whimpered and tried to speak again, but without lips and with a tongue twice as long as a human's, the mess sounded like a foreign language.

Hud sighed. "Sorry, kid. You'll learn how to use your mouth again, too. They'll teach you. Can you stand? If you don't think you can walk, I can carry you, but you'll have to be calm and trust me."

The boy's head bobbled like a newborn's as he stood on shaky legs. With his wings stretched in front of him, he took a tentative step forward.

"That's great." Hud held his hand out although the boy couldn't see it. "Do you mind if I take your wing, uh, your hand to lead you?"

The boy muttered something that sounded like a yes and he nodded slightly, but the weight of his beak still pulled his chin down to his chest.

Hud closed his eyes. "Good. I have a friend here with me. I'm going to talk to her some." He turned to Asheel. "Can I trust you to go back to the cabin?"

The weight of everything that happened settled over Asheel. She'd transformed like this teen had. She was new. She was powerful, but she wasn't in control of it. And whether or not she wanted to admit it, she was scared. If the boy almost accidentally ripped his own arm off, what kind of damage could Asheel do to herself? She considered fleeing home through the Gate but before she could put words to the thought, Doyen's chains tightened around her mind, shooting pain through her skull again, and she stumbled.

She shook her head. She didn't want to be alone, and at least Hud knew what she was going through. Like the boy needed to be with his kind, Asheel needed Hud. But she wouldn't admit that aloud.

Hud ran his hand through his fried hair and looked around them. "I guess I'm supposed to be showing you how this goes anyway. I'll show you to the birds' nest. They're in the giant forest on the other side of Doyen's monolith."

She didn't want to learn what she was supposed to do. She wanted to go back in time when her worst days were using her magic to warn Seshnian families. But this was the best he could offer unless she wanted to be alone at the cabin, which she wanted even less.

"Okay, kid. Let's go." Hud grabbed the boy's uninjured wing and nudged him away from the sludge pit. "Your feet should still work like they did before."

The trudge to the tall trees where the bird monsters lived looped around the sludge swamp and followed a narrow path through forests on the other side. A few of the braver cat-like monsters prowled into view, and the same whispers from the monolith followed them in the shadows.

"The wildcats live in the caves around here," Hud whispered while they walked. "I used to think their tunnels were connected to the ones in the monolith, but they aren't. I don't have to show you where those are, though. When you have someone become a cat, just bring them to this forest. As you can see, a lot of that kind is curious enough to meet you out here and take the new monster off your hands."

With Hud as his human self, everyone knew who the burning skeleton beside him had to be, and they crept around the tree trunks in masses to see two reapers at the same time. Asheel hated them for their curiosity. They'd see enough of her over the next eternity. Couldn't they give her some privacy while she dealt with her new circumstances?

"Hud," Asheel whispered even though the cats' sensitive, flicking ears could probably hear every word, "how do I change back?"

"You just pull it back inside."

She imagined tugging the fire back inside her, but it was already there. It was still on her insides though it had engulfed her outsides as well. She tried to find her human self cowering in her center like where she'd felt the monster bubbling inside her, but that space was empty, too. "How?"

"Just calm down. Forget about whatever pushed you to it."

Asheel focused on not caring, focused on her footsteps crunching the giant dried leaves, but in the back of her mind, she still raged and wanted to kill Doyen, which sent shockwaves of pain down her neck. "It's not working."

Hud sighed while guiding the bird-teen over a rock. "I'll help you when we get back to the cabin."

Asheel dropped her shoulders and groaned. "Give me something less vague to fix it."

"Why does it matter right now? You've already changed. You've accepted it. There's no going back to the old you."

"I feel like a glowing beacon to every monster in here."

Hud shook his head and gave her a pitying look. "Monsters would still stare. Enough have seen you by now that I'm sure the rumors have spread through the realm. Relax. This is part of accepting your new role."

"I thought you told me to forget about accepting it," Asheel muttered.

Hud grimaced and eyed a cluster of monsters they passed. "It's too late now."

When they reached the center of the forest where the giant trees were large enough to hold the entire bird city in their branches, a much larger raven-like creature with the same protruding beak landed in front of them, towering over Asheel.

It controlled its head and mouth better than the boy, and although it had no lips, the way it moved its tongue made its speech understandable. "Reaper? You sound different."

"The kid's all yours." Hud released the teen's wing.

The raven-man turned its head back and forth, picking up where the sound of Hud's voice was compared to the crackling of the embers in Asheel's bones. Before the raven-man could say anything about it, Hud interrupted.

"I couldn't get his name, so you'll have to work with him on it. He bit his wing too." Hud gestured to the limb covered in dried blood though the raven-man couldn't see him. "He's feisty. Good luck."

"Feisty is good." The raven-man ruffled his wings. "We can always use fighters. The cats attacked again just yesterday."

Hud turned and walked away while the raven-man introduced himself to the teen, and Asheel followed him while silently wishing the best for the poor kid. When she'd first been taken to Doyen and shoved in the Stream of Judgment, she could have so easily been stripped of her humanity like that and given to strangers with horrendous features. But was she any luckier to be trapped in the immortal life of a reaper?

Hud picked up his pace, and Asheel jogged beside him. She'd accepted her monster so rashly. How would she get out of the contract now? How long could she take torturous pain if she outright refused to obey?

The whispers continued with each monster they passed, but Hud took her through less populated areas, explaining the monsters that lived there and who the friendlier villagers were, names Asheel couldn't focus on. They passed a small community she hadn't seen before of burrows where plated monsters with curved backs scurried away from them.

When they finally reached his cabin, Hud opened the door and gestured for Asheel to enter, then shut it behind them and sat at the table while Asheel stood awkwardly to the side.

"So how did this happen?" He laced his fingers on the table in front of him. "Did I push you over the edge somehow?" He kept his eyes down, staring at his fingers, not looking at her.

"No, it wasn't you." Asheel waved her hands wildly in front of her.

"That's a relief," he mumbled to himself. He finally looked her in the eye for the first time since they'd left Doyen's lair. "You can sit down."

She shook her hands to try to cool the embers glowing in her fingers. "Help me turn this off." She gestured to her body.

Hud stood and walked to her. "You have to calm down. But here, let me help."

He reached for her hands, but she pulled them away and stepped back. "I don't know how to control the heat."

He smirked. "You're saying that to a guy who has fire inside him, too." He took her glowing hands in his nearly human ones. "You're still part human. What makes you human?"

"Mistakes."

"Not the answer I was looking for. Compassion is an easy one. Feeling remorse for your actions."

"I have to feel bad about what I've done every time I want to be human again? What kind of self-torture is that?"

Hud chewed the inside of his cheek. "It's hard at first, but it gets easier. You'll eventually get to where you don't even have to think about it. You'll just feel what you need to feel."

Asheel dropped her gaze to their hands. If Hud flipped back and forth between reaper and human every day, he had to have turned off the part of him that told him how he truly felt. He had even more right than her to be vengeful and full of rage, but he'd given up. Doyen had defeated him.

"What are you thinking?" he asked.

Asheel shook her head and didn't look up. She didn't want to tell him how she pitied him. She couldn't admit how her lifelong anger had shifted from him to Doyen so easily the past two months. Hud's actions in taking her hadn't been personal. He hadn't taken her for himself. He'd just been doing what he'd been desensitized to long ago. She wanted to help him but not in the mindless drive she'd felt after he'd mentioned a new deal with Doyen. At least he'd be free soon.

Hud tightened his grip on her fingers. "Want me to use my magic?"

She'd forgotten he was a Physiqal like the monster who'd tried to lure her away months ago. The magic had left her lightheaded and confused, but it could be just the escape she needed right now. She nodded, focusing on their hands, trying to beat her monster back inside her.

Instantly, her worries and stress calmed, replaced with peace that wasn't her own. Her own thoughts sank into oblivion, and all she cared about were the hands that held hers and not letting go of them. Hud extinguished the fire like fizz tickling through her gut, filling her with cooled peace.

The smoke floating along Asheel's limbs tightened over her bones, weaving back into place. Tendon, muscle, and flesh returned but not the same as it had been before. Scorch marks and ash laced over her skin. A mirror of the hands that held hers.

"Better?"

She nodded, a loopy grin plastered on her face.

He stared at their matching hands before dropping them and wrapping his arms around her, pulling her to his chest like he had right before she changed. His magic was already leaving her system, leaving her with a hollowness.

"I'm sorry," he said into her hair.

With her face buried in the firebreather leather, tears finally fell. "There's no way out of this is there?"

Hud set his chin on her head. "If there were, I would have figured it out by now. If you'd just waited, I could have made the new deal with Doyen. He'd sent me to the human realm before I had a chance to explain it to him. I could have gotten him to accept it."

Asheel left her arms hanging at her sides while the tears continued to smear between her cheeks and the leather. "I failed. I wanted to make this place better for everyone. I couldn't do that back home and now I'm stuck in the same cycle here." She sniffed and pressed her face harder against Hud's chest. "All I ever do is fail."

"It's okay." Hud shushed her. "You'll be fine. It'll all be fine. You still have your incense, right? You'll have friends over here that I never had." He ran his fingers through her fried hair. "You'll be fine."

After a couple of minutes letting her cry into his chest, he led her to the table and had her sit. She rubbed her eyes while Hud stared at her.

"Can I know how this happened?" he asked. "What triggered it?"

"I don't want to talk about it."

"Did someone else get to you after I left?"

She shook her head again.

"Please, I'm curious."

"Do I have to tell you?" She held the recent memory back, embarrassed by the rage she let flow unabated.

"No, but I'd like to know. I only know about my change."

Asheel fiddled with an empty cup. "I kind of . . . exploded when I thought you were about to give up your freedom for me." She couldn't meet his eyes. "Even if you're a little less lonely now. No one deserves to be a slave for centuries, and everyone here has been forced into it. I mean, not as enslaved as you, but they're all stuck here. And even the humans on the other side. They don't even know it, but he controls them too, able to pull them into this place. They aren't free either."

Hud frowned. "It's been that way forever. Why did it suddenly push you?"

"I'd finally decided to act on my pain, the pain I was feeling for both of us. No one even seems to be trying to free themselves from him." Asheel clenched her fists on the table. "I want to make him pay for what he's done." Pain ricocheted across her forehead, and she pressed her palms to it.

"Shh." Hud grabbed her hand to pull it back to the table, his coarse palm pressing her hand against the cool stone. "We can't kill him. Believe me. I've tried. I think every reaper has tried, maybe just not as soon as you did."

That information would have been helpful earlier, but she couldn't get mad about the oversight. "It has to be possible." Asheel finally met his gaze. "This can't be how things are supposed to be."

"I agree, but all of this was decided before our time. It's not up to us."

"Maybe it can be. Where did he come from anyway?"

Hud stroked Asheel's hand, trying to soothe her. "He's always been here, a part of this realm. It's been like this longer than recorded history. Whoever made it made him to rule it."

She crossed her arms. "There has to be a way to stop him." She squinted through the pain from Doyen's magic.

"Asheel," Hud said softly, "we can't. The best you can do is keep the human realm clean."

The truth of the situation hit her then. He'd said "you," not "we." Hud would be freed from Doyen's magic in a few days, leaving her alone to deal with the mess she'd fallen into. Would he vanish as soon as he was released? "What'll happen to you?"

"I'll finally have peace." He looked over her shoulder out the window with the centuries of his life pulling his cheeks down, finally looking as old as he was.

"But will you turn to dust? Age centuries right there?"

"No." He still gazed out the window. "No, I'll let the Stream of Judgment take what's left of my humanity, and then Doyen will finally kill me. Probably swallow me whole. I wonder what that will feel like without his magic healing me."

Asheel hadn't considered how his plan to move on would work, but being slaughtered by the beast that enslaved him so brutally hadn't been what she imagined. "That's horrible."

"He'll make it fast." Hud reached for her hand again and stroked it, this time seemingly to soothe himself instead of her. "I won't care for long anyway. I'll be dead."

He didn't deserve a short gruesome death . . . or maybe he did deserve it after centuries of kidnappings, even if Doyen had forced him to. Did he deserve it if the actions hadn't been his choice?

It wasn't what she wanted for him. She wanted him free in the monster realm where he'd stay with her, help her. He was the one who brought her to the realm, shouldn't he stay at least for a while to help her figure out how to break free of Doyen? She frowned. She thought she'd changed so much since leaving her home, but she hadn't. She was still just as selfish.

"I don't want that for you," she told him honestly. "I want you to experience a real life. I want to stop Doyen so everyone can have a real life."

"We can't kill him," Hud repeated and rummaged through his shelves. When he revealed a hidden incense stick from underneath a tattered book, Asheel realized he hadn't burned all of it. "Monsters try all the time, and you're restrained by his magic now. Forget about killing him. I'll teach you how to find the humans growing inner monsters and how to make it easier on yourself."

The fumes from the incense tickled through Asheel, calming her, shoving the anger at everything deep into her gut. The others had been right about the effect of the incense. The magic that swirled from the burning tip intoxicated her and dulled her frustrations. She only had herself to blame for her situation. She'd chosen to take Coby's place. She'd chosen the reaper's life even after Hud told her to forget about it.

"I'll find a way to escape his magic myself," she muttered. She'd made the decisions that got her there and she'd find the way to get out, but pain washed across her forehead again at the thought.

Hud spent the rest of the morning explaining where each of

the monster types lived across the realm, where she'd need to take the freshly changed monsters each day, but Asheel barely listened. She wouldn't need to know it for long, not after she figured out how to stop Doyen. The determination rippled under her skin, begging to be let out in scorching fire. Only the incense imbued with her magic kept her human.

CHAPTER
25

Asheel stayed in bed, moping under the firebreather blanket, until Hud prodded her to tell her she'd be going into the human realm as a reaper for the first time.

When she didn't respond, Hud tugged the blanket off her. "We need to talk before we go to Doyen's lair. At least sit up and listen."

"I'm listening." Asheel jerked the cover back over her shoulders.

"Sit up," Hud demanded and poked at her shoulder again.

Asheel only glared at him.

"Okay, fine, but if you're not listening and any of this is a surprise, that's on you." He spun a chair around to face Asheel. She pulled her knees to her chest while he slouched into the chair with his arms crossed and picked at a hole in the leather of his vest. "Doyen will seal our mouths, so I won't be able to give you much instruction when we're on the other side."

"Why does he do that?" Asheel interrupted.

Hud shrugged with one shoulder. "To keep us from revealing his secrets to the humans."

"That seems pointless. What threat could humans be to him? We can't even capture you. Besides, you could write it down for them." As she considered the idea herself, Doyen's magic shot pain through her hands. Writing anything legible with the tremors would be difficult.

"Yeah, letters . . ." He let the thought trail and pursed his lips. His eyebrows rose in the middle. "It's not 'we' for you anymore. You're not human."

That stung, and Asheel closed her eyes. The chains around her heart weighed on her, an ache like a sore muscle. Would her mouth ache, too? "Does it hurt?"

"Not particularly, but it's uncomfortable." Hud chewed on his bottom lip while he thought. "I'll try to convince him to let us keep our voices since there'll be two of us out there, but he probably won't agree to it. If we can't talk, make sure you stay close to me. Most humans like to fight back."

Asheel remembered the time she'd pretended to be a reaper and was stopped by the Seshnian Reaper Guard. "What happens if we get caught?"

"Most of the time they're trying to kill you, not catch you. You're powerful. A spear to the chest is uncomfortable but temporary. Doyen's magic will keep you alive through anything, weave you back together. You've seen that happen to me." He rubbed his neck where she'd sliced him and looked at the ceiling. "If you get caught . . . well, again, you're powerful. Just burn the place down. I've never met a material I couldn't melt. You're strong enough to break stone." He sighed and looked back to her. "This might not be the best first time for you. The city we're going to is one of the largest in the realm. They were almost finished building a huge metal wall last time I was there, and they'll fight back."

Asheel closed her eyes again. "Novoshna." Of course it would be her hometown's capitol. "You're taking me to Novoshna."

"Is that a problem?"

"This whole thing's a problem!" She flung her hands up and let them fall beside her to the bed. "Please don't tell me we're breaking into the palace, too."

"I won't know until we get to the other side."

Maybe she could avoid the reaping one more night, but with that thought, a wave of pain rippled through her head. "If you don't know who you're going to take, how do you know where to go?"

"It's on a schedule."

Asheel sat up rigid. It was. And the next town after Novoshna was Seshnia. She'd have to abduct someone from her home. She couldn't do that. A sharp pain drove through her skull, and she clutched the sides of her head with her fingers in her hair. Hud looked at her with pity but continued talking without asking what was wrong. If he'd lived with this pain for so long, he knew exactly what she was feeling.

"The Gate has twenty-two access points into the human world. A few of them are used for multiple cities. I had the schedule written down, but I haven't used it in centuries. I'll write it down for you when we're back. You simply have your destination in mind, and the spirits in the Gate will guide you to the right one."

Hud explained how their sight worked to find the human whose inner monster had grown the most since the last visit, then he explained how best to hold different sizes and shapes of people to keep them from struggling too much and hurting themselves.

She imagined running through Seshnia, finding a human, and dragging them through the Gate with her. "I don't think I can do it."

"You'll get used to it fast."

Asheel grasped the blanket. "That's not something I want to get comfortable with doing."

A knock on the door startled both of them, and Hud frowned at it. The knock sounded a second time, then louder the third.

"A guard?" Asheel asked.

"Maybe." He stood and walked to the door. "But everyone should know you don't need guarding by now."

When he opened the door, Mama B peered around him into the single room. "I heard what happened. Are you okay?"

The presence of the kindest monster in the whole forsaken place pulled Asheel from her slump. She sat upright and let the blanket fall from her shoulders, and when Hud didn't move, Mama B shoved past him, walked right to Asheel, and pulled her into a hug.

"You poor thing." Mama B traced a black vein across Asheel's cheek. "I thought if anyone had a chance against Reaper and Doyen, it was you."

Asheel carefully hugged Mama B's waist, avoiding the quills. "I'm sorry."

"Shh, don't apologize to me. You apologize to yourself." Mama B turned her head so her lips brushed Asheel's ear. "You can still choose not to," she whispered. "Fight it."

Asheel wished that were true, but she'd already chosen. Every time she tried to imagine ignoring Doyen's contract, his magic ricocheted through her with excruciating, searing pain.

Hud crossed his arms and glared at them. "You never showed me any sympathy."

"Of course not. You've always had a choice in this too."

Hud scoffed. "She needs to get ready for her job, and she won't be able to with you here."

"She wants me to stay, right?"

"Right," Asheel agreed, then remembered what she'd have to do, "but I don't want you to see what I've become."

"I've seen worse." Mama B squeezed her shoulders.

"It'll make it harder. I'll be fine."

Mama B's hooded eyes darted between Asheel's. "If that is what you want. Just remember, you can still choose." She gave Asheel's shoulder one last squeeze then strolled out of the room with her head held high, bringing a smile to Asheel's face, but her amusement vanished when Hud turned back to her.

"Be ready at sundown," he said. "We have a long night ahead of us."

He walked out of the cabin and let the door close quietly behind him. Asheel stretched and stood. Sundown was less than an hour away. Why had he left her there? She already had her firebreather leather on and wouldn't be going outside where greedy eyes waited to see the realm's new reaper, so she paced the small cabin. It was messy, rundown, maybe not where she wanted to spend the next hundred years, but the monsters who'd helped patch the place might finish renovating it for more incense. It'd be hers soon, empty and lonely.

No, not lonely. Mama B had stopped by. She'd hugged Asheel even though she knew what she was. Asheel had at least one friend still. Mama B's words echoed through her thoughts. *You can still choose not to.* Did she really have a choice? If she refused to enter the human realm, how much pain from Doyen's magic could she take before she broke?

A burn in her chest, the monster inside her, had been building steadily since the last of the incense burned out, and it had grown from unpleasant to searing, joining the pain from considering disobeying Doyen. She couldn't think through the itch along her skin, needing relief from it. A relief she'd received the night before from a particularly confusing creature. But it was also a relief similar to what she'd felt from a certain beverage. She wouldn't drink it unless in dire need, would she? Was she in dire need? She found the stash of pink vials in the kitchen. Disgusting. Gross. Surely she wasn't considering drinking it. But she was, and she took one of the flasks of pink and sipped on the floral concoction, like ice running down her throat in a cooling, soothing, metallic effect. After another few minutes, Hud returned in his reaper form.

He looked her up and down with his coal eyes. "Why aren't you ready?"

"Oh. You meant I needed to change into a reaper?"

"Yeah. I thought it might be easier if I weren't here. What did you think I meant?"

Asheel clambered from the seat she'd been lounging in. "I don't know. To mentally prepare myself?" She held her hands in front of her face. "Wait, how am I supposed to do this now that I've changed before? Do I need to feel like I did last time?"

"Not really. It should be easier now." He gestured to his body and ran his hand from his gut to his chest. "You should feel the fire building inside you, begging to get out. Give in to it, and it should be easy. The pain doesn't last as long the second time. It gets easier to let the monster slip out with each change."

She'd felt the fire. Asheel gulped. And she had extinguished it with the pink drink. "What do I need to do if I don't feel it?"

"What are you talking about? If you've accepted your monster, you should feel it."

Asheel pointed to the table, and when his eyes found the empty vial, his bones glowed brighter. "Why would you drink that?"

"I was burning inside. I didn't feel good!"

Hud ran a bony hand down his face. "Asheel, those extinguish monstrous desires. They make it harder to let the reaper out. Why do you think I drink it so much?"

"I didn't realize that." Asheel crossed her arms. "What am I supposed to do now?" Then a smile crept over her face. "I guess you just have to leave me here. Have fun!" She shooed him even as the pain of her magical chains crushed through her.

"I'm dragging you along either way, and trust me, if you get hit with a blade, you'll wish you were in this form." He stepped around the table to pick up the vial and toss it in the sink. "Can you at least try? Do you feel any fire along your limbs? Any at all?"

Asheel closed her eyes to focus, but the only burning was from the ache of Doyen's magic. She shook her head. "Cold as ice."

"Nothing? Not even a tiny spark?"

"Nothing."

Hud sat on the bed and fell backwards. "I'm serious that I'm taking you through whether you change or not. Doyen wouldn't let leaving you here slide, but I don't want you to have to deal with this in a human body."

"Let's just wait on taking me through until tomorrow." Magical shockwaves radiated across her back, but she stayed upright. She could take it. "We have a few days left, right?"

"We have two if you count today, and that's barely enough."

They stayed in silence for a few minutes while Hud thought to himself and Asheel kept trying to pull up the fire inside her. She still had residual anger about everything, but with a cool gut, she just couldn't find it in her to care anymore.

While Asheel stared at her hands, Hud sighed and stood.

"I have an idea," he closed the distance between them, "but you might hate me for it."

"What is it?"

"Since you've become the reaper on your own, I can use my magic to reignite your fire. Make you heated. But it'll make you feel worse than the false good feelings I fed you to help you change back."

Asheel lowered her hands. The memory of the hollowness his magic left her with, of losing her own thoughts, shivered up her spine. "I don't like that idea."

"It's the only one I have."

Doyen's magic sent painful pulses through the top of her scalp and down her legs as if a knife had split the skin there, urging her toward the monolith, pulling her like a magnet. Asheel's stomach twisted, and another jolt shocked through her legs, dropping her to the floor with a grunt. "Okay, fine." She held out her hand. "Let me have it."

Hud knelt beside her, ignored her hand, and placed his palm over her forehead, his fingertips grazing her temple. "This will hurt a little." He let out a slow breath, then the magic hit her.

Like the other times she'd felt Physiqal magic, her own thoughts and feelings slipped away, shoved by the intrusion Hud pushed into her. Anger flared through her. Frustration at things she didn't know she cared about, at people she never knew. Hud's own suffering becoming her own.

The rage ate through the comfort the liquid humanity had given her, and her inner monster reignited. She pushed Hud's hand away, but he grabbed her face and shoved another cascade of pain through her. She screamed as her flames scorched her insides, blazing through her in torrents until it devoured her flesh.

Despite the forcefulness of it, changing the second time *was* easier, and as soon as Asheel's flesh had burned, Hud dropped his hand from her face, keeping the other on her back to hold her upright.

Asheel rubbed her face, her finger bones scraping against an exposed cheekbone. "Did you have to make it that awful?"

"Physiqals can only influence people with things they've felt before, only use what we know. That's what triggered my first change. I'm sorry. I know it hurts." He leaned forward and brushed what remained of his scorched lips across her forehead, leaving a thin trail of his magic, happier feelings, to ease what he'd done. And as soon as his lips left her, the hollowness returned, allowing her own feelings back to the surface. Before she could register his action, he helped her off the floor. "Come on. Let's get this over with."

He hurried out the door, and Asheel jogged to keep up with him, grazing her fingertips above her eyebrow where flakes of his ash remained.

"Wait. What was that about?" she asked.

"What?" He picked up his pace.

"You kissed me."

"It was nothing."

"That wasn't nothing." They cut through a field to the next path. "People don't just kiss other people's foreheads where I come from."

"You did the same to your brother when you said goodbye to him." His bones glowed in the night, and he kept his gaze ahead, unreadable.

Asheel slowed, letting him run ahead of her. He was saying goodbye to her like she had with Coby. She wasn't ready for that, but the plan was for him to die soon so maybe now was the time for their goodbyes. What was she supposed to say? She didn't want to thank him for the past two months, though she'd somewhat forgiven him for the actions he didn't have a choice in. She wasn't ready to say goodbye.

Monsters stared at them as they passed, and she kept her head down with the tendrils of smoke encircling her to hide her from their prying eyes. Some observed along the sides of the road, some silent and others shouting to leave their still human families alone. Hud ignored them, used to the jeering, but she wanted to shout back with words she'd said in her past. It wasn't her fault. She didn't have control over it. Put the blame on Doyen where it belonged.

In the monolith, the snake-like worshipers acted as doting as always. Some ran their fingers, limbs, tails through the reapers' smoke. Asheel sidestepped a few, but the snakes trailed along their path to breathe in their fumes. Their glorification nauseated Asheel. She gagged, and her anger flared up.

"Get lost!" she spun and yelled at them.

But that only riled them up more. They cheered at her hatred of them.

Hud grabbed her wrist and gently tugged her forward. "Ignore them. They never stop."

She followed Hud, and he dropped her wrist. She needed to get used to it. She'd have to do this every night. March past these monsters and their slimy caresses. She didn't want to grow numb to how wrong it all was.

In Doyen's lair, the scaled monstrosity waited for them.

"My most prized citizens!"

Asheel stood rigid with her fists clenched.

Hud wrung his hands while he spoke. "I've proven myself loyal—"

"No you haven't." Doyen snorted. "I know how often my magic keeps you in check. Don't flatter yourself."

With clenched teeth, Hud continued. "I'd like to request to keep our voices for this journey into the human realm."

"Ha! Why?"

"I don't believe I've explained the process thoroughly enough, yet. I'd like to be able to explain it to her as we go. I've never had to teach someone before."

"No!"

"Why not?" Asheel tried to sound confident through the chains stabbing at her throat from questioning him. "What could we say that . . ." she wheezed against the pain, "that you fear so much?"

Doyen's scaly lips rose in some semblance of a smile, and his pulsing eyes narrowed on her. "It's not fear, little one. What do I have to fear if nothing can harm me?"

"That's why I'm asking." If she planned to change how it all worked, if she planned to convince Doyen that things could be better, she should start planting seeds doubt into him now.

Doyen licked his fangs. "I fear nothing! Nothing is stronger than me." His shoulders shuddered, while he muttered to himself too low for Asheel to hear, and his lumpy tongue flopped across his teeth before he turned back to the two reapers. "Your lives are mine including your voices, and while you're away from me, you'll have none." He rose and walked toward them. "Do you remember when the previous reaper took you back into the human realm?"

"Barely." Hud glanced from Asheel to Doyen, as if he hadn't expected Asheel to be so forward with him.

"Barely is enough to know you don't need your voice."

Doyen arched his spine and slapped his hands together then drew them apart. Blue dust flecked with glittering specks swirled between his scaly palms. The smoke congregated around his clawed fingers, and he skimmed one smokey ribbon across Hud's mouth, the tendrils weaving between Hud's partially exposed teeth.

Asheel braced herself when Doyen moved his other hand to her mouth. The tendrils slipped between her teeth like corn silks, smelling of death and defeat. Chalky wisps pooled in her throat; she could breathe past them, but just like how the smoke locked her jaw, it locked her voice as well. The specks in the smoke moved past where it had pooled and latched like ticks onto something deeper, a place unseen but was more her than any part of her physical body. They latched onto her soul like parasites and embedded themselves within the bits of humanity still left in her. She couldn't sense it anymore. She was stuck as a reaper until Doyen called the flecks back to him.

"Now go my little favorites. The faster you return, the faster you can have your voices back."

Hud led them from Doyen's presence, the magic guiding their feet. They darted, through the town, past the monsters, and too soon, the Gate rippled in front of them. If she couldn't feel her humanity, would the Gate be able to sense it? Did she still have enough humanity to get through, or would it consume her, trap her to join the other spirits forever? Would that be so bad if it did? She paused at it.

Hud tilted his head and glanced from the Gate to where

Asheel had paused midstride. He sighed, placed his hand in the Gate, and stepped through backwards, holding her gaze until his face disappeared in the oily surface. Only his other hand remained outstretched into the monster realm. An offering instead of dragging her like he'd been doing. Maybe he meant it as a reminder that they were in this together, but she knew if she didn't take his hand willingly, he'd step back out and drag her through anyway. The pain of Doyen's magic stroked the back of her skull at the thought of protesting. She reached for the bony fingers and intertwined hers with his. The only other of her kind. At least for now. Until she could find the next reaper and get out of this place.

Together, they walked through the Gate, and the same horrors as the first time surrounded her. Hud bowed his head as he walked, but Asheel examined it with her new eyes of coal. The haze ebbed around them, swirling with their movements, giving her vertigo, and something that looked like yellow stained glass supported her steps and gave way where rippling spirits, like disturbed water, rose from the depths. The hands danced across the two reapers, and maybe it was because she'd changed and could see them better through monster eyes, but this time they were attached to faces of horned monsters, emaciated humans, and furry beasts that materialized in the silt. After the hands inspected them, they moved away from Hud and Asheel like a congealed soup of misery.

Light flashed ahead of them, then the Gate opened and dropped them into the human realm. Asheel fell to the ground from the jarring change, shivering and brushing off her bones, the remnants of the spirits' hands ghosting along her spine. Her breaths brought in fresh air, replacing the stifling haze, and even though the Gate scared her, she wished they'd have snatched her and held her in the nothingness forever rather than deal with the eternity ahead of her. Anything to stop her from committing such unforgivable acts, but pain trickled across her shoulders at the thought.

Her knees scraped against stone, and she looked up to see the barren circle that had been her last glimpse of the human realm. Her home was close. A long hike down the mountainside. Her bony fingers reached out, and the sight of her own hand reminded her of what she'd become. She was no longer welcome there.

She turned to Hud who was squatting at the edge of the circle, setting a large rock on a clump of weeds. He stood and motioned for her, and Asheel stood too, peering at the rock where the edge of a pink-tinted paper stuck out. Was it something to help them find their way back to the Gate? She'd ask him about it when they returned.

Hints of the inner monsters' distinct smells called to her, and like they had with Doyen in her vision, the dusty magic laid across the ground with a second layer of glittering yellow flecks. The flecks congregated along the trail pointing her to where the people were. Hud stretched and bounced on his feet before nodding away from Seshnia, to Novoshna. The trip between the two places normally took from dawn through most of the night on horseback, but their reaper speed would take a fraction of that. With one last hop, Hud dashed into the trees, and the magic forced Asheel to follow.

She'd lost all control of her body, as if Doyen held puppet strings above her. Something inside her shifted and bitterness consumed her mind. Somewhere deep under that, the still caring parts of her stirred, struggling against the magic and bitterness, but the magic drowned it out. She could take them, those darkest wretches. She would be rewarded for bringing a struggling human back on her first night. Doyen would give her a vial of humanity all her own to cool the flames in her core.

She shook her head. What was she thinking? The humanity in her heart clawed at its chains to be released, but Doyen's magic was as tangibly strong as iron.

The trees whipped by Asheel in a blur of shadows, the pine needles shriveling as they brushed against them. Her human clumsiness was only a memory. Now her own monstrous strength and Doyen's magic guided each step, her feet barely grazing the ground.

After less than an hour of running, Hud jogged to a stop, motioning Asheel to a large tree. The bark sizzled as he ran his finger over it to score letters into the wood: *army, stay close.*

Asheel had heard and seen what a reaper was capable of, but two against an army weren't odds she was comfortable with. Hud pointed to the trails of dusty magic, the thickened yellow one indicating their target, and motioned for her to follow again.

After a few more minutes of jogging, a trumpet erupted through the air. They'd been spotted. Hud picked up his pace and led Asheel out of the trees to a towering unpolished metal wall. Their glow reflected in it as human-shaped blobs, and Asheel had to tilt her head back to see the top. Novoshna had made itself a fortress. No wonder new farming tools had been hard to find in Seshnia. Every ounce of ore for the past year or more had gone to build the city's shield.

Hud jogged to the wall, his hand alit in flame, and shoved his fingers into it as if it were butter. He did the same with his other hand, then lifted himself, shoving his fingers into the metal again and again, climbing. Asheel stared after him. Novoshna had wasted so many resources on a wall that hadn't even come close to keeping the reaper out.

The magic forced her forward, and her fingers and feet found the handholds Hud had made.

"There's two!" a soldier at the top of the wall shouted.

"Two?"

"They'll take all of us."

"Stand your ground."

Arrows flew past the reapers then one pierced into Asheel's shoulder. Her grip slipped, but the magic kept her going, weaving the torn joint back into place. Another stuck into the top of her skull, and yet another scraped her kneecap. She looked up to see even more sticking out of Hud. He was taking the brunt of the onslaught, but it didn't slow him. Melted metal dripped onto Asheel's wrist from where his fingers touched the wall, but she shook it off, the heat nothing compared to the fire inside her.

"It's not working!"

"I told you the wall wouldn't work."

Another trumpet sounded three quick bursts as Hud pulled himself over the edge with a blast of fire, pushing back the soldiers. With the wall of fire flared around him, he turned back and offered a hand to Asheel who took it and let him lift her to the top of the wall. The inferno Hud had conjured on either side of them blocked her view of the soldiers, but behind Hud, Novoshna stretched out for miles below them, shadowed, soldiers with lamps running through the street and trumpets alerting them to where the reapers were.

The wall's metal was about a foot thick, but stone and wood widened the top to allow the soldiers to stand three across, shoulder to shoulder. Hud lowered his inferno, and the soldiers charged with their swords drawn, a mass of smelly humans.

Hud grabbed Asheel's hand then jumped off the wall, dragging her with him. She tried to scream through the magic smoke holding her mouth closed but nothing came out, and too quickly, the ground rose to meet the two reapers who crumpled in a heap of broken bones and dislocated joints. Dust from the impact scattered through the air while the soldiers on the wall stared down at them. The scream of fear writhing in Asheel's chest turned into a sob of pain while a blue haze encircled the broken reapers and jerked them back into their forms. Doyen's magic wouldn't let them die, even from their own actions.

Before Asheel had regained her bearings, Hud was up and barreling through the streets, shoving soldiers away and throwing the arrows from his body to the ground. She half-heartedly followed, forced by her invisible chains, and shoved a few of the soldiers away while trying to find the humanity left in her heart. The officials who'd invited her to the palace could have been amongst the soldiers. Maybe people from Seshnia had joined their ranks. These were people she might know.

A soldier with a rageful expression stabbed through the smoke at Asheel's gut, and Asheel pulled the spear from the woman's grasp to smack her helmet with the pole. These people were just defending their families and didn't deserve her wrath. But what would they do if she stopped fighting? Could they kill her through Doyen's magic?

Three soldiers jumped on Asheel's back, stabbing her and trying to tie a thick chain around her neck.

The two sides of her warred in her chest, but the monster side eclipsed the human again. What had she done to deserve their wrath? She'd not even taken one of their people yet. Her fire flared out, blasting back the group of warriors, and she ran after Hud, who hadn't glanced back to check on her, until the soldiers lost her in the maze of buildings in the cramped city.

Hud jumped up the steps of an elevated house and ripped open the door. A woman shrieked and threw a pan at him, which he dodged, but the pan hit Asheel broadside in the face, knocking her back down the steps.

She lay on the stone street, dazed, staring into the cloudless sky overhead, stars winking at her through the heatwaves rising from her body. Sobs of a child nearby, maybe in the house, reminded her of the bleating lambs back home. Even locked in a body of bones with no voice, she could lie under the stars until she wasted away, letting the soldiers stab, slice, bury her, torture her until they were satisfied. She'd rather that type of torture, than go back to the imprisonment of Doyen and the hate of an entire realm. Of course, those thoughts of disobedience sent sharp blades of pain through her limbs, worse than the magic-numbed jabs of the soldiers' swords, but she could take it. No matter how bad Doyen's pain got, she would stay in the human realm, unmoving, letting the humans have the revenge they so greatly needed.

The soldiers' shouts broke through her morose thoughts, and Asheel sat up with a sense of clarity from the strike to her face. Doyen's chains tugged at her limbs, urging her to climb the house's steps, but Mama B's last words to her made sense now. Even with everything ripped away from her, even if she spent an eternity in agony from Doyen's magic, tortured, she still had her mind and her choice.

Doyen hadn't taken that away. He'd just made certain choices harder.

Hud appeared in the doorway with a young woman thrown over his shoulder. He tilted his head and gestured at Asheel on the ground then made a shooing motion and leapt over her. She grabbed his ankle and jerked him back to the ground. Pain jolted up her arm like lightning. The woman cried out while Hud rearranged her on his shoulder, then he shook his foot out of Asheel's grasp and lifted her to her feet. With light tugs, he pulled her back toward the wall. Doyen's pain flared in her legs and she gave in, trotting a few paces after Hud to relieve the cramps, but before they reached the next street, she lifted the woman, as light as a newborn, from his shoulder and set her on her feet. The woman quivered with fear while pain seared through Asheel. She stumbled to one knee but stared back at the woman's round, amber eyes to regain her focus. She could choose this. She could become numb to this pain instead of horrid acts.

The woman whispered something Asheel couldn't hear through the ringing in her ears, then squealed, pointed over Asheel's shoulder, and ran back to her house.

Hud slammed into Asheel like a bull, grabbing at her limbs to pin them behind her back. She struggled free and turned to face him, his glare more frustrated than enraged. He had to understand. They could fight back together. She shook her head hard and crouched, ready to defend the city, ready to defend the entire world.

A group of soldiers finally found them but paused in their pursuit at the odd sight of two reapers fighting. Asheel would save them. She would help them all. She would become an idol to humans, and they would worship her. With her humanity locked away, the thoughts of power and ruling them poisoned her mind. She was glad that they'd witness her first acts as their protector.

Hud's gaze darted from Asheel to the woman to the soldiers, back to Asheel, back to the woman. Asheel shook her head again and stepped towards him. This wasn't up for debate. She was strong now. She could drag Hud back to the monster realm and hold him in the Stream of Judgment, let it strip him of his remaining humanity so that he could never return.

Hud dashed to the side to recapture the woman, but Asheel was faster, fueled by the searing pain rather than restricted by it, the reminder of who she truly fought. She tackled him to the ground and stretched her jaw against the magic that held it shut. Impeded by the pain of disobeying Doyen, she wrestled with Hud, but he had centuries of experience on her and flipped her onto her stomach with her face pressed into the ground, scraping charred bits of the remaining flesh from her cheek.

Doyen's pain grew inside her and combined with the feeling of failure to fuel a new hatred for their roles in the world. She stretched her jaw again, fighting the magic, letting her rage thrash against the agony, letting the physical pain feed the emotional pain, letting it consume her. She had magic too, magic powerful enough to make a monster feel human again. It could change people, and if it was inside her, if it was hers, it could change her too. She writhed as Doyen's pain seared back up through her spine, her rage eating his magic until the invisible chains grasping her throat shattered, and the smokey silks between her teeth stretched and splintered.

"No!" she shouted and coughed up chalky blue dust. "This isn't right."

CHAPTER 26

Hud jumped off her, his eyes wide, and she flipped onto her back, panting, to plead with him.

"We can refuse," Asheel said. "Even if Doyen tortures us, we can refuse."

Hud tilted his head, and Asheel sat up, ready to fight, her own rage pulsing through her limbs, keeping Doyen's pain away.

"What's preventing us from staying on this side? Look at me. I can talk. Doyen's magic isn't as strong as you think. We don't ever have to go back."

Hud lifted his hands to his jaw to pull and claw at the intangible bindings, but the smoke still wove between his teeth to keep his mouth stitched closed. He pointed to his mouth and splayed his hands in defeat.

"We'll figure it out. You won't be alone on this side."

Hud looked from Asheel to his hands, then his body convulsed. He clenched his fists and dashed in ridged jerks to the woman. Maybe Doyen's hold was too strong on him, or maybe he didn't care anymore because he'd be released from his contract soon. But she was sure he wouldn't take the woman if he wasn't under Doyen's spell. If only Asheel could be more powerful than that monster. She could free everyone. She just needed to be stronger. She needed to be the strongest.

The picture of power settled in her mind, buoyed by her growing anger and hatred of Doyen, and a new craving pierced through her heart, a desire for power, for her own realm where she could selfishly make life what she wanted. She could lead the monster realm better than that abomination. She could take it from him and give the monsters the ruler they deserved. She could release Hud, and he could choose to be a protector like her. She'd take the realm from Doyen to make it safe, to force everyone to be better. The new desires oozed thick and black from her mouth and dribbled down her chin like drool. Her magic was stronger than Doyen's. She had overcome his spell. She was powerful enough to overthrow him and take his realm.

The craving coiled inside her and coursed through her bones, lying to her, telling her that her strength couldn't be stopped, that she was the strongest, the best, that she deserved more. The power was so tempting. She could have everything Doyen had. She could have more! Hud could take the Novish woman for all she cared; she had a kingdom to take instead.

More chalky smoke rose from her gut but flecked with purple instead of Doyen's blues. She vomited the heavy smoke onto the ground. Piles of it pooled at her feet, dredged up her legs, and wove back into her bones. They sizzled and popped, echoing in the night, and blackened until they turned to dust themselves. The purple smoke slid into the spots where her bones had been, fleshing her, adding bulk. It mixed with the ashes of her bones and plated like scales over the swirling mass that had become her new body. The black ooze that had dripped from her mouth now seeped between the scales, coating her in an oily slime.

Her teeth elongated unevenly, following no pattern. The coals of her eyes became black pits, and a sickly green glow shuddered from her throat when she spoke. "I can stop Doyen," she said in a growly, reverberating voice to the tiny reaper staring up at her. "I can free everyone from him." She turned her massive body away, intoxicated with new desire. "I will destroy him." Her voice, deep and hoarse, boomed across the rooftops.

Following her instinct, she opened her jaws wide and coughed up a slimy glob that hovered in the air before her. It pulsated, growing until it had stretched thin and translucent petals held it in place in the air. It opened to her, and she dove into the oily surface, welcomed by the spirits like an old friend.

It guided her back into the monster realm, and when let out on the other side, she launched toward the monolith. Two tiny snake-like monsters, Doyen's worshipers, stopped on the road when they heard her thundering towards them, but they were too slow to flee while her clawed hand came down on them, splatting their innards onto the ground.

Good riddance. She didn't want the slimy things in her realm. She'd make it what she wanted: a home for herself with the adoration she deserved. She barked out a laugh, and more chalky smoke poured into the air.

The faintest scents filled her, calling for her attention. Sweet spice to her right. Flowers and mint to her left—humanity still hiding amongst the monsters—but the rancid, unmistakable fumes of Doyen kept her on her path. She yelled to the sky. The power in her new body was incredible. Unstoppable. She would win this land for herself. Finally, a place she'd belong.

She leapt over smaller buildings, decimated clumps of trees, and tore deep rivets in the ground with her claws. This would be her land, and she could do whatever she wanted. Many of the monsters fled from her as she passed but a few unlucky ones met gruesome ends, and by the time she reached the monolith, blood, fur, and feathers coated the bottoms of her feet. She hit the side of the cavern's entryway, and the monsters inside scattered into corridors and chambers away from her. Doyen's chamber glowed like a beacon in her sight. Her prize. A throne stained with fear and humanity.

Asheel's laughter rang from the walls when she skidded into the room, and Doyen shimmied around his throne and puffed himself up like a cornered kitten while peering around the edge. The snake monsters ran to the edges of the room, their heads swiveling between their master and the newcomer.

"Another me?" Doyen whispered. "It can't be."

Asheel, still laughing high-pitched and crazed, prowled towards him.

Doyen squinted and calculated. "New Reaper? What have you done to yourself?" Doyen stepped back in front of his throne but drew himself tall, threatened.

"It's someone else's turn to sit on that throne." Asheel sneered, and black drool dribbled from her mouth.

"I can't give it up." He shook his great head, sending blue dust to the ground.

"You can by my hand!"

"No." He held up his clawed hands. "If I die, this realm dies with me. You'd kill everyone in it."

Asheel paused and tilted her head. "Lies. This realm . . ." The legends from home about Cay and the Gate tickled somewhere behind her blind rage, but she ignored it. "You're abusing it."

"Yes, but I can do that because this place is me." He dipped his hand into the pool. The bubbles ignored him, and he pulled it out and watched the water drip from his claws with pulsing, oil-like eyes. "I am the realm, and the realm is me. I created it!"

Asheel's crazed mind couldn't comprehend it, couldn't make the connections.

"If you destroy me, you destroy the realm and everyone inside," he repeated and flicked the water at her where it splattered and bubbled across her snout, reacting to her though it hadn't so much as sizzled on Doyen.

She hesitated. If he were telling the truth, was destruction of the entire realm what she wanted? Not exactly, but if it freed her, freed every human and monster from the cruel monster's reign, then that was what she'd do.

She lunged and collided into Doyen. His head only came to her shoulders and his stomach bulged from his gluttony, but like Hud, he'd been around longer. He knew his body better. They wrestled across the floor, fangs and claws shredding each other's scales, which were quickly replaced by their smoke. Some of the snakes fled the chamber, and others hissed from the edges.

Asheel leapt over Doyen, kicked off the back wall, and slammed into his chest. They tumbled back to the ground with Asheel on top, pinning him to the quaking stone. Great tremors twisted her legs around each other, but Asheel kept her weight on the cruel creature and opened her mouth wide to press her teeth against his neck. But before she could bite down, Doyen flipped around under her and clamped onto her leg with his own ragged fangs. He crushed the smokey bones at her knee and ripped it off.

The shriek she released shook the stone walls and reverberated through the realm. She couldn't lose. She had to be stronger. She had to win. She needed to be praised for freeing everyone and becoming their new ruler, to be worshiped like she deserved by human and monster alike. Her smoke exploded from her, pushing Doyen back against a wall along with the few remaining snakes, then like a cord stretched too tight, it snapped back to her and swirled around her like a whirlwind. Her shrieking continued, broke off, became a sob, then split tones until the smoke twisted back down her throat.

She'd doubled in size, her head brushing against the lair's ceiling. A purple, grooved tongue lolled out between missing fangs and dripped oily black sludge while a gold, stone-like eye bulged from one socket, and in a slice of pain, a single, skinless wing jutted from her back. The scales along her limbs had vanished, replaced by grey human flesh that squirmed like worms.

Her writhing skin shifted back to smoke with a thought, and she dove at Doyen and engulfed him in the purple-smoke tornado of her body.

He threw his arms over his head, but nothing could stop smoke. Her ethereal body entered his and shredded him from the inside while he clawed at his arms, his legs, his stomach. He tore great gashes into his face and across his scalp, but he couldn't reach her. She slaughtered his innards until she found the last deeply hidden clump of his own humanity and grasped it in her claws, then the raging storm in Doyen's body suddenly quieted.

She found herself floating as her human self in a place that seemed like the inside of the Gate but emptier. It both looked like it went on forever and felt like it was constricting her, and in front of her floated a dainty man, with thin arms and legs and a sallow face. Scraggly prickles of a beard grew patchy on his chin, and his clothes hung tattered and worn.

His eyes dipped at the sides, and his smile was sad. He almost reminded Asheel of her father, so small, but where her father was pale like her, this man was brown, tinged a bit grey maybe from being in whatever this place was for so long.

"I guess this is the end at last for me," he said.

Asheel glanced around them, and her human hair drifted across her vision. Was she dying, too? "Are you Doyen?"

"Yes, kind of." The man nodded, his eyes reflecting blues,

greens, and purples like Doyen's. "I became him, but that's not who I was. That's not who I meant to be. I lost my way."

It made sense. Doyen had to have been human once. Monsters were only humans with their worst traits on display.

"I need you to make this realm what I meant it to be."

"What do you mean?" She looked around again. The place was empty. What realm was this?

He gestured to the emptiness. "Not here. I need you to take care of the monster and human realms. I'd divided them to make a sanctuary for both. A place where people could learn to be human again and a reprieve to the humans to live their lives without fear. I meant to send the monsters back when they had found their humanity again." He glanced down at his hands and flexed his fingers like he hadn't moved them in centuries. "But I became jealous when I realized I could never return. I grew selfish. To find the power to split the worlds, I had to accept such a horrible act—stripping people of their freedom. Realizing that even if I could overcome what I'd become, become human again, I still wouldn't be able to return like them . . ."

He looked back up to Asheel, his hair floating around him like a halo. "I'd used too much of my magic to create the monster realm. I'd split myself too much, my heart pumping magic through the realm to keep it alive, my eyes in too many places away from me. Spend too long watching everyone else and you'll forget to watch yourself."

Asheel couldn't believe it. This man was Cay. He'd spent millennia as that beast, trapped, just as much imprisoned as the other monsters. "You kept them from regrowing their humanity."

"Yes." He smiled at her. "Selfish, I know, taking from them what I couldn't have. I was so jealous." The emptiness constricted tighter, and he drifted to her to place his hands on her cheeks. The shifting colors in his pupils whirled and glowed and filled the space between them. "Make this realm what it was meant to be. Let the Stream of Judgment decide your fate."

Cay faded, dematerializing like a dream, and the emptiness contracted even tighter until her hands and feet felt like they were about to burst.

Then she was thrown back into her enraged and grotesque form with her hands still clamped onto Doyen's dead humanity. She ripped it from his body as she exploded from his chest, and it draped from her claws like the fresh pink humanity Doyen had stripped from his captive humans. But his hung wilted, already colorless and dead. She tossed it into the pool where it swirled up the waterfall and disappeared into the crack in the ceiling.

The smoke holding Doyen's body together dissipated, leaving behind the solid bits, his scales, teeth, and a few condensed flaky pieces.

Her rage coiled through her unhindered, wiping away the discussion with Cay and cloaking her in ignorance. She'd done it. She'd defeated Doyen. She roared to the ceiling, scaring the remaining snakes from the chamber, then swept most of the remainder of his scales and dust into the pool. Pink consumed humanity that had leaked from him smeared across the floor and a few of his scales skittered out of her reach, but the pieces in the pool dissolved and swirled up the waterfall and through the crack where his wilted humanity had vanished.

The waterfall quivered and stuttered, and the ground quaked even harder than during their fight. Parts of the cavern crumbled. She looked to the ground then to the crumbling walls, then her memories of what Cay had said jolted through her.

The realm was him. It was a living entity and with its host destroyed, it was dying. She scurried in a circle trying to figure out what to do, slipping and stumbling into the walls. She'd just won. She hadn't gotten to enjoy her own freedom yet. She hadn't gotten to relish in worshiping monsters.

A large stone slab crashed into the pool and drenched Asheel. The water stung her and bubbled across her skin, but it hadn't bothered Doyen. It had been like he controlled it, like his magic was fed from it. Flashes of the dreamlike realm came back to her in her panic. He'd mentioned the Stream . . . Following her instinct again, she dove over the pool, straight into the waterfall.

Bright flashes blinded her, and water filled her insides, choking and drowning her, weighing her limbs and holding her in place. Her crazed mind blurred. This hadn't been the answer to stabilizing the realm. She was drowning, dying.

CHAPTER 27

After several minutes, Asheel was still aware of the water funneling through her. It swirled through her gut and her limbs, it cooled the fire in her belly, and slowly, she became one with it until she no longer choked. She flowed with it throughout the realm, the pink veins creeping under the surface of the world, slipping unseen through the waters, lacing through the leaves of every plant, tracing the lava fields, and reaching invisible into the sky. The veins wove through her with the water, funneling her own magic through the land.

The water and veins restructured her, taking the magic from her and returning it with bits of life from the realm, and finally, the waterfall coaxed her back to shore and returned to its lazy trickle from the pool to the crack in the ceiling. The realm stopped quaking. The energy that had vibrated through the air stilled. And she gasped what felt like the first deep breath she'd taken in her life.

She'd done it. Power straightened her back and strengthened

her limbs, and she extended her solitary wing, the useless thing. This was her world now. The monsters scampering through the realm . . . she could feel each of their feet, paws, hooves running across the ground like fleas scuttling across her skin. She could feel the wings of the beaked monsters soaring through the air like a cough tickling to escape her lungs. She knew the twinges were the monsters as easily as she knew how to move her fingers and toes. With a single thought, she could banish them. They only existed because she allowed them. They were her innerworkings, her outer scales. She carried them inside her. They owed her for keeping them safe.

And she'd make sure she got repaid.

The realm was hers, and she was the realm.

The chamber door flew open, and she spun to face her first subject, who happened to be the reason she was there at all. Hud ran into the lair, gasping for breath with a hand over his chest. He glanced at the carnage on the ground, to the snake carcasses along the walls, then at the new monster before him.

"Look at me now, Hud," Asheel said, her voice still metallic and high-pitched. "I've freed you!"

He dropped to his knees and gasped as if something had knocked the wind out of him. "It was you." He drew in a ragged breath. "All the pain vanished." He lifted his burnt coal eyes and tilted his head. "What are you?"

Asheel lifted herself to her full height, and the top of her head pressed into the ceiling. "The realm's new ruler."

Hud lifted his hands and examined the milky pink remains dripping from them. "You killed Doyen?"

"Easily."

"How?"

"I took what he owed this world. His humanity." Asheel stepped to the throne and crouched over it, too large to sit in the seat she'd fought for. Power buzzed in her head, drowning out all other thoughts, numbing her to anything but her own greatness. "I ripped it from his body and tossed it in the pool." A bubble of laughter escaped her in a short burst. "His power is mine now!"

Hud picked up an orphan scale. "And what are you going to do with the power?"

"Revenge everyone who always feared me. Show them they truly have something to fear now! Watch as they bow at my feet pleading for mercy and praising my greatness." Fire shot from her mouth and poured over Hud.

He lifted an arm to shield his eyes, but for someone made of fire, the shower did nothing. "What about all of the monsters you pitied who were ripped from their families? What about the humans? I thought you wanted to protect them."

"What have any of them done for me?" Asheel roared. "What has anyone in either realm done for me?" She stomped her foot, which shook the ground causing another chunk of rock to fall from the ceiling. It shattered, releasing a glittering pink vein that floated through the air and slipped through her writhing flesh to join the smoke in her body.

Hud stepped toward her and shook his head. "Why have you changed your mind? I thought you'd gotten over those feelings. You couldn't even bring out your inner reaper with them."

Flashes of her old life surfaced, and something between a sob and a shriek erupted from Asheel. "It still hurts! The memories hurt!" She scraped her claws along the ground, leaving deep scars in the stone like the scars on her heart. "I will finally have peace."

"This isn't you. Have you forgotten how many friends you've made the past month?"

Asheel stopped shrieking and snapped her head to him. Hud took another step, and she jerked back from him and the painful memories, stifling them with her rage. Anger was her comfort now. Anger was an emotion she controlled, not the pain caused by others.

Hud kept his gaze on her feet and spoke softly. "You were right about the Stream of Judgment being wrong. It showed me some things I would do . . . those moments arrived . . . and I . . . I didn't do them. I thought maybe it was because I'd already accepted the monster I am, but I realize now it was always in my control. I had decided not to. You helped me see those were my decisions, not an inescapable fate."

Asheel clamped her jaw shut, but a ribbon of black drool dribbled down her chin. She coughed through her teeth, and black gunk sprayed between them. "My decision is made!" she screamed and dropped her forearms to the stone.

Hud lifted his gaze to the beast, ignoring the fire building in her throat. "I decided not to! Do you hear me?" he screamed back. "I was able to walk away from that woman in Novoshna. I had a choice all along, and neither the old reaper nor Doyen gave me a chance to reject their plans." He paused and looked away. "I still had the option to reject it, and you do, too!"

Asheel shrieked and lunged at him with her mouth agape.

Hud leapt onto her snout, slipped on the writhing flesh until he found footing, and stared straight into her bulging eye. Asheel shook her head and tried to swipe him off her face, but he blasted her hand back with a stream of fire.

"I know the girl who sacrificed herself for her brother is somewhere in there. If you found Doyen's decrepit humanity after so long, you still have it, too. I'm sorry I came into your home and took you, for not protecting you from the monsters here. I'm even sorry your home took you for granted. But I left Novoshna without the woman. I felt like my insides were being pulverized, but I had a choice. That means you have a choice, too. Even now. Even after becoming whatever this is," he pointed at her hulking body, "you can still choose not to. The power is delicious, I know, but if that's what you want, think about how much more power you'd have by controlling it. Having power over yourself, your own thoughts, not letting it have power over you."

Asheel shook her massive head and tried to snatch him, but he dropped back to the ground and ducked.

"Think of your little brother! If you stop this, you could see him again!"

The word "brother" reminded her of families—families that despised her, spat on her, and slapped her in the streets. Families were pain. She had no family, only fleas on her back, and she would squash the one in front of her.

Hud jumped out of the way, wrapped his arms around her wrist, and tried to pin it to the ground. She slipped on her remaining leg, off balanced, falling to her knee.

"If you stop this, I'll stay with you instead of dying. You won't be alone," Hud pleaded with her.

Those words sounded familiar too, but she roared loud enough to drown out her thoughts and jerked her hand up, Hud still clinging to it. He let go and dropped to the floor on his back. Asheel saw her chance to rid herself of the creature who'd haunted her life and drove her claw down, through his center, and pierced into the stone under him.

Hud gasped once, his hands clutching and tugging at hers before they fell limp. His smoke swirled around him, changing back to flesh, and the boy she'd grown so close to stared up at her with blank eyes.

She'd finally destroyed them both, the reaper that had caused her so much misery through her life and the creature who'd started the whole thing, Doyen, Cay, whatever he went by. She sat back on her haunches and let her tongue loll out of her mouth. The boy continued to stare at her, unmoving. Black muck, flecked with ash, poured from the hole in his stomach. She licked her claw clean of the gunk and looked around the cavern. Hers. All hers. Nothing made a sound except the thin trickle of the Stream of Judgment, which flowed in time with her own heartbeat.

She'd been victorious, but she'd expended so much energy. She was hungry, needed to replenish her magic. She needed to settle her insides, like how the pink drink had before.

She nudged the corpse on the floor. If only she'd forced the humanity from the reaper before killing him, but she still had plenty of beasts to feed from, the sweeter smelling ones who unknowingly were growing their humanity back. She closed her eyes and explored her world. There, one of the bats hanging on the monolith.

Her magical tendrils, invisible to everyone but her, creeped up the stone mountainside and prodded the bat to join her in the lair, and instantly it dropped from the stone and glided inside the mountain. It entered her cavern and lurched to a stop at the gore around Asheel's feet.

"I won't kill you." Asheel beckoned the bat forward.

The muscular creature squealed at losing control of her legs, and when she was close enough Asheel grabbed her, shoved her into the pool, and held her below the surface while the wisps of regrowing humanity slipped out of her like ribbons. When the ribbons cut off, Asheel released the bat who fled the lair whimpering, not looking back. Only the slightest amount of humanity hung from her claws like streams of snot.

"That's disappointing," she muttered and slurped the scant meal. No wonder Doyen had sent Hud into the human realm daily. She'd need more than a dozen monsters to feed her if that was all she could get from them.

Over and over, she pulled monsters into her lair and forced the humanity from them until she'd had her fill. She sealed the door and curled beside the pool to rest, but her remaining leg grazed something cold and stiff. The body. The corpse of the reaper who'd thought he could control her, force her to be something she wasn't just like everyone else. She sent her magical tendrils through the corpse, preserving him in that state, a reminder of what she'd conquered, then kicked it to the side and laid her head on her hands.

CHAPTER 28

The next day passed similarly. She pulled monsters into her cavern and fed from them, laughing when they cowered from her and snapping their necks when they dared to consider fighting her. The snake-like attendants finally returned and catered to her, cleaning her claws, and removing the carcasses of their fallen companions. All except the reaper laying near her throne on the cold stone, the muck beneath him dried.

And the next day passed, then the next.

She grew bored of the constant need to feed, and more than once, when the fleas on her back started fighting, she had sent a shiver through the land to make them stop. It itched along her skin. They weren't enough. She needed new inhabitants, better food. She snarled at the reaper's corpse. He was supposed to be bringing her more.

On the fourth day, the door to her lair creaked open, and Virgil stepped into her cavern, the snakes startling from the unexpected guest.

"Asheel?" he asked tentatively, his gaze narrowing at the new monster with squirming skin and coiling smoke. His eyes darted to the corpse by her throne, and he gagged and turned his face away.

"My friend!" Asheel lunged from where she'd been sitting, and her tongue flicked out of her mouth.

Virgil stepped back. "What are . . ." He looked away from her. "Where's Doyen? I'd heard—"

"Dead!" She slipped on her missing leg and plopped back onto her haunches. "I've freed you from him. Praise me!"

"Is that . . . did Reaper . . ." He gagged again.

"We despised him, and I killed him. For all of us. No one has to hate him anymore because he's gone!"

"Gone . . ." Virgil whispered and took a half step toward the corpse, but Asheel placed her clawed hand between them.

"He's m—"

"No! I needed him!" Virgil shoved at her hand, but when she moved it so he could see the corpse again, he heaved and fell to his knees.

Asheel tilted her massive head and rolled her bulging gold eye at the translucent man kneeling toward the reaper instead of her. "You hated him. I killed him. Bow to *me*."

Virgil shook his head and looked her in the eye. "Why'd you have to kill *him*?"

"He was trying to control me." Asheel glanced at the corpse. The rippling pink veins glittering over his body reflected off the smooth stone throne. He'd tried to tell her to give up this power, but she finally had the notoriety and strength she deserved.

"I doubt that." Virgil scoffed.

"You question me?" Asheel snarled and brought her head inches from Virgil's face. He couldn't harm her. Not when the energy flowing through the realm would heal her in seconds.

"Yeah, what are you going to do about it? Kill me, too?" He

thumped her nose, and she jerked back while the snake-like monsters hissed. "Go ahead!" He shouted. "I'd rather die because without him going back to the human realm, I have nothing left to live for!"

"I've killed your enemy!" She reared back. "You dare—"

"I dare!" Virgil stomped forward, more emboldened than anyone yet who'd visited her. He wiped his hand across the back of hers then licked his palm. His eyes widened, dropped to his palm, then slid back to her.

He was a curiosity. He didn't flinch from her. He wanted to die, but she'd given him what he wanted. He'd hated Hud. Tolerated him, but hated him. "Why?" she asked, pulled from her boredom.

"He was my link back to my dad. Without Reaper, I can't send him any letters." Tears lined his eyes but didn't fall. "You've cut us off from our families, and for some of us, that's all we had left."

"You were already cut off."

"No," Virgil shook his head. "We could still write to them, but we couldn't let Doyen find out, even the humans. People like my dad," he finally lowered the hand he'd licked, "were willing to live in near solitude to stay in touch." Virgil's translucent forehead crinkled where his eyebrows rose in the middle. "Reaper didn't tell you that? That part of the job was to be a messenger?"

Asheel glared at the corpse. He'd reacted when she'd mentioned letters but hadn't told her why. The paper he'd stuffed under a rock at the Gate . . . What else had he kept from her? Had he been saving it for the last day or had he not trusted her to keep that secret? It didn't make sense. If Doyen were as connected with the realm as she was now, he would have known. He could have heard any conversation he wanted to, read the letters over Virgil's shoulder. Maybe he did know and his humanity wasn't as dead as she thought, feigning ignorance to give them a little peace.

"How will you keep in touch with your family now? Huh? How will you find out how your little brother grows up?"

With her initial rage passed, the word "brother" didn't cause the pain it had when Hud said it. Virgil was right. She was supposed to be watching him grow up from a distance. She'd only been in the cavern for a few days, but already she was bored with this life. She wanted to look forward to a monthly visit to her family, even if just peeking through their window as a fiery skeleton.

She crawled to where the reaper's corpse lay. What other secrets had he not told her? Why . . . why did the sight of that body bring a tightness to her chest now? Why, with a whole realm of creatures at her control, did emptiness echo hollow inside her?

Why was she crying with images of a curly-haired little boy and a black-veined young man pressing in her mind?

"Hud." Asheel reached toward the corpse. His life had been important to her for some reason. "Hud."

She blinked the bulging golden eye back into her head, then shook and looked down to see Hud lifeless in front of her, lying in his dried blood, unmoving. The milky pink vomit of humanity had mixed with the black murk of his blood in a brown mess, and her claws scraped flakes of the dried mixture while she tried to lift him to sit up. "Hud!" Her claws, too large and clumsy to slip under him, rolled his corpse beyond her reach.

The memory of the past few days returned to her with clarity. She'd done what she'd intended—she'd found the power to kill Doyen—but she'd also attacked Hud. The film of the humanity she'd consumed coated her mouth and she flicked out her tongue to scrape it with her claws. She'd hurt dozens, killed just as many.

"No . . . NO!" she shouted. The snake-like monsters hissed at her curiously, and she shouted at them to leave, putting the full force of her magic behind the command. They fled, leaving Asheel alone with Virgil and Hud's body.

She slipped again from her missing leg. She had to help him, but she couldn't in this form. She knew how to change back, how to find her humanity again. She'd gone from reaper to human and back. She could do it again, at least change back to the reaper.

Asheel closed her eyes. The desire to rule the monsters and steal the regrowing humanity from them still pulsed through her along with the power to do it, and that pulse quivered in her hands. She could rip the Gates apart and meld the realms together. She could slam her hands into the ground and release the fires in the depths of the planet. It was all in her grasp. No one would ever have to suffer like this again.

But she had to help Hud.

She closed her eyes even tighter. This wasn't her.

The tornado of purple smoke evacuated her body and spiraled around her until only burning bone and scorched flesh remained, except for the leg Doyen had bitten off. Her clothes had shredded at some point during her transformations, but being a monster of fire and bones with only scraps of flesh, she didn't worry about her appearance. She collapsed, off balance from her leg still gone at the knee. Smoke seeped from the jagged bone and pain radiated up her thigh, but she was Hud's only hope. She scrambled across the ground and flipped him back onto his back, waving off the pink veins that had preserved him.

"Hud!" she cried. He couldn't die. Doyen's magic should have been weaving him back together, but she'd killed Doyen. His magic was gone. She had it now, knew how to use it from memories inherited from Doyen through the Stream. She could use it to fix the hole in his stomach.

She placed her hand over the hole, unable to cover the entirety of it, and willed the strongest magic she could find into it. She imagined her purple smoke replacing his skin like she'd seen Doyen's do before. But the dust merely filled the hole then faded, not even removing the gore.

"NO!" she shrieked. "Hud!" What had she done? She pulled

his shoulders into her lap and wept, great tears of lava streaking down her cheeks. "I can't do this without you."

She rocked him and a drop of lava fell onto his flesh with a sizzle, leaving a burnt streak across his forehead. Surely something in the magic-filled cavern could heal him.

"Virgil, help!" she screamed, and he was by her side in an instant, whether from her own magic forcing him or his own free will, she didn't know, but he was there. "Humanity. Humanity can heal him." It had healed her wounds when she almost died. "The vials." She pointed to two remaining vials of humanity that she'd vomited to give to the snakes like she'd seen Doyen do.

Virgil retrieved them, and Asheel opened one and dribbled the entire vial into Hud's mouth like he'd done for her months ago.

He didn't move, and she unstopped the second and poured it in, too. "Come on. Come back." A few drops missed his mouth and slid down his cheek.

She'd poured so much into him. It had to work. His eyes stared past her up to the ceiling, and a small bubble escaped the pooling pink humanity in his throat, giving her hope. "Breathe," she whispered and jostled his shoulders. "Wake up. I need you."

But he lay limp, as cold as the stone beneath them, the fire in him long gone.

"No!" A weight plummeted through her chest, tightening her throat, and her arms shook. "NO!"

CHAPTER 29

"It's too late," Virgil said and placed a hand on her scalding shoulder, jolting away when it burned him.

"I didn't mean to. I . . . he . . . I just wanted to stop Doyen." Sobs shuddered through her chest, which tightened around her heart, squeezing it, breaking it. "Please help him. Bring him back. I can't—" Her voice hitched. "I can't do this without him," she mouthed inaudibly, her throat too tight to speak.

"You can." He held his blistered palm to his chest, averting his eyes from Hud. "He wasn't your only friend."

She clutched her arms around Hud's head. He was more than a friend. He'd understood her better than even Lana had. This wasn't the death he deserved. Not a vengeful, mindless murder. She kissed the scorch mark her tear had left on his forehead. She wasn't saying goodbye. She'd been figuring out how to say it, and this wasn't how she'd pictured it.

"Come on." Virgil put his uninjured hand on her shoulder

again, lightly, testing if she'd burn him again. "We can't help him now."

"I can't." Asheel shook her head, the exposed bone of her chin brushing against Hud's skin. "I can't leave him."

"Why didn't the wound heal?"

"That was Doyen's magic," Asheel's voice broke again, "and it's gone. It's my fault."

Virgil finally dropped his gaze to the corpse, and he drew his own shaky breath. "Asheel, it's okay." He touched her elbow and knelt beside her in the grime. "This was what he wanted, remember?"

"Not like this." Asheel shook her head and met Virgil's eyes. She remembered everything so clearly now. "He changed his mind. He said he wanted to stay."

Virgil's eyebrows rose, and he held the sides of her face in his cool palms, forcing her to control her pain or risk burning him worse. "It doesn't matter. It's too late, darling." He glanced away from her gaze. "Let's go somewhere else, get away from here and let you get your bearings back."

Asheel clutched tighter to Hud's head. "I deserve to rot here."

"You've been through more than your mind can handle and you're injured. I don't know if that smoke," he pointed at her weeping leg, "means you're bleeding, but we need to get you taken care of."

She glanced to the smoke oozing from her leg. It wasn't draining her, though she wished it was. Virgil forced her face back to look at him.

"There's more for you."

"No, there's not." Asheel shook her head, wishing she could close her eyes and pretend Hud was still with her, but Virgil kept her face in his grasp. A sob burst from her chest. "You don't understand. You have Ziyiel and Ratel."

"What about the human realm? Your family?"

"I can't go back there." Asheel clenched her exposed teeth,

disgusted by the scraps of lips that wouldn't close. Even if she could change back to human after being such a beast, the black veins and scorched smudges under her eyes would frighten everyone back home. She'd probably become so monstrous that the Gate would never let her back through, imprisoning her here like it had with Cay.

Virgil's eyes pleaded with her, and he lifted her chin to keep her eyes off the corpse. "Can we go somewhere else, please?"

"What about Hud?"

Virgil gently tugged at her arms, prying them from where she hugged Hud's head against her stomach. "This isn't him anymore," he said. "It's just a shell."

"We can't leave him here."

Virgil sighed but nodded. "We can do whatever you think he needs."

The fight in her arms faded when Virgil finally freed Hud from her grasp. She had nothing left. No reason to stay with the monsters, and she couldn't go back home. She was hollow, the grief more than what her body knew what to do with. None of this was real. A pain like this . . . it couldn't be real, not even in the monster realm. "I don't know what to do."

"We'll figure it out, okay?" Virgil slipped an arm behind her back and pulled her out from under Hud's shoulders. "We'll figure it out together."

"I'm not leaving him here."

His eyes flicked to her missing leg then to Hud. "Can you walk? I don't think I can carry him, let alone both of you."

She struggled to stand with Virgil's help, but without leaning most of her weight on him, she was immobile.

"We'll never make it back to my place like this." Virgil helped her lower back to the ground. "I need to go find someone who can help."

Asheel picked up a chunk of rubble from where a slab had

fallen from the ceiling and stared at it in her palm where the rough edges scratched her embers. "You can leave me here," she mumbled. She didn't fear the creatures in her world. The magic she'd found to defeat Doyen still coursed through her, and using it was as instinctual as breathing. She could stop them with a mere thought.

"You're injured, though. I'm not leaving you here without help."

She didn't respond. She wouldn't die from the injury to her leg. She wouldn't let it kill her because giving in, dying, would kill everyone in the realm with her. The monsters were clueless they were a part of her, even Virgil kneeling beside her. Yet, she could feel them, every single one.

The snake creatures paddled in the sludge like twitches in the lava that flowed through her bones. Bat creatures clung to the monolith, like mites to her scalp. The realm was truly hers. She could only assume Doyen had felt the same life along his scales like she did now.

Virgil eyed Asheel's leg. "Won't that grow back?"

"Not anymore." She rolled the rubble between her fingers. The realm, her magic, would heal any new wounds, but the damage Doyen had done between when she broke free from him and when she gained the realm for herself would always scar her. Hud's stomach wouldn't heal either, like a wound from the realm itself. She clenched her teeth, the weight of his death still pulling at her, wanting to come out in ways she feared.

"I guess we can't wait for that then." He stared at it as if willing it to heal. "How are we going to get you out of here? And don't say to leave you again."

Asheel tightened her fist around the rubble, leaned her head back, and let the black specks in her vision block out her sight while she focused on the nearby city, rumbling like a knot of activity in her stomach. She found the flea she wanted and sent an urge through the tendrils of her world for the humanity peddler to come to the monolith with her cart.

"I could try to convince a snake to fetch someone for us," Virgil picked at his hair while he considered their options.

"Someone's coming to help." Asheel stared at the rubble in her hand again, weary and losing hope that the whole thing was a nightmare.

"What? How?"

"I . . ." She didn't want to explain it. "It's complicated. Just wait."

With a little reluctance, Virgil lowered himself to the ground facing away from Hud's corpse and stretched his legs in front of him. The cart's smoothed wheels from years of rolling across stone and dirt skimmed across her skin at a hastened pace. It exited the city and began the easy trek to the monolith.

Virgil examined a pink vein's glittering remains in a piece of rubble before tossing it into the pool. Asheel winced as the plunk fluttered in her chest. He fiddled with his hair, oblivious to her.

"So how did you change back from whatever you were? I've never heard of Doyen doing that before."

"Weren't you trying to get me to change back?"

"Not really. I was just trying to get you to see reason."

How did she do it? "I thought I was too far gone to ever return, but . . ." She'd needed to change to save Hud, which she'd failed to do. She gritted her teeth to hold back the sob flexing her chest. Deep down, beyond the feeling of the realm, a coil of purple smoke searched for any crack in her determination to slip out and blanket her in ignorance. She took a few deep breaths to steady herself.

"I decided to." That was it. It sounded so simple, but the power she'd felt, the temptations, she'd wanted to choose them. It would have been so easy. She could have drowned herself in the power, never looking back, ruling the realm and feeding off the monsters in it. She still could.

But without Hud and with her becoming such a monstrous beast that the Gate surely wouldn't let her through to the human realm, no one would be able to replenish this place, and in a few short years, she'd be alone, fading away.

"You decided to," Virgil repeated, side-eyeing her skeptically.

Mama B had told her she had a choice, that she always had a choice, and that's what she chose. "You reminded me why I didn't need to be that mindless beast."

"Well, I'm glad you 'decided to' instead of eating me."

They fell into silence after that with tension at their backs where Hud's body lay. Virgil watched the Stream of Judgment, refusing to look at Asheel now that she'd calmed down, but he occasionally peeked over his shoulder at Hud.

Still loosely holding the chunk of rubble, Asheel looped her arms over her bent knee and rested her forehead on them, hiding her face and the lava that seeped down her cheeks without pause. Her heart twisted and ached, and unleashing the ignorance that she could lose herself in became more tempting until, outside the monolith, the humanity peddler's cart finally rolled to a stop.

"Our ride is here." Asheel wiped her cheeks on her forearms and looked up.

Virgil stood and offered her a hand. "How . . ."

She shook her head and motioned over her shoulder. "Take Hud . . . take the body first."

He scowled and stretched his hand closer to her. "I'll find someone stronger to come get him."

Asheel glared at his hand, letting her sorrow come out in frustration, then finally took it. "If something happens to him—"

"I'm sure they'll regret it." Virgil hefted her from the ground, and she looped an arm around his waist to hold herself upright. He grunted while they took their first steps together. "I'll be right back down."

They slowly hobbled through the cavern.

"I'm sorry," Asheel finally whispered when the glow from outside appeared through the main chamber. "I messed up, and there's no way to fix it."

"It's okay." Virgil patted her ribs where his arm looped around her, holding some of her weight. "I mean, it's not really okay, but we'll figure it out."

"I didn't know he meant that much to you." She adjusted her grip on his now soiled shirt. "You always seemed to tolerate him just for vials of humanity. I didn't know."

They stepped into the light, and just where Asheel had felt the cart stop, the peddler, Yory, stood with her long limbs and brown-grey hair sprouted all over her body, looking confused at her decision to visit the monolith.

Virgil paused and narrowed his gaze at Asheel. "How did you know?"

She shook her head, still clutching the rubble she'd taken from the cavern.

Yory studied the two but stumbled back when she caught sight of Asheel's face. "The eyes—"

"Can you help us?" Virgil rushed his words, cutting her off.

"My eyes?" Asheel glanced to Virgil who was avoiding looking at her with clenched teeth. "What's wrong with my eyes?"

"They're fine." Virgil still wouldn't look at her. "They just look a little different."

"They're like Doyen's," Yory said.

The oil-like eyes from her nightmares swirled through Asheel's memory. Was that why Virgil wouldn't look at her? Losing her human body was awful, but having to carry those eyes, having to see Doyen in her reflection. She let go of Virgil's waist and reached to her face to rub, to claw at her eyes, but Virgil grasped her wrist and pulled it back around him, securing her hand with his smooth one.

"Can you help us get to my mansion?" Virgil repeated, changing the subject. His thumb rubbed the back of Asheel's hand in gentle strokes, forcing her focus from her own plight.

Yory pursed her lips while glancing into the monolith. "There was a reason I came here, but I'm not sure why."

"That was me," Asheel said.

"You?"

Asheel ignored the question. "I can't walk, and he can't carry me. We need help getting to his home." She had nowhere else to go. Hud's cabin was out of the question, and she was too ashamed to cower in Mama B's hut.

Realization hit the peddler. "You're the one with the magic sticks. The incense." The monster tapped her fingers against her thigh. "No. I don't give lifts to people who steal my customers."

Asheel clenched the rubble chunk for a moment then loosened her grip. This was nothing new. Her magic had always caused her problems. "If you give me a lift, I'll supply you with enough incense to make up for whatever business I stole." If she still had that magic in her, if she hadn't lost that with her humanity. "I know you didn't want it before, but there's been a shift in the market." Asheel recalled an explanation from her dad from her childhood. "If you can't shift with it, it'll leave you behind with your pride."

The peddler chewed her lip while she thought. "People do love your incense. Fine." Yory turned to Virgil and looked him up and down. "But I'll need this lad's help to pull you."

CHAPTER 30

Y ory agreed to take them to the lava fields first to send Hud's remains into the fires that raged like his body had.

They settled Asheel in the cart on top of Hud's torn vest, among Yory's meager supply of humanity, which Yory said she'd only just started reselling when the incense supply had been cut off a week ago. Her customers had returned, frantic for it. Virgil had found a thick blanket in one of the side chambers of the monolith and wrapped most of Hud's body in the shroud. His feet, cold and lifeless, stuck out of the wrappings beside Asheel, and if she didn't focus on them, she could pretend they weren't real. Still, she curled in the bottom of the cart and let the lava tears flow into the gaps of her scorched flesh and cracked bones. The sound of gravel crunching under the cart's wheels lulled her into a trance.

Yory and Virgil chatted quietly while they walked. The air stilled with Asheel's mood, with her repressed thoughts that could reawaken the beast in her. Most monsters had fled the eerie stillness, and the ones that remained in the open slunk quietly along the streets, gazing at their feet as if Asheel's mood repressed theirs, too.

They reached the outskirts of the lava fields, stopping closer than Yory liked, her fur singeing on the ends. Asheel hadn't visited this land yet, but she reached out through the magic veins like she had for her feedings and to find Yory and called the closest colony of firebreathers to her. Virgil narrowed his eyes at her while she pretended not to notice. A confused procession of six fiery orange creatures with their own skins tied loosely around their waists ambled across the field of heatwaves.

"Will you be okay on your own?" Virgil asked for the second time, fiddling with the curling ends of his silky hair.

Asheel nodded, still holding back the sobs that tugged at her throat.

A mid-sized firebreather tilted his head at Asheel, glanced at her missing leg, and smacked his thick lips as if to moisten them in the dry air before speaking. "What's happened, Reaper?"

"I'm Asheel." She pointed without looking at the mass beside her. "That's the reaper you knew."

The firebreather stared at it, expressionless.

"He's dead." Virgil clarified.

"Pity," the firebreather smacked again, then looked to Asheel and eyed her. "Are you here for the clothes? We have two sets ready, small like he requested."

"I . . ." Asheel did need more clothes. Some of Hud's old items would fit, but they'd sag off her uncomfortably. "Yes, but we also want to have a . . . funeral . . . for the reaper."

"A firebreather funeral?" The man tilted his head and smacked. "He has no skin to reuse. His organs are worthless to us."

"His bones?" Asheel prodded.

The man scuffed his bare feet in the black, volcanic soil while he thought. "The bones of fire, yes. Come with me." He turned and took a step, and a woman clambered forward to lift Hud from the cart.

"Wait, I can't walk," Asheel muttered, embarrassed but without another choice to assist her.

The man turned back around, gathered Asheel in his arms that smelled of soot and stone, and nodded to his companions who began the trudge back to their homes. Tents of darkened orange skin came into view with posts of bleached white bones. Freshly stretched skins were drawn taught over small glowing pools of lava. Several more firebreathers joined them as they walked through the small village to an expansive lake of lava that bubbled and spewed noxious fumes into the air. If Asheel weren't a monster made of fire herself, her human skin would have been scorched beyond recognition, probably dead before they'd even reached the town.

At the lake, the man halted and belched out a slew of words in a language she didn't recognize. The surrounding firebreathers repeated the last word, then the man bowed his head slightly and spoke to the lake. His words flowed smooth, well-rehearsed. While he spoke, the woman carrying Hud unwrapped him from the remaining scraps of blanket that hadn't burned away yet and lifted him above her with his head lolled back and arms hanging stiffly down.

A sob burst out of Asheel's chest, and the lava lake bubbled, roiling with her internal pain. With him prone like that, feet away, she couldn't pretend he hadn't died. It ripped the denial from her. She let the black flecks in her vision swirl closed to block out the sight, but a tiny pinhole remained, just large enough to see Hud's blank eyes staring back at her. Her body shook, fighting the pain, trying to escape into the form she could lose herself in, but she fought back. The pain was good. The pain meant she was still human enough to feel sorrow. She couldn't let it drown her, though. Mama B had said that was a reason she'd been brought to the monster realm.

The man ignored the sobbing reaper in his arms and said the

last few lines of his eulogy. Then the woman laid Hud's body in the edge of the pool where lava ignited his grey skin and ate away everything but his bones, which the woman scooped out one by one, blackened from years of burning.

Asheel looked away from the charred remains, and something deep inside her blackened and died with him.

CHAPTER
31

In Virgil's mansion a full day since Hud's funeral, Asheel rested in a vacant room with blankets from Hud's cabin protecting the bed from her embers. She'd figured out how to keep them cooled enough not to singe everything, but her grief returned at random times, rippling through the realm and flaring her fires.

Mama B sat on a stool beside Asheel's bed, watching her eat a plate of ringas. Virgil lounged across a long chair, plucking at his hair.

"Something's different," he said, his eyes narrowed at the singed ends he continued grooming.

Everything was different, Asheel's new struggles, her understandings, the way everything fit together. She didn't want to talk about any of it, but she wanted to know what difference he was noticing. "What do you mean?"

He shrugged. "I'm not sure. It feels like I had something gripping around my waist for the past twenty years and now it's suddenly vanished."

"I feel it, too." Mama B nodded. "I feel . . . lighter. Hopeful? And Doyen's eyes are gone." She glanced at Asheel, guiltily. Doyen's eyes were still there, on her face, keeping everyone from examining her too closely, but she kept them to herself as much as she could, staying out of their dreams.

"Yeah, I don't see him in my dreams anymore either." Virgil smiled at his hair. "I think we can thank our little reaper for that."

Asheel glanced to the table beside her, eyeing the rubble she'd brought from the monolith. She needed to talk about what had happened. Who else in this realm could she trust if not the two kind monsters before her? She kept her eyes on the rubble while she spoke. "I need to tell you something."

"Yeah?" Virgil didn't look up from his hair, avoiding her eyes, but his grooming paused.

She opened her mouth to tell them everything, to explain how she'd lost control, how she'd become the realm, that she could feel them sitting on their chairs as real as if they were perched on her shoulders, but she couldn't voice it. She shook her head.

He sighed. "I'm trying to give you the time you need, but I'd like to know. How did you become like Doyen?" He raised his hand to stop her before she could say anything. "Take your time, all that you need, but talking about it might also help you get back to your human form."

"I . . . I have a feeling if he'd left me in the Stream of Judgment it would have shown me becoming like him, beyond a reaper, but no one expected that since it's never happened before. And I think . . . I don't think I can be human again," Asheel admitted and fiddled with a ringa, accidentally toasting the fish paste.

"Why not?" Mama B asked. "You're a reaper. Reapers can change back."

But Asheel had gone as monstrous as Cay had, and he'd lost his humanity, unable to grow it back, stealing what he could from others. She was lucky she'd even been able to return to a reaper. "After abusing so many monsters in my rage, I've lost that part of me." The part she most desperately wanted. "I don't think I can."

Mama B placed a hand over hers, flinching only a little from the heat. "You have a choice."

"If I still have a choice, you have one, too." Her grieving for her lost side came out snappier than she'd meant it to, but she couldn't hold it back. "Change back to human," she demanded of her.

Mama B shook her head, her quills clinking quietly. "Our human forms were stolen. Yours was not. You have a choice."

"I think Doyen lied to everyone about that." Asheel wrung her hands. "If he'd taken all of it . . . Everyone still has a choice, and that's why he fed from everyone in the realm even after the pool had stripped their humanity. Why the ones who fought it the most were fed from so frequently. It's not something that you can fully lose. It can be regrown." He'd said as much to her when she'd seen the true Cay.

Virgil sat up abruptly. "So everyone can return to their homes, to the human realm? We could be human again?"

Asheel shrugged. "Maybe. But I doubt all of them could. Some wouldn't want to change even if they had the choice." She'd smelled their awful feelings. Some seemed too far gone, but she had to believe they had hope. If they didn't, how could she? "Sure, we all got here for a reason, consumed by pain we couldn't escape, but maybe some could go home."

"I could go home," Virgil muttered, then frowned at her. "Well, if we have hope then you can definitely change back to a human." He let his hair fall over his shoulders. "You've done it before, right?"

"Once." Asheel grimaced. "And I wasn't able to change myself. I had help."

"Needing help is okay," Mama B said. "What help do you need?"

Asheel kept her head down, watching her bony hands, willing them to grow normal human flesh again, but the glowing embers crackling and sizzling in her knuckle bones only flared brighter with her effort and frustration. They didn't have the help she needed.

"Asheel," Virgil said. She glanced up at him, and for the first time since he'd found her in Doyen's lair, he didn't flinch from her eyes. "We want to help, but we can't if you don't tell us what you need. How did you change back before?"

She sighed. "Hud used his magic on me, okay?" She looked away, heat flaring through her cheekbones. "The only thing that made me feel anything like that was human essence, and I'm not shoving anyone into the Stream of Judgment to get any."

"So it's either a Physiqal or human essence you need." Virgil scratched his chin. "I don't know any Physiqals that would want to help, do you?" He glanced at Mama B, who shook her head and shrugged. "My Lingual magic can't do what they can," he continued. "But I . . ."

He ran his fingers through his hair, tapped them against his knee, then stood and left the room. Asheel and Mama B waited in silence, and he returned quickly with his hand shoved in his pocket. He shuffled to the bed, sighed, and pulled a full vial of humanity from his pocket.

"Here." He placed the vial on the plate of ringas when she didn't grab it. "I was saving it, but if it helps you get your humanity back, you need it more."

The pink liquid glistened in the lamplight, but Asheel didn't touch it. "I don't want to take the last of your humanity." She cringed at her poor choice of words. "You won't be able to replenish your supply."

"If it makes you feel better about taking it, I'm also offering it for my own selfish purposes until I can figure out how to get back through the Gate, too." He sat back on the lounge chair and began pruning the ends of his hair again. "If the last of my stash helps you do that, then I'll gladly give it to you. But if it still makes you sick like last time, don't ruin the carpet."

Debating with herself, Asheel watched bubbles slide up the sides of the glass. She'd craved the liquid humanity while she'd ravaged the realm from Doyen's cavern. She'd been cruel, stripping the smallest amounts from the monsters she pulled into the monolith. Would taking a sip make her slip back into that beast?

Mama B took the dwindling plate of ringas from Asheel and set the vial from it into her hand. "Drink it," she said and pulled Virgil from the lounge and out the door with her, leaving Asheel alone in the room to decide.

What if it didn't work? Cay couldn't go back through the Gate, and she'd been just as awful as him. Or maybe she'd escaped the spiraling misery he'd lost himself in soon enough, escaped her misery decades before Cay had tried to escape his. She hadn't lost herself as entirely as he had.

She had hope and a choice. Getting help to be human was an option, and her decision glistened and bubbled at her as she removed the stopper and raised it to her lips.

CHAPTER 32

T he next week was chaos. Some monsters fought over a new hierarchy, wrestling in the caverns and throwing each other into the pool in Doyen's lair, which she felt even at a distance and shoved them out, fighting the urge to let the bubbles drown them.

Some monsters tried to run through the Gate, which was when Asheel learned she could see through it. The first one who entered it felt like a twinge in her eye, and when she blinked, she could see into the human realm, like looking through multifaceted eyes. Several layers of images flitted over her regular sight. They had no sound, but the images spun quickly from person to person, cities overlayed with cities, millions of swirling trails like what she saw as a reaper. She could understand a little why Doyen was so adamant about not letting them into the human realm with their voices if he'd watched them for so long soundlessly.

She'd blinked the images away after trying to sort through the cities to find her family, but by then, the whir of sights left her with a migraine that rivaled the pain Doyen's contract had caused. The strain kept her from looking back through often, but when the twinges of monsters entering the Gate returned, she'd peer for a moment to see if anyone got through. Only one survived to the other side, but she came back quickly when she realized her friend had gotten stuck in the Gate's fog. The report led everyone to believe that most still couldn't go to the human realm.

Asheel made incense again. Virgil, Ratel, and Mama B all confirmed her magic still imbued it, and Ziyiel delivered batches to Yory, now the sole incense seller with more customers than she could supply. The more they burned, the more peace it brought them, and each of them slowly started to smell better and better, less monstrous and more human.

But none of the monsters changed back to their human forms. That part of them had been torn from them forever even if their internal humanity returned.

Asheel wasn't sure if she was one of the ones that could get back through the Gate or not. Her grey, black-veined flesh proved she still had some humanity in her, enough to stave off her reaper form. But how could someone who had become such a monster . . . someone who murdered and worse . . . how could she be allowed back through?

She stood inches from the Gate, leaning on a crutch, taunting her fate.

"You'll be fine." Virgil put a hand on her shoulder. "Trust me."

"You can't know that." Asheel didn't turn from the murky oil splotch that matched her eyes. It pulsed in the air, beckoning her.

"Hush." He flicked her shoulder. "It has no reason to keep you from going through. You're more human than anyone else here."

She glanced down to her grey hands where she clutched a crinkled, pink-tinted letter. She had to get through the Gate. She needed to get through to keep healing.

"You ready?" Virgil squeezed her shoulder. This would also be his first time going back through, and his confidence in Asheel's judgment that he would survive it made her nervous enough for the both of them.

Mama B and Kady stood several feet back, and Ziyiel stood even farther, just as nervous as Asheel about Virgil's attempt.

"Good luck!" Kady screamed and waved. Asheel had promised to take Kady back through the Gate to her family if the girl could release her own bitterness, her thorniness, and learn to forgive to heal herself. That hope of seeing her family again shifted Kady's demeanor overnight.

Asheel smiled over her shoulder and nodded. "Let's go."

She and Virgil stepped into the Gate, which engulfed them instantly, and the ghostly hands welcomed them. The yellow haze thickened and filled Asheel's lungs, and when two hands brushed across her shoulders, she stiffened. They would grab her. They'd hold her in the Gate's mist forever, and she reached out for Virgil's hand and held it tight. He was tense too, and they clutched each other while the hands fluttered around them. At least she'd have a friend in her eternity in the Gate. Would they recognize each other when they dissolved to join the hands? But after a few more passes, the hands nudged them onward and guided them through to the other side while the glowing, soulless eyes watched from afar.

On the other side of the Gate, in the human realm, Virgil paused and took a deep breath.

"That wasn't nearly as bad as I remember my first time through it," he said and stretched his arms out with his head tilted back. "I never thought I'd be back here." Sunlight glinting through the trees shone through his translucent skin in splotches, but he'd refused to hide under a cloak like Asheel.

She'd been able to stay in a human body with a little help from her realm's magic, but the black veins and scorched, rough patches of skin still revealed her for what she was. She pulled her cloak's hood over her head to hide what she could, but a few scales still decorated her forehead and the bottomless pits under her eyes sometimes seeped liquid fire. Permanent stains that nothing could cleanse.

She and Virgil walked down the mountain together while she imagined how her meetings would go. It wasn't too late; she could change her mind and go back to the monster realm. No one on this side would know any better of it.

But she wanted to see her family. Let them know she was okay.

At the edge of Seshnia where the forest met farmland, Virgil nudged Asheel ahead. This part was up to her, but he would wait for her in the shadows.

She held the hood tightly around her face and hobbled toward her house. The streets were packed with faces she didn't recognize, and after eavesdropping on a few conversations, she figured out a lot of people had fled Novoshna because of the new Reaper Gate that'd opened in the center of the city a month ago. Someone blamed the wall for it, saying they'd angered the reaper and he'd put the Gate there to mock them. Other whispered conversations mentioned how the reaper had vanished. No towns had reported him visiting since the night that two had appeared.

A few children ran across her path, one of them with the distinct smell of a monster growing inside them, and Asheel smiled. She could finally smell past the pain that seeped out in fumes to notice the sweetness that still poured from them. That child still had a future here. Still had a chance to feel their pain and decide to let it fester or fade. The reaper wasn't coming for them.

Her smile faded. But what if the child let it consume them? What happened if the child turned into a beast and destroyed Seshnia?

Most people ignored her journey through town, and after a few more minutes, when her house appeared, she hesitated. She was still Asheel. Her parents would still love her. Surely, they would see she was their daughter beyond the gruesome marks. Maybe her little brother would be afraid of her appearance. That would be understandable. But her parents, they'd still love her.

She knocked on the door, something she'd never thought she would do at her home, and kept the hood tight around her face.

Her mother answered and narrowed her eyes, her black hair twisted into a messy bun. "Who are you?"

"It's me, Mom. It's Asheel."

"Asheel?" Her mother, skeptical, tried to peer under the cloak, but Asheel kept it tight. "You can't be."

"Can I come in?"

Willa narrowed the opening, blocking the entry, preventing her from slipping inside.

"Is that Berice?" Coby's voice called from behind their mother. "I want to play!" His curly head shoved between their mom and the door, and he glowered at the hooded figure when he realized it wasn't his friend.

"It's me, curly."

Coby's face broke out in the biggest smile. He was missing another tooth, but it was the smile she'd missed so much. He dashed to her and threw his arms around her neck. Fumes of sweetness rose from him, only the faintest hints of the rot she'd smelled the last she'd seen him remained. He'd been healing himself. He'd been growing, becoming a better person, someone who wanted to be good and kind.

He tightened his hug, accidentally pulling her hood back, revealing Asheel's face to their mother.

"I missed you!" Coby cried while their mother gasped and tugged him back from Asheel.

"Get away!" Willa tried to close the door, but Coby grabbed the frame and his eyes finally met Asheel's.

"What's wrong with your face?" He frowned.

Asheel pulled the hood back up. "It's from some bad choices, but it's better than it was. Is it scary?"

His thin eyebrows furrowed. "A little."

"Help!" their mom shouted into the street where a couple of teens paused with their cart of vegetables.

"Mom, it's okay. It's me," Asheel muttered half-heartedly. "The legends about the monsters and Cay are true, but we forgot people change into them and could change back."

Her mom tugged at Coby again, and the couple started across the street. Asheel was out of time if she didn't want to start a scene.

"Leave my family alone!" Willa shouted at her.

The heat of sadness burned behind Asheel's eyes. She took a step forward even though she knew her mom needed space. "It's still me." She reached out one hand. Her sleeve slid back from her wrist and revealed the ashen skin over her hands, the blackened veins that glowed with lava as blood.

"You're not my daughter!" Willa's voice shook. "You've possessed her body."

"What's going on here?" a teen from the cart asked.

The rejection pierced Asheel's heart even though she'd expected it. She understood. She would feel the same way, distrusting of someone so horrid. But her reunion was over. "Bye, curly." She gave a small wave to her little brother. "You're safe now. The reaper will never take you." She looked up at her mom. "Tell Dad that I'm alive and well, that I miss you both." She paused, knowing this was the last thing she'd say to her mother. She couldn't see her father after her mother's reaction, couldn't take him rejecting her, too. With one last glance at Coby, she turned away from them, her back to the teens who were squeezing their way between her and her home, and hobbled away on her crutch.

The next person to find was Lana, but Asheel couldn't take

more rejection just yet. Surely Lana wouldn't be as horrified as Asheel's mom had been, but if Asheel's aura were completely gone, she wasn't ready to find out.

Virgil opened his arms when he saw her tearstained face, but she limped past him deeper into the trees until she couldn't smell Seshnia anymore. He didn't have to ask how it went. He put his arms around her and patted her back while she sobbed both normal tears and lava.

"My mom hates me. She hated me on sight and thought I wasn't me."

"What about your dad?" Virgil asked. "Your brother?"

"Coby was a little scared, and I didn't even look for my dad. It was too much." Asheel sniffed. "Even if Mom hates me, at least I can pretend Dad doesn't."

"Maybe it's better to let her believe that you weren't her daughter. Let her remember you how she wants to."

"I miss them."

Virgil twisted his mouth while he thought. "You always will, but it'll get easier."

Asheel sobbed quietly a few minutes before Virgil spoke again. "Did you find your friend?" he asked.

"I couldn't face her after my mom. I need another minute."

Virgil let go of her and stepped back. "Want to help me with my reunion while you wait?"

She nodded. Though Virgil had come to support her, he'd really risked the Gate for his own errand, and her excitement for him overshadowed her grieving.

Virgil didn't know the way, so Asheel led them through the corn fields and up the cliffs to the long expanses of plateau above the tree line. He followed in silence, nervous but ready. When Asheel's crutch slipped over the loose gravel, he caught her before she fell, but most of the slope was gentle enough to make the hike easy. Birds twittered and danced in the brilliant blue sky, and lizards sunning themselves on the rocks skittered away when they passed.

A lone lamb greeted them when they stepped onto the plateau. It blinked at Asheel then bleated feebly. Its flock was nowhere in sight. Most shepherds didn't bring their flocks this close to the plateau's edge, but she knew one shepherd who did.

"Hey, little guy." Asheel knelt to check the branding in its ear. The blocky mark wasn't fresh, the lamb probably old enough to be weaned. "One of Jean's flock. It's your lucky day." She scratched its chin, and it closed its eyes. "We can take you back to your family." She turned to Virgil. "Can you help carry him? I don't want to drop him."

He lifted it into an awkward cradle in his arms, uncomfortable handling the squirming lamb. Asheel bit her lips to keep from snickering at his struggle, but she couldn't hide her smirk.

He rolled his eyes. "You seem better now."

"Animals are easier than people."

"Easy for you to say." He flipped his silky hair.

Asheel led them through the field to where Jean liked to keep his flock, at a lake hidden below a short ridge.

They fell into comfortable silence again with only the occasional bleating from the lamb in Virgil's arms. A few clumsy steps over the ridge, and the familiar flock she'd spent only a few weeks with grazed in the pasture below them. The lamb bleated, and the sheep closest to the ridge glanced up at the two people spying on them. A few ambled towards the middle of the flock, which filled the pasture between the ridge and the lake.

And on a stone bench sat the gentle man who had nudged Asheel into her wild journey.

She stepped off the ridge, and Virgil set the lamb on the spongy grass, its little legs kicking to get back to its family as if it had suddenly lost all trust in the pair. This could be Asheel's new purpose, bringing the broken families back together. She'd bring the monsters back one at a time in her arms until they were all back where they belonged. Maybe some of them would be human enough again one day.

Jean turned at the disturbed bleating of his sheep and spied the two of them. His eyes narrowed, and Asheel could almost hear the man complain about how age kept sneaking in at night and stealing more of his senses. She waved, which seemed to pacify Jean, and he turned back to the lake where a family of ducks dove under the water and bobbed back up.

"Are you ready?" Asheel asked.

Virgil shook his head, his confidence waning. "I shouldn't have come."

"Jean's great." Asheel glanced between Virgil and the old man and held out her hand. "He won't be like my mom."

But Virgil ignored Asheel's hand and started across the field of sheep with her at his heels. Most of the flock stepped out of their way, hesitant of their presence, but a few seemed to remember her even through her hideous form and followed her for a few steps before returning to grazing. She pulled the hood tight around her face as she got closer while Virgil held his head high.

"You haven't retired yet?" she asked the old man.

Jean ignored her question and asked one of his own. "So were you too stubborn for even the reaper and he let you go?"

The warmth and peace she'd found in these fields came flooding back to her at the sound of his voice. She wanted to stay here, on the plateau, and ignore the world. Just her and the sheep. No one would have to see her or fear her or demand her to use the talents she never wanted.

But she'd have to see someone eventually to sell the wool or deliver a plump ram for a wedding feast. It wasn't the fairytale ending she was imagining. It'd still have its own problems.

"Can we have a seat?" Virgil asked.

"I don't own the bench." Jean squinted again at the translucent creature, studying him, unbothered by the strange skin but his eyes catching on little details, pausing, recognizing. "Son?"

The translucent monster nodded.

Jean hefted himself from the bench, and the two stared at each other before Jean stepped forward with his arms open. And for the first time in decades, the father and son embraced.

Asheel might not be able to carry every monster through the Gate yet, but one was a start.

Virgil sat beside Jean, and Asheel lowered herself onto the bench with an arm's length between them. This was their moment. She'd only known Jean a short time, and though he was accepting of his own son, she wasn't sure how he'd react to her strange skin. Jean and Virgil stared at each other in silence, neither knowing what to say after so long apart.

"Sorry my letter was so short last month," Virgil finally said. "Asheel really upheaved all our lives over there."

"Well," Jean patted Virgil's leg, "I'd say this makes up for it." He coughed into his elbow then peered across Virgil to Asheel. "I have a feeling there's a story behind how my son is here, and I suspect it has something to do with my old apprentice."

"Sorry to leave my apprenticeship so suddenly."

Jean smiled, and his eyes disappeared under the folds of skin. "No harm done. Life goes on."

"I found the powerful Cay," Asheel explained, "from our legends. He was so far gone that he couldn't get back through the Gate that he'd created. And he stayed there thriving on the stolen humans, eventually forgetting why he still dragged them through the Gate."

Jean didn't seem shocked by the information. He simply nodded along. "Anyone can lose themselves if they forget to keep a check on their priorities."

Asheel knew that so much better than Jean could have

realized. He was such an understanding man and hadn't cringed away from either of the two monsters beside him. She let the hood loosen from her face but kept it pulled forward, still wanting to hide the signs that she'd lost herself. "He'd had a little humanity left in him," she said while the two men listened. She hadn't told Virgil this part. "His intentions were good at first, but they fed into his monstrous side, his need for immortality and power."

"Power is seductive." Jean closed his eyes. "But it's also fleeting, so fleeting." He cleared his throat though mumbled his complaints. "I wish I could have some of my old strength back." He lifted a twisted hand from his staff and examined it.

"No one has to worry about being taken anymore. He's gone now. Everyone is free." She glanced at Virgil who smiled at the last bit.

Jean turned back toward Asheel, his gnarled hand still hovering where he'd been studying it. "I'm proud of you."

"Why?"

"You'd given up on everyone last time I saw you, but now you tell me you've freed everyone. That tells me you care about people again."

It was like Jean could see her heart just as clearly as she could see those around her. He leaned forward to try to peer under Asheel's hood, but she looked away. She was ashamed to let her mentor know how far she'd fallen, how much she'd lost herself. How much she still reeked.

"You're different. You've found your strength," he said with smug satisfaction. Even though she was certain he'd point out her monster side, he saw beyond that.

"Don't think well of me." She stole a glimpse sideways at him. "I've lost myself just as much as the powerful man."

"Nonsense. You said he couldn't get back through the Gate. Yet, you did. I conclude that you aren't in the slightest like that monster."

Asheel let go of the hood and let the wind brush it back from her head. "But I'm a monster now. I look more human than the others, but I've become what we've always feared."

He looked back out towards the lake and scoffed. "Just because you look like one doesn't mean you are one. You're still Asheel just like this is still my Virgil. Even my weary eyes can see that."

This was beyond the kindness she expected from this elder who'd spent his time in solitude in the wilderness. "I wish my family understood that."

They sat in silence for several minutes, Jean patting Virgil's knee, Virgil twisting the ends of his hair awkwardly. Asheel didn't want to leave the peace of the lake yet, and Virgil was slowly relaxing enough to enjoy his short time with his father.

Jean cleared his throat. "I was thinking," he said, "if the Reaper Gate was created, surely it can be destroyed."

It wasn't a question, but Asheel answered anyway. "No. Well, maybe." She lifted a pebble from the ground and tossed it into the lake. The sheep that were drinking on the banks scattered back, startled. Even on this side of the Gate, she could still feel the monsters roaming the monster realm, the footsteps along her arms, the squirming in her stomach, the quivers in her chest. They were safely a part of her, a realm she carried with her wherever she wandered. "But I won't let that happen." If she destroyed the Gate, what would happen to her?

"Oh?" Jean leaned on his staff to study her.

Virgil turned to look at her, too.

"It'll remain for anyone who becomes a monster, who chooses to let that side of themself consume them." She decided. "They'll answer to me. I'll drag them back through, and they'll live out their days in the monster realm."

"Even the children?" Jean leaned on his staff.

"They're still learning and flipping so fast between how they feel and what they should do. They aren't monsters, but if any change, I'll take them through and try to help them come back."

Jean sighed. "Don't let the power go to your head. I like the idea of those glowing footprints never returning."

Another few minutes stretched between them while the father and son caught up in ways letters couldn't provide. The sun slipped through the sky, and the afternoon bugs began their chorus.

"Do you have plans to retire in Seshnia?" Asheel asked, worried that Jean didn't have a new apprentice by his side.

Before he could answer, a figure appeared on the horizon on the other side of the lake, jogging around the banks toward them. Asheel pulled her hood up and held it around her mouth again, and Virgil jerked up and away from the approaching figure.

"Yes," Jean answered. "But between you and me, the flock liked you better." He winked then put a finger to his lips.

The figure reached them and bent forward with her hands on her knees to catch her breath. Her brown hair was cropped to her scalp. Her hazel eyes were harsh, but a plumpness around her cheeks softened her appearance.

"I couldn't find the lamb, sir," the girl said between wheezes.

Jean lightly thumped her arm with his staff. "Did you check everywhere?"

She nodded. "Yes, sir. I—" Her gaze fell on Virgil, and she gasped and stepped back.

"Ignore him," Jean said. "Where did you look?"

The girl quivered, her gaze darting between Jean and Virgil, but she answered, Jean's own calmness easing her panic. "From the ridge here across the pastures. I even jogged through the forest and asked the other shepherds if they'd seen him. I ran all the way to the meadow."

Jean thumped her again. "There's a lesson to be learned here."

The girl waited expectantly.

"Asheel, please explain where you found the lamb."

The girl jolted at Asheel's name, her eyes finally tearing away from the translucent monster, and she took another step away from the ghost she must have assumed stood cloaked in front of her.

"The lamb was sniffing around at the edge of the cliff." Not much of an explanation, but what more was there to it than that?

"That's right." He nodded as if she'd bestowed great wisdom on them. "Danger is always just behind us, and we need to search there first, always be aware of it. And when it creeps up too close, sometimes we need someone's help to bring us back to safety."

The girl's gaze continued darting between Virgil's eerie form and Asheel's cloaked mystique. Asheel smiled to herself, enjoying Jean's unusual mannerisms, but it was time for them to go. She wanted to find Lana before returning to her realm, which needed to be soon. The ache and a new hollowness had been growing inside her. She wasn't meant to be on this side for so long.

Asheel and Virgil said their goodbyes, promising to visit again when they were able. Virgil could have stayed, but they expected most people to respond to him like Jean's apprentice had, fear and disgust; plus, he'd built a life in the monster realm, even though he'd said he had nothing left over there.

Asheel let her hood loose while they walked in the dark back toward town, through the fields she'd dashed through to save Coby.

"Ready to go back to the Gate or find your friend?"

Asheel tilted her head back to the sky, reinvigorated and encouraged. "Lana. I need to tell her I'm okay. I need to give her a job."

Virgil fiddled with his hair, and his steps bounced with a new energy from visiting his dad. "Job?"

Asheel smiled to herself. Even if Lana feared her or rejected her, this was a job she could do.

CHAPTER
33

S he found Lana right where she expected, at the care-home, nursing those who needed extra help to live comfortably. Asheel watched her through a window, wrestling with herself between Lana rejecting her new stains or accepting her as she was. This was Lana, her friend. She wouldn't reject her, but if she did, maybe it was time for them to move on from each other. Maybe Lana already had.

A bearded man ambled by Asheel, and she pulled her hood lower.

"Excuse me," she said, standing by the care-home's garden, and the man paused at the door. "Can you ask Lana to step outside to see an old friend?"

"Who?"

"The girl with the eye patch."

He agreed, and Asheel peered back through the window to watch the exchange. Lana turned to the door and stepped toward it, a painstakingly slow movement. Asheel still had time to hobble away.

Lana, halfway to the door, caught a glimpse of Asheel in the window, and Asheel ducked, then peeked over the windowsill to find Lana reaching for the door. It was too late to run.

And then the door opened, and the sweet scent of Lana's heart smacked into Asheel, stronger than Asheel's memory could do it justice. A floral perfume that shot up her nose, opening her airways and causing her to inhale deeply.

"Hello?" Lana's high voice pierced Asheel's ears, and all of her happiest memories crashed through her, as painful as the Stream of Judgment had been. She could live in her voice forever. "You asked for me?"

Asheel opened her mouth, but the words wouldn't come out. Lana might reject her. This might be goodbye.

"He said you were a friend?" Lana crossed her arms with a quizzical gaze just over Asheel's head where her aura would be strongest.

"It's me," Asheel whispered.

Without another word, Lana darted down the steps and wrapped her arms around Asheel, jostling her enough to loosen Asheel's cloak, which she clutched at instead of returning the hug.

"Can we go behind the care-home?"

Lana glanced over her shoulder at the people inside and flicked her wrist toward them. "Of course. They'll be fine without me for a few minutes." She reached for Asheel's hands, but she buried them in her sleeves before Lana could notice the blackened veins.

Behind the home, hidden in the back, shadowed edge of the care-home's garden, Lana hugged Asheel again, her fingers snatching the back of Asheel's hood and pulling it back. "How are you back here?" Lana asked and leaned out of the hug to look at her friend, but when her eyes found Asheel's, she stumbled back a few steps.

Asheel froze, terrified, the same shock reflecting in both girls' faces. Lana's gaze drifted above Asheel's head again.

"It's bad. I know." Asheel grabbed her hood to lift it back over her head, but Lana placed a hand over her ashen one and her eyebrows rose in the middle, pulling her eye patch up slightly.

"What happened?" Lana kept a few paces between them and crossed her arms again, rubbing at her sleeves.

"A lot." Asheel wanted to tell Lana everything from the moment she went through the Gate to her mom's rejection of her, but they didn't have time. So many thoughts fought to escape. "I'm sorry," Asheel finally mumbled. "I'm sorry for leaving you. For abandoning Seshnia. All of it."

Lana dropped her arms and shook her head, her curls bouncing with the movement. "You did what you had to do, and somehow you came back so that doesn't seem like you abandoned us."

"I guess that's true," Asheel rummaged in her pocket and pulled out the rumpled letter. "Everyone should be safe now, but they need your help."

"My help?"

"I found out why the reaper took smelly people with him. They were in danger of becoming monsters to terrorize humans." Asheel held out the letter to Lana.

She took it. "So the legends are true? We become monsters? What's this?"

"Can you give that to Kady's mom for me? It's from her."

"Kady's alive?" Lana straightened and clutched the letter to her chest. "Is everyone alive?"

Asheel shook her head and dropped her gaze. She never asked Hud who from her town was still in the monster realm, and now she couldn't. "Some are. Some didn't survive. But they don't have to go through it anymore. That's what I need you to do. The monsters that grow inside them, it has a cause, but it also has a cure. Any painful feelings can become so overwhelming that it consumes them. But I think you can show them the way out of it. Your magic," Asheel spun her hand in the air above her head, "seeing people's auras, I think you can help them through their pain."

"How am I supposed to do that?"

"The other people with sensory magic that live in Novoshna's palace figured out how to use their magic on people. They can help you, maybe, but you might have to reveal yourself to the queen to get to them." Asheel blinked to bring the swirling views of the world into her sight. "There's several people on the other side who've figured it out, but I'll try to find others over here, too."

"I don't want to influence people's auras. That can't be okay for them to be forced to change."

"No, don't force them. You'll just be guiding them. There's no harm in helping them understand what they're going through."

Lana scratched the edge of her eye patch, unconvinced. "But how will I know who needs help?"

"Definitely anyone whose aura starts to fade, but other than that, you'll have to talk to them, make connections even if you think they don't like you. I'll try to find some people like me who can figure out who's most in danger. I'll help keep an eye on everyone, but I don't want to bring people through the Gate anymore if I don't have to."

"I can try, but I still don't want to change people. It has to be their own doing." Lana slowly touched Asheel's cheek. "What happened to you?"

"I . . ." Asheel tucked her hair behind her ear, revealing the veins along her cheeks. "A lot, but I'm okay now. I have . . . I have friends helping me." She tested the word, worried what her *friends* would say if they found out she'd called them that, worried if Lana might be jealous that Asheel had moved on from her.

A smile crept up Lana's face. "Good." She closed the distance between them, pecked Asheel's cheek despite the gruesome appearance, and pulled her into another hug, this time Asheel returning the gesture. When they parted, Lana was still smiling. "Good," she repeated. "You deserve them. I'm glad you got your friends back." Her gaze drifted back above Asheel's head.

"Is it . . . Am I . . . Can I ask?"

Lana smirked. "All I'll say is don't worry about it. Don't ask." But she continued staring at the air above Asheel, and that was all the answer Asheel needed.

They spent a few minutes catching up, Asheel promising to visit again soon, and they walked back to the side of the building for Lana to return to work.

"I'll see you again." Asheel turned to her friend. "I promise."

"Soon, please," Lana whispered, giving her a last wave while stepping back into the care-home.

Asheel hobbled to the edge of town and found Virgil still hiding in the trees, and together, they returned to the Gate in much better moods, ready to return home. They'd both visit Seshnia again, and Asheel would whisper encouragement to them and stories about how the reaper saved them all.

CHAPTER
34

After returning to the monster realm, Asheel convinced Virgil to let her visit Hud's cabin alone. She wandered up the street, breathing in the clearing scents of her realm. Her destruction had been cleaned up, and homes were slowly being rebuilt.

Pine needles bunched around her crutch while she limped up the path to Hud's cabin, abandoned since the night he died. At the edge of the rock garden, she paused and pulled the piece of rubble she'd taken from the monolith from her pocket. He'd had his hurried funeral, but this was something she needed to do for herself. The lives lost, she couldn't shake responsibility for them, and to make it up to them, she'd work hard not to make the same mistakes Cay had.

She stared at the rubble in her palm. A few faint shimmers of pink, a damaged vein of magic, pulsed through it. This was for the creatures she'd trampled in her rage; for those who'd never gotten the chance to recover; and for Hud, who gave his life to try to save her. She let it fall from her hand to join the ocean of rocks.

It landed with a clatter and split into three pieces. A broken tombstone for a colony of broken lives.

With a deep breath, she turned from the cabin instead of going inside and trudged toward the monolith. She couldn't go back in the cabin yet. She wasn't ready to face the emptiness there, but she needed to visit the heart of her realm. Her heart. Where the magic flowed through.

In Doyen's lair, filthier than she'd ever seen it, a cluster of antlered monsters hovered around the edge of the pool.

"Get out of here!" Asheel flared into her reaper form for the first time since drinking Virgil's last vial of human essence. The fire in her had been growing for days, but she wasn't scared to let it out anymore. She wouldn't let it consume her. She'd feel it, let the pain burn out, and then return to her new life. She flared her embers and shooed the monsters.

They scattered quickly from the new reaper, the truth about what happened to Doyen having reached all ears. They scampered and stumbled on their hooved feet, but eventually they were all out the entrance and clomping back through the tunnels.

Asheel rolled her shoulders and tilted her head from side to side. She'd been afraid of returning, that revisiting the memories would crush her. She had been afraid to lose control again and that she might not return from it the next time. But she didn't fear her fiery form now, a form she'd use to protect those struggling through their own pain, a form that made her own pain tangible. Asheel knew how to choose her path and stay far from the line of no return.

She walked to the throne, its smooth stone glowing with pink veins that swirled through it like marble. The monster realm couldn't survive without a leader. Even if she hid in the shadows, keeping secret her role of maintaining the realm, the monsters would keep warring over who was in charge and eventually destroy themselves. She ran her hand along the stone armrest then slowly lowered herself into the seat. The throne dwarfed her. She didn't even come halfway up the backrest. Not a single monster in the realm could fill the seat.

Except maybe her, if she became the smokey purple beast again.

But she wouldn't do that. She didn't need to do that. With a mental shove, she pushed the memory of power from her mind.

She stood and walked to the pool. The waterfall ran clear, but the water that splashed on the banks reached for her. Called for her. She knelt and scraped her finger along the bank where the thinnest ribbon of humanity had washed up. She lifted it from the water, the ribbon hanging like a slimy thread from her fingertip. It glistened in the light from the pink veins lining the cavern.

This was how Cay had stayed around for so many millennia, taking life from humans, stealing the faint trails of magic that flowed through each of them. His own magic flowing into the Stream of Judgment and feeding the realm, a magic that now resided in her.

The humanity ribbon dangled in front of her face. Something so small but held so much power. Power that shouldn't be wasted. She placed the ribbon in her mouth and swallowed, letting it cool her, support her. But instead of soothing her, consuming it filled her with guilt. She had her own humanity—it wasn't something they could lose entirely, each of them having dredges of it fighting in their hearts like fragile blossoms against vines.

She could sense every monster in the realm, and some of them smelled sweet.

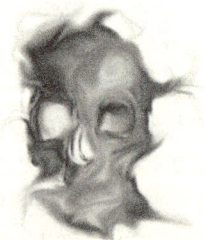

Acknowledgments

Thank you, the reader, for giving this book a chance. Whether you loved it or hated it, I'd love if you could review it and let me know what you thought!

Thank you to everyone who supported me through this project!

Moe and Audrey for valuable input during drafting, for not kicking me out of our group for my weird ideas, and for being all around great humans.

Michelle for reading an early draft, helping with my weaker areas, and encouraging me through my doubts. Jennifer for reading an early draft and suffering through the errors. Sara for being such a cheerleader and keeping me sane.

Huge thank you to my beta readers for critical eyes, honesty, enthusiasm, and encouragement: Tanni, PJ, Sara (yes, I'm thanking you twice!), Megan, and Court.

And of course thank you to the best husband who couldn't be more supportive. <3